'Utter genius.'

'A bittersweet domestic drama . . . sharply funny . . . occasionally very moving' *Marie Claire*

'This should be compulsory reading for all working couples with small children, since it encapsulates precisely, but with plenty of humour, the madness of the modern working family.'
Sarah Vine, *The Times*

'Sharp, funny and deliciously rude.' *Daily Mail*

'This is a fascinating exposé of chaotic relationships, the demands of modern life, and societal preoccupation with youth. A fast-paced and entertaining read.' *Image*

'A great comic novel on marriage and motherhood . . . very funny.'
**** *Red*

'A well-written, absorbing story, with lots of little touches that make it believable and true to life . . . a great grown-up novel for everyone who's terrified of growing up (that will be all of us, then)!'
Fabulous

'Christina Hopkinson has wittily and very realistically tapped into the zeitgeist – literally the most relevant novel for a working mother since *I Don't Know How She Does It* by Allison Pearson.'
Plum Sykes, author of *Bergdorf Blondes*

WITHDRAWN FROM STORE

'Christina Hopkinson is a talented writer with a gift for observational humour and sharp one-liners.' *Spectator*

'A hugely witty read, which will appeal to almost everyone.'
Lady

'Immensely e   *o.uk*

Also by Christina Hopkinson

Just Like Proper Grown-Ups
The Pile of Stuff at the Bottom of the Stairs
Izobel Brannigan.com

About the author

Christina Hopkinson is an author and journalist whose work has appeared in the *Daily Telegraph, Guardian, The Times, Grazia* and *Red*. She lives in London with her husband and three children.

Visit Christina's website at www.christinahopkinson.com and follow her on Twitter @Xtinahopkinson.

The A-List Family

Christina Hopkinson

HODDER

First published in Great Britain in 2014 by Hodder & Stoughton
An Hachette UK Company

1

Copyright © Christina Hopkinson 2014

The right of Christina Hopkinson to be identified as
the Author of the Work has been asserted by her in accordance
with the Copyright, Designs and Patents Act 1988.

A CIP catalogue record for this title is available
from the British Library.

Paperback ISBN 978 1 444 78528 9
Ebook ISBN 978 1 444 78529 6

Typeset in Monotype Sabon by Palimpsest Book Production Limited,
Falkirk, Stirlingshire

Printed and bound in Great Britain by Clays Ltd, St Ives plc

Hodder & Stoughton policy is to use papers that are natural,
renewable and recyclable products and made from wood grown
in sustainable forests. The logging and manufacturing processes
are expected to conform to the environmental regulations
of the country of origin.

Hodder & Stoughton Ltd
338 Euston Road
London NW1 3BH
www.hodder.co.uk

To Bini Adams, a real-life BFF

My very first photo call was attended to by two stylists, three assistants and one big-name photographer. They used make-up on the baby acne and Photoshopped further when this concealer failed to hide the imperfections. The results were published to a million coos (or, judging by the comments that I've since read on some archived websites, a fair few 'shit, that is one ugly baby for such a hottie mom').

That's not including an even earlier public appearance from the womb. Cally was snapped coming out of the obstetrician's clutching a picture of a baby scan in her hand, which was duly blown up and examined as evidence of her pregnancy. Taking photos of babies isn't enough: you've got to get the foetus too.

Later, I am pictured with my signature frappé, while a tantrum in the park is captured frame by frame and outfits are dissected with labels as to where to 'get the look'. I am carried, never pushed in a buggy like civilian children, across endless airport arrivals areas where my parents have no apparent luggage. I wear sunglasses and a hat. I am a newborn, a one-year-old, then two, three and four. I am already more famous than you'll ever be.

At five, I am still displayed doing ordinary things as if they were extraordinary, except now my face is blurred, as if someone has taken a thumb to the photos and smudged hard. I am a little well-dressed body with well-brushed hair, but no facial features. The bottom half is aspiration; the top is as if my picture is illustrating a news item about international child trafficking.

By six my face had become unblurred once more, but my expression remains unreadable.

I'm sure you've all looked at photos of famous fathers whooshing their children around in the playgrounds of expensive areas of London, New York or Los Angeles. It all looks so sweet and wholesome. Now imagine the camera swinging 180-degrees away from the cutie kid and hands-on dad to capture the ranks of small-faced men with big cameras who are snapping away like zoo visitors at the lion enclosure. Don't think it's just one of them; they travel in packs. Not so wholesome then, is it? It's a man with his child in a public place with a lot of other men thrusting hardware at them, shouting 'Antigone, oi, Ant, Ant, over here', and promising sweets, which they never give, especially since they know my mother's view on how sugar is 'white crack' (isn't crack white too? I wouldn't know, maybe it's brown like unrefined sugar. Not that I was allowed much of that either).

I've got so many sources to draw on. I call myself a historian because I'm majoring in history (first year Grade Point Average 3.92 – despite being the youngest by some margin – nothing less than an A- on any of my assignments, generally acknowledged to be the only summa-cum-laude dead cert). I liked the paucity of evidence for ancient history, but now that I'm investigating my own life, I find I have too much documentation. My name was trending and hash-tagged before I was even old enough to speak, let alone type. There were accounts in the name of my cashmere tights, the frappés regularly snapped in my hand, the full head of hair that I sported at birth. There are whole sites devoted to me and my play-date companions, imagining who I will marry in the future, like some modern-day dynastic unions, as if I am the infanta and those little boys with their styled hair and fashion jeans are the dauphins.

I would be able to research myself thoroughly if the quality of the material were better. I am a snob, I know, but a well-educated one. Cally makes much of having graduated from the university of life, but she was at great pains to ensure that I attended a more bona-fide establishment, as my father had done before me.

I look so sweet in those early photos, so lacking in self-consciousness. But now when I load them, I can see the irritation flashing across his face and the way that Cally has her head pushed out with her chin down as she later taught me I should do when the cameras were on. Even when carrying me through airport security or out shopping, she has contrived to always be standing with one leg in front of the other, and her body in a three-quarters profile, so that a quarter of her disappears. She is a big name trapped in a tiny body; she wants to both appear and disappear.

There is a real art to ignoring photographers. Most people, I'd guess, can't help but reflexively look towards the flashlight or cover their face with their hands or push out their hands to block the lens or make some goofy face. My parents steer a path between the two. She has mastered the art of looking nonchalant, as if the cameras are not there, but at the same time still seem like a nice person. She has to receive the attention yet never seem to revel in it. Only D-listers smile back or wave. Only bad-boy stars scowl or hit the man carrying the camera.

At about eight or nine, that sweet indifference to cameras melts and I bury my face in my dad's chest or pull my hat down over it. There's that moment for children, isn't there, when, instead of being unaware of what others might think about them (or if they are aware, it is safe in the knowledge that they are adored), all children become acutely self-conscious. Teens are known for being paranoid that everyone's looking at them. But I know everyone is looking at me. Just by meeting someone, by existing in the same air as them, I become central to an anecdote that they will tell and retell. My everyday is their once-in-a-lifetime, their oft-repeated, 'I saw that Antigone once, in the children's department – she's not at all pretty in real life.' I know because I used to hear them start forming the anecdote while I was still there as though I were deaf. It's as though I've got two heads but no ears.

I should start at the beginning. I expect you think you know it all anyway. That I was born in a beautiful water birth in London's finest low-tech private hospital, that

Cally took no drugs to ease the pain because all the yoga really helped her to breathe me out. That I was breastfed because it's what god intended breasts to be for. Although I was a healthy birth weight, her body sprang back into shape a mere three weeks later, which she attributed, laughingly, to some good control underwear and being so busy running after a newborn. Because we all know, don't we, how much those pesky newborns run?

That birth didn't happen. Conception didn't happen, or at least not the conception that you might imagine, all linen sheets and candlelight, befitting one of the world's most photographed couples. As for the breast-feeding, you should realise that you've probably seen her breasts in as much detail as I have, what with those risqué early works she did in an attempt to throw off her child star past. (She's mortified by those movies, by the way – not because of the sex scenes, but because she's, in her words, 'so fat, I'd kill myself if I ever get that fat again'. To put that remark in context, I haven't weighed as little as that since I was 12.)

I want to start at the beginning, or even before then, but I find I can't stop thinking about the spring and summer when I was eight. That's when everything changed.

I

A Most Accomplished Young Lady

There's an old joke that goes: what do you say to a Classics graduate (or History or Literature or Media Studies, delete as appropriate)? Big Mac and fries please.

It's wrong, Anna had discovered, because what you actually say, to this one at least, is absolutely nothing. You do your very best to avoid her eyes, you swerve to give her a three-metre berth; at most you might mutter 'sorry'.

'Excuse me,' Anna shouted to a woman pushing a buggy, although she knew from experience that they were the most unlikely to stop. She did at least look at her and then nod towards her baby as if the very act of being a mother was an outstanding act of charity in itself.

'Can you spare a minute to hear about cancer support?' she said to a young man who ignored her. The blankers, they agreed, were the worst. Anna was wearing a fluorescent high-vis tabard and yet was seemingly invisible.

Her head filled with the humiliating stories she'd collected in her six months as a street charity fundraiser. There was the woman who ran over her foot with her mobility scooter. Anna wouldn't have minded, she was very sympathetic to the needs of people with disabilities,

6

after all, but the driver told her to 'move her fat arse' as she sped past. Again, Anna would have tolerated this, were it not that it was shouted to her by a person who must have weighed over 30 stone.

Then there was also the elderly man who'd stopped to listen politely, seemingly on the verge of making a monthly debit payment, before groping her as she bent down to pick up the paperwork. Or the boy who'd signed up to donate with the name 'Mr Richard Head' of Flat 2P Enis House.

She turned to the next pedestrian.

'Excuse me, but I'd like to tell you—'

The woman didn't even look at her, but said loudly in a well-bred voice, 'fucking chuggers'. Anna's eyes welled up. We're wrong, she thought: blankers aren't the worst, after all. She tried to shake off how hurt she was, to bank it up as anecdote to share with the others, her fellow charity collectors forming what they dubbed the 'gauntlet of guilt' down the high street of Anna's small town, a place slap-bang in the middle of England, both in geography and attitudes. Its only claim to fame was that Elizabeth Taylor and Richard Burton had once planned to stay the night in the hotel on the market place. In the end, they'd just stopped for a cup of tea.

'Can you spare a minute to hear about cancer support?' she said quietly to the next pedestrian, continuing to read from her script.

The mistake Anna made was in thinking accomplishments mattered. She wished she had been born into a Jane Austen novel where her many ancient and modern languages, artistic pursuits, academic excellence and musical ability would properly be appreciated.

Her position as first clarinet in the local youth orchestra didn't impress the Job Centre, nor her position as Goal Attack in the netball team and her progression through to the semi-finals of the county under-14s tennis tournament. Her most impressive attribute, both the Job Centre and the temping agencies agreed, was her typing speed, though these days everybody could type that well. Some people, she was told, could do 70 words a minute on their phones. Anna didn't think that one of those ferociously well-educated women of history, your Ada Lovelace or your Lady Jane Grey, were praised for their ability to text, like, really fast.

At school she'd dreamt of university, where her life would finally begin. She read biographies of women writers, where they'd describe being feted by fey young men and debating the intellectual questions of the day. But on arriving at Oxford, she found that there were no pretty boys to punt her down the Cherwell while reciting *The Waste Land*. Her fellow students were either too busy washing down their legal highs with alcopops, or were treating their degree as an extended job interview, collecting internships and CV points like a scout covering his shirt in badges.

OK, so Oxford had disappointed, but the hopeful, hungry women of those 20th-century novels she had read then moved to London, where they were pushed up against Agas by hairy married men wearing hairy fisherman's jumpers. But, on graduating, she'd fallen down a rabbit-hole into a world where everything she'd once believed had been turned on its head. She was now 'too clever' to get a job.

The only friends with employment were the ones who had an uncle in Parliament or parents they could live with in London, the ones who'd always intimidated her with their confidence and connections. It didn't matter that they hadn't edited the college newspaper, since their stepfather edited a national one. It didn't matter that they'd once camped in tatty tents outside evil corporations demanding that they pay fair taxes, when there was a nice opening in banking that their uncle eased them into, which they were only going to do, they vowed, until they'd made enough money to give it up and write a book about the venality of the financial world.

'Nobody cares about fancy degrees,' her old friend from college, Toby, said to her over the phone, 'except for the parents who want to pay me to tutor their children to get into academically tip-top schools so that they can get into the best universities and then find themselves unemployable except to be paid to get others to do what they've done.'

'Great, so going to Oxford has merely qualified me to teach other people to get into Oxford who will then only be useful in teaching other kids to go to Oxford?' Anna said.

'Pretty much. But it's not just Oxford, there's Cambridge too.' He was so cheerful it was as though he was whistling as he spoke. But then, what wasn't there to be happy about? Since graduating two years before Anna, the tutoring agency he'd founded in London, Brideshead Revision, was flourishing. He charged the sort of hourly rates for his stable of pretty and well-educated graduates that were normally associated with the most mercenary of lawyers. Super-tutors, they were dubbed, and Toby was getting 30 per cent of every super-pound his tutors were earning through his pitch-perfect marketing. He had every reason to be super-happy.

'I still don't understand, how come you don't need a proper teaching qualification to do it?' she asked him.

'What, some certificate in education from a crappy college in Luton? Nah, all the parents care about is the old Oxon and Cantab at the end of your name, darling. I promise I can get you enough work for you to live off in London, while you save for your doctorate or poncy job. Yesterday, I had some parents wanting someone fluent in Latin to help their four-year-old get into the right pre-prep.'

'I am not "fluent" in Latin, as you put it, and I don't want to be a tutor.' Anna was holding out for a proper job in publishing (she liked books), a museum (she often visited them) or charity (she was a nice person). In the nine months since graduating she'd managed two fortnight-long stints in London doing unpaid 'internships' – one at a magazine, inputting subscription information, and the other at a charity that – and the irony was not lost on her – campaigned against modern slavery.

'But darling,' said Toby, 'you don't need to do it forever, just for a few months, a year, tops, and then only for a few hours a day. How much money are you making with your chugging?'

'My charitable work, you mean. Enough.'

'Just think about it,' said Toby, like a well-spoken drug dealer offering a first hit of heroin.

Anna found herself browsing through the Brideshead Revision website that evening. 'First-class minds for first-class children', it announced. She opened the 'Who We Are' page and examined the gallery of faces and names that it revealed. Every girl in the arty black-and-white photos was long haired and had a name ending in 'a'. It felt like a posh escort agency. 'Allegra's speciality is Common Entrance' it read, and her flirty, flicky-fringed look to camera made it sound as though that was a euphemism for some filthy sex act. Common entrance my arse, thought Anna, and giggled out loud.

Yes, Anna's mistake was to think that accomplishments mattered, so that when Toby emailed her the one job advertisement that actually seemed to think that all her achievements were just that, achievements, it piqued her interest. If only the ad had asked for a bit less, she'd never have been tempted to offer so much.

'High-profile couple seek Oxbridge/Ivy League graduate or postgraduate (first/summa cum laude),' the advertisement read, 'with knowledge of Latin, Greek, plus one or two modern languages; ability to sketch; musical aptitude (preferably piano and violin); understanding of modern maths teaching; proficiency at tennis and further sports. The successful applicant will be given their own accommodation, be expected to supervise homework and create valuable extension exercises for three hours a day (and up to eight in the holidays and some weekends) and be as entertaining as they are educative. Facility with children a bonus.'

Toby's office was small but with a perfectly formed address in Knightsbridge. 'My Russian clients love that,' he explained. He was giving her a last-minute pep talk before she went to her interview for that most super of super-tutor positions. 'Promise me you'll be nice,' he implored, desperate for his commission. 'Remember, you could be earning a huge wodge with all accommodation paid for, a bit of foreign travel, a lot of glamour – and all you have to do is the whole *Amo Amas Amat* thing for a couple of hours a day and paint a picture.'

'But if it really is as little as you say it is, a bit of reading and painting with a dollop of Latin, why can't the parents do it themselves?' Anna asked. She thought back to her mother dragging her round museums and the little projects she'd set her every holidays.

'Oh Anna, you really have no idea.' He sighed with all the world-weary wisdom he'd acquired in the extra two years he'd had since graduation. 'Rich people subcontract out everything, and there's no area that's more open to subcontracting than parenting. There are people that potty-train your child, people who'll make up a perfect balance of first solid foods and others who'll teach them to ride a bicycle. If you're giving your child fish oils and sending them to an expensive school, why will you leave to chance the casual intellectual stimulation that a clever parent would give them if they had the time? You don't want the kids of that bitch stay-at-home mother with the PhD getting ahead, so you subcontract out the reading and the numeracy too, because the nanny, bless her, is sweet with children but dots her Is with a smiley face and puts an apostrophe S in potatoes. And then your neighbour with the PhD finds out about the tutor you're using and she calls me up and then the first one hears so she gets a maths tutor as well as the English one, and so and so on.'

'Like an arms race?'

'Exactly,' said Toby with satisfaction. 'And you're my Trident missile.'

'Can I go now?' said Anna.

'A couple more things,' he said. 'Remember: no one's child is average. They're never badly behaved either – no, the reason they set fire to the school is because they're very bright and not being sufficiently challenged.'

'OK, OK,' said Anna.

'And rich people have this weird attitude towards their employees. They either like to boast about their butler and get him to bring them a banana on a silver platter. Or they like to pretend that they don't have servants at all; that these people scrubbing the floor are just friends who are helping out. Try to work out which sort this lot are and behave accordingly. Now get out there and get me my commission.' With these words, he gave her a patronising pat on the bottom.

The receptionist of the smart London hotel around the corner from Toby's office ushered Anna to the corner of the foyer. There, a woman was pouring herself a cup of tea from a china pot. She stood up on seeing her and put out her hand.

'Anna? I'm so pleased to meet you.'

Anna now realised what people meant when they described others as polished – everything about this woman looked as though someone had taken a buffing cloth to her and rubbed efficiently. Her hair was shoulder length and shiny; it seemed to rise from her forehead as if lifted by invisible butterflies, while Anna's merely grew. The nails of the proffered hand were varnished the sort of neutral greyish shade that smart people painted their hallways. Her skin shone as if she lived on a permanent holiday, the Caribbean in winter, the Med in summer.

Anna looked at her own dress, which had once been black, but now was that just-off shade that suggests a bad washing machine. Looks weren't important, obviously, but she wished she too had an aubergine-coloured shift with a quirky cut that denoted both personality and professionalism.

She put out her hand quickly, hoping that her own bitten nails would go unnoticed. 'Yes, Anna Thomas. From Brideshead Revision.'

'Janey,' the paragon said, as if that were enough to identify her. The ad had said that the parents were high profile, and Anna felt that perhaps this woman did look familiar, while at the same time very unfamiliar to her world of chugging and pubbing and dreaming about an entry-level office job in arts administration. 'Thank you so much for coming.'

'A pleasure,' said Anna, and something about the woman's graciousness made her think that it was in fact a privilege.

'So, I expect you'd like to hear more about the job? I hope you understand that I obviously won't be able to name the child,' said Janey. 'But she is a girl and she's eight. She is at what is considered to be one of the best preparatory schools in the capital, nay the country, but it has been found to be insufficiently classical or rigorous in its approach to education. There seems to be a lot of learning through play – you know, foam letters and funny little experiments.' She laughed. 'And she is not a child for whom this approach is necessarily optimal. It's all very sweet, but it is thought that she would benefit from a sound knowledge of the ancient languages. As a highly intelligent child, she'd find this fun. She's G and T.'

Gin and Tonic? thought Anna.

'Gifted and Talented,' Janey clarified. 'It is thought that the school is not stretching her sufficiently.'

Anna conjured up an image of a child in expensive clothes being laid out on a medieval torture rack, with her winding the wheels as the child was lengthened, screaming all the while. 'Yes, absolutely. Stretching. Yes. So important.'

'But at the same time, the successful applicant will not merely be strong in the academics and the classics. No, it's not all about work. They should also be able to oversee her piano practice and set interesting art projects. It is also thought that she would benefit from a healthy role model with regards to sporting achievement and outdoor pursuits.' She looked down at her notes. 'I believe that you excel at tennis.'

'I play it. I'm quite good.' Someone as competitive as Anna should never go for interviews for jobs she didn't want. 'I was in the college team at Oxford.'

'And you've a double first and you play the piano, but not the violin . . .'

'I know the basics, plus I play the clarinet.'

Janey continued looking at her CV, which had been Toby-fied with hyperbole. 'I believe you've also had an exhibition of your paintings?'

In a pub. Back home. Anna shrugged, faux-modestly.

'I must say you are one of the most impressive candidates we've come across.'

Janey had a perfect smile. Looking at those white teeth was like staring at the sun which, combined with the praise, made Anna glow red. She could do nothing but grin back, while attempting to hide her own less than dazzling teeth. She'd rather forgotten her stroppiness at being talked into this by Toby, but was enjoying the luxurious civility of a cake-stand laden with cucumber sandwiches and a beautiful woman asking her about her tennis levels and the details of her finals.

'I think my employers will be impressed too.'

Anna frowned in confusion. 'Sorry?'

'Her parents. The child's parents,' Janey said.

'But I thought . . . I thought that . . . I'm a little confused as to your position.'

'I'm the clients' administrator, right-hand woman, girl Friday, whatever you want to call it.'

The phone that was lying on the table between them rung. Anna saw the initial C flash up on the screen. 'Excuse me,' said Janey, picking it up. 'Hello, darling.' Her face creased in exaggerated sympathy. 'Poor you, what a nightmare.' She glanced down at her watch. 'It's four a.m. at the moment, but I can't see why they wouldn't be answering, it's supposed to be twenty-four hour. Give me five and I'll sort it out for you.'

She stood up and moved away from Anna, scrolling through her contacts to make a call. 'Yes, yes,' she was saying in a brittle tone very different from the one she'd employed to the last caller, 'but why wasn't the call dealt with immediately? It's not what we expect and I'm sure it wouldn't happen at the Wilshire. Yes, no yolks, obviously, and with chives. Two with varying degrees of doneness so she's got a choice. Goodbye.' She made another call and her voice became warm again. 'Done. It will be with you shortly. Any time. You too.'

She sat down again with a look of satisfaction. 'Sorry, we were saying . . .'

'That you think that the parents might be impressed with – you know – me.'

'Indeed. I'll be in touch with the agency to arrange a further meeting.'

Being from the countryside, Anna could never quite get over her prejudice that houses that were attached to other houses weren't for rich people, even if they were in Belgravia or Hampstead. Or indeed, St John's Wood, which is where she now stood, outside the address of her putative employers on a crescent-shaped road called Lorston Gardens. The house was a stucco-fronted, white-columned building forming the end of a terrace, set back from the road by a carriage driveway and fronted by a high glass wall with a gate. As she said her name into the intercom, the gate slowly opened and she walked in, feeling the cameras that balanced around the property fixed upon her. A stout woman in a tracksuit came to meet her.

'I'm Martina,' she said in an accented voice. 'I take you to Janey.'

Anna was ushered into a black-and-white tiled hall with a sweeping staircase. You couldn't look at such a cantilevered structure without imagining yourself coming down to the ball with everyone gasping at you in admiration. The hallway had a confusion of doors leading off it and she realised that her sense of it being modest in comparison to the stout suburban houses she was used to was wrong. This house was as large within as any country pile.

Janey bustled in with that walking-and-talking efficiency of a high-powered lawyer in a TV programme, swapping papers as she did so with a woman who had also nailed that chic grown-up look in tailored trousers and a silk T-shirt. 'Hello again,' said Janey. 'Anna, this is Priya. She's just going. She's my right-hand woman.'

The right-hand woman's right-hand woman, thought Anna. This is all getting confusing.

'All right,' said Priya to Anna in a voice that was pure East End in contrast to her West End appearance. Anna realised that she was as young or even younger than she was, despite her sophisticated air. She felt herself blush at her own clothes.

'So,' said Janey. 'Would you like a quick tour? And then we can find Antigone for a little play.'

Anna nodded. Antigone, Antigone, why did the name ring a bell, beyond the classical reference to the daughter of Oedipus and Jocasta's inadvertently incestuous union? And what sort of people would call their daughter Antigone?

'We've two kitchens,' said Janey. 'This is the one that the family hangs out in. Antigone's mum just loves to spend time whizzing up cakes and juices with her daughter.' Anna stared at the chrome-covered island surrounded by pale green open shelves across the room's vast walls. Actually, island was too small a word for it: it was a kitchen continent. To the side was an area of sofas slumped elegantly like tipsy aristocrats, flanked by large glass doors that led out to the almost synthetic green of the lawns of the vast garden beyond. 'Through there is the kitchen used by staff when there is more large-scale catering to be done,' said Janey, pointing to a room beyond open double doors. Anna could see an industrial-sized cooker and fridge, alongside what she knew from her watching of TV cooking shows to be a prepping area. 'Beyond that is the utility room. You've met Martina.'

'Yes, but I'm not quite sure . . . ?'

'She's the housekeeper. And you'll also meet Beatriz, who works with Martina, with special responsibility for Antigone.'

'Her nanny?'

'We don't use the word "nanny" here. Bea's been here since Antigone was born, more or less, and they get on very well, but she's not a nanny as such.' She pronounced the name with full Hispanic flourish, *Bay-a*. 'My employer manages to maintain her very busy career and look after Antigone herself without the use of a nanny. No, Bea is here to help Antigone reach fluency in Spanish. My employer doesn't feel comfortable leaving her own child's upbringing in the hands of somebody else. It's remarkable how she fits it all in. You'll realise that when you discover who she is.' A pause as Janey looked her up and down. 'If it comes to that.'

Anna felt stung by the warning. Clearly the job was not yet hers.

'The successful applicant will live in self-contained accommodation above the garage to the right as you came in,' continued Janey. 'The other members of staff live in their quarters.'

'And you?'

'I have a separate flat nearby. I expect you'd like to see the rest of the downstairs.'

'And meet Antigone,' said Anna.

'Of course.' Janey crossed the hallway towards some large double doors that opened out into a room where everything seemed to have been stretched upwards. It was high ceilinged, with tall, rigid-backed sofas that faced each other in perfect symmetry, as if about to begin a formal dance. 'The living room,' said Janey, with an almost audible 'ta-da'.

Anna felt that she was expected to gasp, so she tried to do so, though the sound was more of a squeal. She couldn't respond to the room as if it were in somebody's home, because it looked far more like the communal areas of the sort of hotel she couldn't afford to visit, right to the unopened glossy magazines and art books that were piled neatly on the coffee table. For a living room, it was remarkably unlived in.

'I know,' said Janey, looking at Anna's feigned appreciation, her cool presence at last warmed up by pride. 'I think of interior decoration as an art form and this room as one of its masterpieces. Shall we go through to the playroom?'

Anna would have guessed the playroom would be near the place that Janey had called the family kitchen (as opposed to the kitchen kitchen, where the actual work seemed to take place), but they went down a long corridor and down some stairs to a basement that seemed conjured up out of nowhere, before entering a large, low-ceilinged room with windows out onto an internal patio.

Another member of staff was sitting at a miniature desk as a girl painted with a whole spectrum of colours and brushes from a large case of oils. The woman glanced at them with a shy smile, while the child carried on painting. Janey cleared her throat, but still the child ignored her, as if entirely absorbed in her task.

'Antigone, I'd like you to meet Anna. And that's Bea,' she added, pointing at the woman.

The girl eventually looked up without surprise or curiosity. Toby had thought that the parents might work in cinema and it would be appropriate if she did come from movie-making stock, since she looked like every creepy horror-film child, viewing them with the pale-eyed stare of a Midwich Cuckoo and the knowing superiority of the boy from *The Omen*.

Anna panicked. She'd never been good with children, not even when she'd been a child herself.

'I like your picture,' she opened.

'Thank you,' said Antigone.

'What it is it?'

'You're not supposed to ask that.'

'Sorry, what do you mean?' Anna felt herself blush. She was being made to feel an idiot by an eight year old, which was a new low, even by her own standards of easily being made to feel foolish.

'You're not meant to ask children what their picture is supposed to be. You should say "tell me about it", as an open statement. It's rude to say that you don't know what the picture is, as that sounds like it's not very good,' the girl said.

'Not very figurative, perhaps,' said Anna, before wondering if she was using inappropriately adult vocabulary. But Antigone's face was turned to her expectantly and with no hint of incomprehension, so she continued. 'But what if it's an abstract that needs some title for it to be evident?'

'Like a Rothko?' said the girl. 'He's my favourite artist actually. Have you seen his rooms at the Tate Modern?'

'I have. And your drawing reminds me of his work. You need some explanation to enjoy the Rothkos, don't you?'

'*I* don't,' she said, staring hard at Anna. 'They speak to me directly. Daddy takes me there. Sometimes we go when there's nobody else there because he knows the director of the gallery. Do you know him too? It's much easier to look at paintings without anybody getting in the way.'

'Antigone,' interrupted Janey. 'Have you shown Anna your lovely new shoes?'

Antigone frowned. 'I did not choose my shoes.'

'You're a poet and you don't know it,' rhymed Anna, in an attempt at playfulness.

Antigone frowned. 'But I do know it. Would you like to see some of my poems? Mummy had them bound in leather. I wrote them last year, so they're a bit babyish.'

'I'd love to. Shall we sit down?'

Anna sat beside Antigone on one of the three sofas in the playroom.

'This one's good,' said Anna, pointing to one of the pages. '"The leaves say goodbye to the tree. He leaves and says goodbye to me". It reminds me of Gerard Manley Hopkins – do you know his work? "Margaret are you grieving/Over Goldengrove unleaving?" Is it about someone you know?'

Antigone frowned. 'I prefer this one.' She flipped over the pages to find a poem about the solar system, which imbued each planet with a personality based on their size and attributes.

'Venus thinks a lot of herself, doesn't she? I like the idea of planets being like people. Do you think numbers have different characters too?' asked Anna. 'I like odd numbers and have always thought that even numbers are smug. Especially the number twelve.'

'Because it's a product of two, three, four and six? Some people might think that makes it admirable, but I agree it makes it a bit annoying. I think prime numbers are naughty but clever too. Seventy-three is my favourite double-digit one because it's the highest one that's made up of two single-digit prime numbers. My day is always good when I see the number seventy-three bus.'

'Have you been on the number seventy-three?' asked Anna, remembering the thrill of sitting on the top deck on visits to London as a child.

'Oh no,' said Antigone. 'I've never been allowed.'

'Perhaps we could go on it together one day?'

Antigone's face lit up and morphed from weird to weirdly beautiful. 'I'd *love* to do that. We could go all the way from Stoke Newington to Victoria. And back again. That would be amazing.' She turned to look at Janey, who shook her head as if she'd asked to bicycle the wrong way up a motorway. Her shoulders slumped.

'What other numbers do you like?' asked Anna. 'I don't think about them as much as I used to. The longest one I know is my phone number.'

'What is it?' said Antigone, apparently over her disappointment at not being allowed to plan a bus trip.

Anna recited the eleven digits, which Antigone repeated back perfectly. 'Hmm,' she said, 'it ends in ninety-one so it might be a prime number, I suppose.'

'Can you work out primes to a billion?' Anna joked.

'No, of course not.' Antigone looked at her as if she were a very slow child.

'Yup, yup,' said a voice from behind them. It was then that Anna noticed Janey was wearing an earpiece and seemed to be nodding in response to it. 'Sailing,' she said to Anna. 'We'd like to know if you can sail.'

'Yes, of course,' said Anna. She crossed her fingers, since her only proficiency at that moment was in sailing close to the wind. Her maritime experience was limited to a pedalo on holiday in Spain.

Janey nodded again. 'OK, got it. That's enough. We've seen enough.' She turned around. 'Anna, shall we go?'

'OK.' She turned to Antigone and put her hand out towards her. She thought that a formal gesture would suit this most formal of children. Antigone looked at her proffered hand with blank disdain, so Anna moved forward to try to make it more evident what she was doing and reached for Antigone's hand. When she grasped it, the child jumped back as if scorched.

'Don't you dare touch me!' she shouted, backing away from Anna. 'Nobody touches me without permission.'

'I'm so sorry.' Anna knew she'd misjudged it, but wasn't sure quite why, so she twisted her hand up in order to try for a high-five instead. Antigone looked puzzled, so

Anna turned into it a wave, trying hard to look as though that had been her intention all along, but feeling as though her limb was a disobedient ventriloquist's dummy intent on humiliating her.

Janey and Beatriz were staring at her to see what she'd do next. She made a slight bow, as if in a business meeting in a foreign land. Their eyes swivelled to Antigone for the next shot. There was silence and then she did a little bow in return before returning to her desk, whereupon she did not look at either Janey or Anna again.

'Yes that will definitely be all,' said Janey.

I've blown it, Anna thought. 'Am I not going to meet Antigone's parents?'

'They're not in the country. No, they were meeting you, so to speak,' said Janey, glancing at the wall.

Anna had followed her gaze and saw a small embedded security camera. She looked away quickly, as though she was the one who'd been caught staring.

Later she felt failure prickle her skin as she tried to enjoy the soft leather of the car that had been tasked to return her to Toby's office. She hadn't wanted the job anyway, but now that she had so messed up the interview, she found herself strangely disappointed.

'So what did you think of Lady Antigone then?' the driver Dan asked, once he'd finished telling her about how he'd trialled for Arsenal in his youth. He mispronounced the name 'An-tiggy-o-nee'.

'She seemed rather amazing.'

He laughed. 'Is that posh for weird? I think she's got

something wrong with her. That's what we all reckon. You know, one of those kids who's – what's it called – agnostic or something.'

'Autistic you mean? I think she's very bright.' And, thought Anna, I doubt she's agnostic. I suspect she's examined all the evidence and writings and is now as firmly atheist as Richard Dawkins. Or she'll have created her own belief system based on unique theories of evolution.

'Gives me the creeps,' Dan continued.

Anna's eyes flicked around the car interior, looking for cameras, wondering if this was some sort of a test. She looked at his eyes, captured in the driver's mirror, and then quickly turned away as they stared back at her with a dark lack of self-consciousness.

'She's called Antigone, the little girl, and she's rather sweet actually,' said Anna to Toby at her post-interview debrief.

'Of course.' He slapped his forehead and started typing into Google. 'Was this the house you went to?' Anna looked at the screen and nodded. 'And this the girl?'

'Yes, except her face wasn't pixelated when I met her.'

'Her parents are Cally Steward and Sholto Carpenter.'

'No!' Anna was so impressed she didn't bother to try to hide it. Not so much by the mother's name (she was just an actress she'd always thought of as irksome), but the father, yes oh yes. She had gone up to Oxford convinced that she'd be inundated with suitors who

would be like him, the It-boy of his Cambridge genera-
tion, fiercely intelligent and as attractive as any of the
actors he directed first in the theatre and now on film.
'Now I see where she gets her brains from. Let's face
it, it isn't from her mother, with all those stupid
romcoms.'

'And there was me thinking you were aloof from
celebrity culture.'

'I don't consider her to be a celebrity,' she said haugh-
tily, 'but he's a cultural giant.'

'Now you want it.'

Anna blushed.

'The job I mean,' said Toby. 'What did you think I
meant?'

Back home, Anna had another soul-sapping session of
chugging, followed by a particularly poor pub session.
The head chugger, Finlay, had accosted her as she
returned from the toilets and promised her the best
spot for work, outside the organic bakery, in return
for sexual favours. On turning him down, she knew
she'd be consigned to the pavement by the pound shop
for ever.

She sat in her childhood bedroom, thinking about
Sholto Carpenter. He'd never behave like that. Her eyes
began to fill with tears of self-pity at the contrast between
the life that she had briefly glimpsed and the reality of
her own. The narrow IKEA bed she slept on seemed to
sum up the hopelessness of her existence. A man like
Sholto would never pleasure a woman on a bed like this.

She checked her emails.

'Yay!' read the title of the message from Toby. 'You're in there. Be ready to start your job as tutor to the stars by the end of the month.'

Anna lay back on the bed. My life starts now.

I don't remember much from before Anna's arrival, though I've got all those archived sites, tweets and magazines to help me. That's the thing: everything from before then feels as though I can only remember it as an outsider looking in on myself. I look at that little girl and it doesn't feel like me.

I know there were other children and play-dates, endless play-dates; you'd have thought I was the most popular girl in the school. But if I remember those girls and boys, it's as if they weren't real either, as if I were viewing them on a page or a website, just as I now view myself as I try to research my own life. They used to talk to me and screech at me and I'd see their lips moving and I knew what the words meant but could never understand what they were saying.

My memories of looking out from myself, with the camera in my head instead of trained on me, only begin when Anna arrived.

Most people aren't sure if they have early childhood memories or if what they are seeing is merely their mind's recreation of a cherished family photo. Or at least that's what I'm led to believe. I wouldn't know because the two are almost indistinguishable, the real and the digitally captured. I don't know that there is a moment of my life that hasn't been pictured. Sometimes I have odd flashes of things that don't fit the narrative of all that I have read of myself and I suppose they must be the real thing. I can hear somebody shouting or screaming, but I can never quite work out who it is. My body relives a pain. I don't know whether it's a mental or physical one.

I suppose I was an unusual child. There are some children that educationalists describe as 'twice exceptional' or, in the olden-ungolden days, 'gifted-handicapped'. It means that they have extremely high IQs in addition to some other special need, like Asperger's or Sensory Processing Disorder. Two statements for the price of one, if you like.

I feel like that describes me, except my second extraordinary characteristic – the one that's in addition to my huge intellect – is not that I am dyslexic or dyspraxic, it's my parentage and everything that has brought with it – the focus, the attention, the assumptions. I was exceptional without having to do anything about it. It wasn't me that made it so but everyone else; those who were interested in me for who I was rather than for what I had to say (despite what I had to say being generally pretty fascinating for a small child). I really thought it was normal for an adult to sit down to eat with me at every meal rather than fish fingers being doled out along a breakfast bar while the adults got on with washing up pans or checking their emails. I thought everybody got freshly pulped apple juice, despite the fiddly bits to clean from the juicer. I believed it was standard for the faces of passers-by to be obscured by their camera-phones as they lifted them up to snap me and that these strangers should know my name without us being introduced. I assumed that every child was invited to the parties of every other child in their class, even of children in other classes in the school. I believed that most children had play-dates with the other children of those considered A-list (I suppose that makes me a double-A student as well as twice exceptional).

Despite being genetically likely to be both bright and beautiful, it didn't look as if I was going to turn out that way as a baby. At 18 months, as other mothers excitedly swapped their children's words and even sentences, my mother and Bea would have to remain as silent on the subject as I was at all times. At two years old, I was still mute; worse, not even gabbling. I suppose children speak in order to communicate, but what need did I have to transmit? All my desires were met without me having to ask. All the experts disagreed; some blamed Bea for speaking to me in Spanish (despite being expressly mandated to do so), others said I had global delays; others said all children went at different paces and perhaps I was just a little slow.

Bea was there one day, the next she was gone. Nobody told me why. I suppose they thought that since I couldn't speak, I couldn't understand either. And that's my only true memory of those years – utter misery and confusion at her not being there. I remember hitting myself with my favourite cuddly toy, Blue Bear, to supply new pain to distract me.

That's when they got me my first mentor, an educated woman who looked after me every afternoon – speaking, singing, reading at all times, like a demented radio that I couldn't switch off. At last, I had something that I needed to communicate. 'Stop,' I said, soon after followed by, 'I want Bay-a', as my first sentence.

And just like that Bea was back. Her going was not spoken of and nor was her return. In the evenings, when my parents were away, I'd sneak out of my bed and snuggle up to her as she watched the DVDs of telenovelas sent over from home. She used to watch them with the subtitles on in an effort to improve her English.

I suppose it must have been then that I taught myself to read. That's what Bea and Janey guessed, but never told their bosses for fear of them being angry that I'd been up late watching inappropriate Latin American sagas of love, larceny and incest. Certainly, when I spoke, it became clear that I had not only speech (English and Spanish), but the power to read, having realised that the words on the screen meant something and that this meaning was connected to the shouting actors. '*¡Ay dios mio!*' I used to exclaim. '*¡Puta madre!*'

Cally and Sholto were thrilled that it turned out they had a genius child, just as they had hoped. Then the paediatrician said that it wasn't me being clever, necessarily, but was a possible sign of hyperlexia (symptoms include: late speaking, early reading obsession with numbers and letters, which is frequently – though not exclusively – associated with an autistic spectrum disorder). They watched nervously how I traced letters in the bubbles of my bath and memorised licence plates of cars in the street. I was only three and it seemed as though I was racing through the paediatric diagnoses as fast as I could read them.

The experts prescribed lots of playing with other children, who were easily procured, where I would trot out some pre-rehearsed speeches that I'd done in role play with my ed psych. 'Hello,' I'd say. 'My name is Antigone. Do you like Lego?' Then Myrna and Ryder and Cressy would go off and play with each other and leave me alone.

2

Nobody's Looking At You, Dear

'You've met Martina and Bea,' said Janey, as she ushered Anna into the house at Lorston Gardens that was to be both her home and her place of work. 'And Dan, you know, who drove you the other day. Anything to do with the cars or security, he's your man.'

'Security?' Such an odd word, thought Anna, both comforting and terrifying at the same time. Nice when attached to blankets, not so with homeland or airports.

'Yes, though we call in an external agency for big events and when there are particular issues that need addressing. And outside, you can see Wadim, he does the garden – well, the maintenance, not the planting or planning – as well as fixing anything that breaks or needs doing around the house.' Anna looked through the expanse of glass to see a muscular figure, wearing overalls rolled down to the waist with nothing underneath, as if straight from a casting for a handyman in a retro porn film. He was talking to the young girl she'd met when she'd been interviewed. Janey followed her gaze. 'You've met Priya, haven't you? The one talking to Wadim. She only works here part time, helping me with admin and accounts, so you won't see much of her.' This was a shame, thought

Anna, since she had marked her down as a possible Work Friend. 'What else? You've seen your kitchenette. I don't see why you'd need to prepare any food in either of the kitchens here.' Janey smoothed her own stomach, flat beneath the fitted dress she wore. 'If you need a snack, then I'm sure Martina can get you something. Do help yourself to drinks. That's everyone, I think.'

It evidently was not, thought Anna, as she surveyed the scene around her. There were others bustling whose job descriptions were not revealed to her. 'Is it usually so busy at weekends?' she asked. Women carried flowers or clothes, men heavy bits of furniture. They swooped around each other as if choreographed by Janey in a complicated hallway waltz. Anna yearned to retreat to her eyrie over the garage, with its spacious bedroom, en-suite bathroom and corridor with kettle, small fridge and two-ringed cooker.

'No, it's normally calmer,' said Janey. 'It's because they are back on Monday.' The word 'they' seemed both capitalised and italicised for emphasis.

'And normally I won't be expected to teach . . .' Janey raised an eyebrow. 'I mean, play with Antigone in an educative way at weekends?'

Janey frowned. 'Flexibility is all, Anna, flexibility is all, especially given what you are being paid.'

'Of course, sorry.' Anna looked at the walls to see if her misdemeanour had been captured on camera.

On Monday, she was to venture out with Antigone for the school run or, more accurately, the school gentle stroll with child on a scooter ('obviously, you will be very vigilant when approaching roads, won't you?'). Dan was to accompany them for the first fortnight, she was told. Anna didn't know if this was as some sort of bodyguard or whether it was because she couldn't be trusted with applying the Green Cross Code at busy junctions.

'The walk will take you about fifteen minutes,' said Janey, 'so leave plenty of time. Bea will make sure Antigone is ready, but from now on you will be in charge of her school bag and its contents. Update the central calendar as to any additional homework to be completed, or extracurricular activities. Dan can drive you when it's raining, but generally . . .' She looked at Antigone and said in a voice that wasn't quite quiet enough, 'The exercise will do her good. Cally has asked that this happen unless there are compelling reasons not to. Healthy attitudes to food and exercise are very important to her, so of course you will refrain from eating junk food in front of Antigone, though you are permitted fruit or nuts. Of course, as you're probably aware, Cally makes every effort to do the administration associated with school attendance herself as a hands-on mother, but you will still make sure that Antigone's bag is packed and any permission forms from school have been completed even when she's here. That way, all that will be required of Cally is to actually take her daughter to school. Which, as I say, she does most days, though with the development of her new skincare launch coming up, this may be somewhat compromised in the forthcoming months. Nonetheless, she and Sholto make sure to synchronise their schedules so that Antigone has plenty of time with one or other.'

'Of course.'

'And, even if you go in the car, it is important that Antigone's mind is warmed up in preparation for school and she is fully stimulated.'

Stimulated? It made Anna think of coffee and sex, of drugs and violent computer games. 'I thought I'd play this game where you have to swap times-tables as you walk, and if you miss one you have to start hopping, then skipping and other forfeits.'

'I shall let Dan know. And here she is.'

Antigone was putting on a pair of gloves with the precision of a surgeon, despite it being mild outside.

'Hello,' said Anna, with the breezy tones she was trying to copy from children's television presenters. Everything needed an 'isn't this fun?' subtitle. It wasn't so much that Antigone ignored her, but that she didn't seem to hear the words. She had a trance-like expression.

'Shall we be off then?' she said, louder this time, standing nearer but careful not to touch her.

Antigone looked at her with an expression somewhere between blankness and surprise and shrugged. They walked towards the front gate; as Anna keyed in the exit code, she heard the sound of feet and male voices. As they emerged, she heard a voice say, 'There's Ant,' and two men with cameras across the road began to snap, then put down their cameras with disappointment. Anna looked around herself with an exaggerated 'who me?' gesture and then down at Antigone.

'Oh don't mind them. Are they are annoying you? I try not to notice them any more.'

As Anna took a closer look, she realised that they were not so much men as boys, pasty-faced ones who looked as if they lived off a diet of crisps and orange fizzy drinks, a fact that was corroborated by the pile of rubbish collecting at their feet. They both wore hoodies and their faces were partially obscured by scarves, so that they looked exactly like rioting youths, bar the heavy cameras that they held in their hands in place of bricks. These had concentric black and white circles of long lenses on them, so that they resembled the snout of some exotic aardvark.

'They'll be very angry that you're nobody,' Antigone continued.

'Why, thanks.'

'I expect they'll be here a lot more when Mummy gets back. Just make sure you aren't photographed with Daddy, or there will be a photo of you in the newspaper.'

'What, with the caption "Sholto Carpenter with mystery blonde"?'

Antigone frowned. 'I suppose so. Why would you be in the paper anyway? You're not famous, are you? And your hair isn't really blonde, is it? Not like mine.'

'No, I'm not blonde. Or famous.' But, she thought, I'm beginning to get a sense of what it might be like if I were. 'And I wouldn't want to be famous either.' No, she wouldn't, she really wouldn't, despite the thud of rejection in her stomach.

'I am,' said Antigone, all matter of fact. 'Everyone

knows my name. People are always staring at me and shouting it out. Sometimes they use bad words if I don't look at their phones. You know, like "cunt".'

At the school gates, Anna felt her nervousness increase still further. Janey had told her to follow Antigone to the classroom's line and introduce herself to the teacher and two teaching assistants.

Every adult head in the urban playground swivelled towards them. She didn't know what was more unnerving: the eyes upon them or the impassivity of Antigone's reaction. They were mostly women, and they either stared intently to catch Anna's eye or looked away immediately to appear as if ignoring her. Anna kept on smiling. She repeated her mother's mantra, always said when she'd been consumed by nerves at a party: 'Nobody's looking at *you*, dear.' But they were, they were.

'You must be the new nanny,' said a good-looking woman in a suit. 'Where's Bea got to?'

'I'm a good friend who's helping the family,' she said as drilled. 'I love hanging out with Antigone.'

'Will you be organising her play-dates for this term? I work but I can take time off when Antigone's available.'

According to the schedule of Latin, Greek, physical exercise, music practice and improving museum visits that had been suggested to her, Anna wasn't sure when these so-called play-dates were to take place. She wondered whether they were like real dates, awkward and inter-rogatory, with a feeling of triumph or despair at the end.

It had been a while since she'd had one of those, good or bad: the dating pool back in her home town was pretty limited. She smiled and shrugged at the woman.

'Well, I do hope Antigone can make it to Ilsa's party. With Cally, of course. We're friends too. I'm Rebecca, by the way, do tell Cally that you saw me.'

'This way,' said Antigone, pointing her in the direction of a line of pupils who were as striking in their ignoring of the girl as their parents were in paying her attention. The boys jostled each other in the line, while the girls touched each other's hair and compared the glittery key rings that hung from their bags. But Antigone stood straight-backed, talking to no one, looking neither happy nor unhappy about the fact.

Anna spent the hours that Antigone was at school feeling as though she was frozen like the courtiers in *Sleeping Beauty*, waiting for the princess to wake up. She worked on preparing some educational activities and tried to get the hang of the local geography. The streets around the house were quiet save for the arrival and departure of the vans belonging to the dog walkers, gardeners and cleaners that serviced the neighbourhood. She was relieved when it came to the time to pick up Antigone from school, at last given some purpose.

When she and Antigone got back, the activity at the house was now frenetic, with a side order of panic. Anna didn't dare ask how things actually worked – did all the staff line up facing each other in ranks outside the front door to welcome back the mistress of house? Like most people, her knowledge of servants was based on TV costume dramas.

She and Antigone were having a snack in the kitchen when at last she heard a commotion to suggest that the mistress of the house had returned. While Antigone made no move, Anna looked through the open door to the hall, eager to see the woman whose image she'd so studied.

There she stood, Cally, a celluloid image made flesh. Though in truth, there was not very much flesh and what there was looked nothing like the mottled, flawed skin that Anna was used to.

She was tiny – not short, in fact quite tall, but everything else about her appeared as if it had been vacuum packed. This was a woman who was held up as an athletic alternative to bird-like anorexics, whom websites accused of 'flaunting her curves' when she was papped in a bikini on the beach at Sandy Lane, and yet who looked as though she would be crushed by Janey, whose arm was linked with hers. That was the second surprise: that she and Janey should be so physically relaxed with one another.

Janey called through to Antigone who made her way into the hall with little enthusiasm.

'My baby!' Cally said, in an accent more English than Anna had expected.

'Hello, Mummy,' said Antigone.

Cally put her arms out so that they hovered either side of her daughter's shoulders, then moved them up and down, all the while about four inches away from Antigone's flesh, as though repelled by a force field. It was the sort of national dance from an Eastern European nation with a difficult past that people laugh at on YouTube. Antigone neither stiffened nor relaxed at this greeting. 'I missed you so much, honey. Let's look at you. You've grown two inches and lost two teeth.'

'Only one. Tooth.'

'Did the tooth fairy come?'

'No, but Bea left five pounds under my pillow.'

'Well, you're certainly bigger.' Cally and Janey exchanged glances. 'But you're still my baby.'

'Where's Daddy?'

'He'll be back very soon.'

'Why are you back first? I'd like to see Daddy.'

'Shush, honey, you'll see him. And, in the meantime, you and I can have a special time. I thought we could do some wonderful girly treats tomorrow, go to the spa and have a swim and some treatments. Or get Daria round here to give us matching mani-pedis? Won't that be wonderful?'

'I have to go to school.'

'I'm sure one little day won't hurt. We'll tell them you're having a duvet day with your mom.'

'I want to get my one hundred per cent attendance award. And I've a spelling test.'

'All right, sweetie, at the weekend instead.' Cally's voice rose at the end of the sentence so that Anna didn't know if it was a question or statement. 'Where's your new friend Anna? Oh, but I'm dying for a cuppa.' She said the last word in an exaggeratedly British accent.

'Hello,' said Anna, emerging from the kitchen.

'It's so great to meet you,' said Cally, her teeth so

dazzling that they made Janey's look as snaggled and yellow as any stereotype of English dentistry.

Anna felt herself glow with pleasure as she felt the full wattage of Cally's attention. She was even able to touch the icon when she shook her hand (very smooth and slightly slippery, as if just moisturised, perhaps with a cream from the soon-to-be launched *Callyskinetics*™ range of products that Anna had read about). There was not a trace of fat or hair upon Cally's body, except where you might want some (head, eyebrows, lashes), where it was luxuriant. Her body was toned to hardness everywhere but her breasts which, if they were fake were very well done, and the apples of her cheeks which, like her breasts, were high and round. Her lips, too, were plump in comparison to the firmness elsewhere, and when she smiled the gap between her top lip and nose disappeared.

Her frame was tiny but her eyes huge, as if drawn by Disney animators. She looked like one of those photo-montages that scientists create of the face that the world finds most attractive. Skin a smooth caramel, chestnut hair blocked with butterscotch highlights and lips the shiny red of a glacé cherry – the adjectives that came to Anna were the only things about Cally that were calorific. Her racial make-up was hard to discern, since her skin and hair were darker than the average Caucasian, but her eyes were a yellowy-green. She could, the marketers always said, appear mixed race to a black audience, Hispanic to that group and solidly white to the rest. Whatever the country, she claimed some heritage – Cherokee, Puerto

Rican, maybe some umbrella term like 'Asian' was thrown around too. While promoting a film in Ireland, she claimed to be of Irish descent. She was a racially non-specific child-woman; she crossed all interest groups as if created in a laboratory. Anna tried not to stare but she had never met someone so beautiful and yet so weird looking.

'I hear you've been doing wonderfully with Antigone, thank you,' she said to Anna.

'She's an amazing child.'

'So bright.'

'Yes, exceptionally so.'

Cally turned back to Antigone. 'Let's go into the kitchen and you can tell me all the marvellous things you've been doing.'

Anna hung back, unsure of whether to follow. Cally turned and gave her an exaggerated swoop of her arm to indicate, yes absolutely.

Cally and Janey sat down at the kitchen island, looking for all the world like best friends in an advert for sweetener. Martina offered them all a choice of drinks, with Cally, for all her talk of cuppas, opting for a freshly made juice that emerged a vivid green, while Anna was thrilled with proper cappuccino from the coffee machine, complete with milk frother and espresso shots. She drank too many of them, like a student at a party who discovers that the alcohol is free.

'This is totally divine,' said Cally to Martina. 'I've missed your way with the juicer. Honestly, I swear there's no one in the world who can make me such a perfect extract. Where's my darling girl gone?' Antigone was hanging back in the hall with Bea. 'Bring her in here, now, Bea.' There was a snappiness in her tone that Anna hadn't heard before.

'So honey, what have you been learning with Anna?'

It's been three days, thought Anna, three days.

'She told me about Pompeii and Vesuvius and we made our own mosaic of what we might be able to find if we had a volcano here. I did a swimming pool using different blues and greens.'

'Lovely. I played a Roman empress once, but you probably know that,' she said to Anna. 'You've seen that movie?'

'Yes, it was very entertaining.'

'Janey thinks that it would be good if Antigone did some more sport. It's good to keep healthy, isn't it? Can you timetable that in? Perhaps you could work on her tennis; we're members of the club. And of course, what's the point of having a swimming pool and a gym if it's not used? Jude comes to train me there first thing, but it's available at other times of the day. Except when I have an evening session too. You swim?'

'Of course. I've got my swimming costume.' Anna inwardly cringed at the thought of putting on her quick-dry racing-back outfit in front of these elegant creatures.

Cally laughed. 'Costume. I love it when you Brits say that. Makes me think it comes with a fake nose and glasses or something.'

And swimsuit is so much better, thought Anna, as if

46

it's got a shirt and tie. She forced herself to join in Cally's amusement with as much gusto as Janey.

Cally leant over to Anna and squeezed her arm. 'We're so thrilled you're here. Really we are. I think you and I are going to be such good friends.'

3

No Bombing. No Diving. No Petting.

Anna went to check over her schedule in the morning and found Cally standing in the hall, while Sandi, the hair-dresser slash make-up artist, lightly backcombed the roots of her already enormous mane.

The internet had shown Anna that Cally was an expo-nent of 'school-run-mum chic', a blow-dried look involving chunky cashmere and casually expensive trou-sers, rounded off with an artfully tied scarf and topped with forbidding sunglasses whatever the weather. Today, she was wearing an outfit that gave the vague impression of being the sort of thing one might wear to play a game of football with a child – jeans and a hooded jacket; yet it was clearly expensive, and accessorised with impracti-cally high-heeled boots. Her face was made up in that no-make-up look that seemed to be a lot of work. Sandi got out a stick of something and began to skim it lightly beneath Cally's arched brows and then onto her collar-bone. Highlighter, Anna believed it was called, though to her the word suggested the fluorescent pens for marking up revision notes.

Cally caught her eye in the mirror. 'Hello there.'

'I was just coming to talk to Janey and to wish Antigone

luck in her spelling test today. She's done them perfectly in all our practices. Even the word "anaesthetist".'

'I've played an anaesthetist. Dr Grace Jenkins was her name and she gave someone a disastrous epidural. Not sure I could spell it though.' She laughed and Anna felt herself liking her a lot more. Cally then squealed as a woman wearing a 1970s tour T-shirt and not a lot else approached them. She and Cally carried on making high-pitched noises as they locked each other in a strange embrace where their torsos were pulled tightly together, while leaving Cally's hair and make-up free from mussing.

'Have you met Lysette?' Cally asked Anna, when they finally disentangled. Lysette nodded perfunctorily at Anna before kneeling as supplicant to check the way that her jeans fell above the boots. 'She's my stylist, but also one of my most bestest friends.'

'Yeah, babe,' said Lysette as she stood up to check the whole look, 'love you the most.'

'Love you more,' said Cally. 'Do these jeans make me look fat?'

Lysette was by this time standing behind Cally, pulling at her top and using bulldog clips to pull it tighter. She very obviously rolled her eyes at the question, as if she'd been asked it a thousand times before and been forced to repeat the same answer. 'Are you crazy, girlfriend? You are looking so fit right now.' She pulled a face in Sandi's direction.

'Yeah, smoking,' agreed Sandi.

'Aw, love you too, honey,' said Cally smiling at her.

'Group hug. You guys are my sisters.' The three of them then embraced carefully.

How strange, thought Anna, for your best friends to be in your employment. Did that count as a sort of friendship prostitution?

'Antigone, time to go,' shouted Cally.

Antigone emerged from the kitchen with Bea, her bag already packed by Anna the night before, and her hair in a pair of perfectly symmetrical French plaits. Her uncharacteristic nervousness and old-fashioned school hat made her look like a portrait of a wartime evacuee. A well-fed evacuee.

'I don't want to go.'

Cally's face brightened. 'That's marvellous, let's have our girly day together instead. After I've done my little workout. It will be such a blast, we can paint each other's toenails and make cupcakes and pop out to the park together.'

'But I do want to go to school. I just don't want to go out there.' She nodded towards the front door. 'Please. I hate them. There are so many more of them when you're here. Can't we go in the car?'

'Much healthier to walk. We have to set a good example. Chin up, as your father would say. Mommy will be with you.'

Anna was expecting further resistance, but Antigone began walking towards the door in resignation. Anna loved the way that Antigone's body language was so literal; she was dragging her heels as she sloped off, while her shoulders drooped with unwillingness.

'Good luck,' Anna said.

Antigone looked at her with astonishment and gave a hopeful smile.

'With the spellings,' Anna added.

'Oh, them.' She sounded disappointed. 'It's not like I need luck for them though, is it?'

'That's the spirit.'

'Come on, honey, people are waiting,' called Cally, donning her enormous sunglasses.

As Cally and Antigone went through the front gates to the outside world, accompanied by Dan walking a few paces behind, Anna heard a cacophony of voices and footsteps erupt.

She frowned in puzzlement at Janey.

'Paps,' explained Janey. 'There are at least a dozen of them this morning. The school-run celebrity picture is second only to the return from the gym one these days. They much prefer them to the red-carpet ones for some reason.'

'I suppose they're more natural,' said Anna.

'You think?' said Janey.

'How do they know Cally's going to come out? I mean, yesterday there were only a couple of photographers.'

Janey laughed. 'If somebody wants to avoid having their picture taken, they can.'

'So, are you saying . . . ?'

'I'm not saying anything,' she said. 'What you have to remember, Anna, is that Cally is a brand, and she is in a continual process of self-branding.'

Anna had a vision of that beautiful skin being soldered

with a hot iron like a herd of cattle before going to the slaughterhouse. 'Self-branding?'

'Obviously. She's more than an actress, she's a model, she's got her fashion lines, the bed linen, now the skincare . . . she really is a modern-day Renaissance woman and her success is all predicated on maintaining her image. You know, the way that people say "very Cally", and we all know what it means.'

Anna hadn't, until her extensive research had made it clear to her – Cally's name had become an adjective to describe an intriguing hybrid of hard-scrabble beginnings combined with her upscale ends, a cheap bourbon and vintage champagne cocktail. The gorgeous good taste was made all the more so by the contrast she drew to her childhood. More than once, she had been quoted as saying that her shoe closet was bigger than the whole of the trailer she grew up in, which was clever because it meant that nobody could resent her good fortune.

'We're always saying things are very Cally,' said Lysette, 'aren't we Sandi?'

'Yeah,' said Sandi. 'It was a right *callymity* when Jude got the wrong-flavoured protein drink.'

'Not as bad a *callymity* as when you used crimped rather than straight Kirby grips.'

Sandi and Lysette high-fived each other, giggling.

'Now, now,' said Janey. 'May I remind you that your wages are reliant on the success of this branding. Especially the forthcoming launches, the skincare . . .'

'And don't forget the exercise programme. Which,' said

Lysette to Anna, 'is going to be called "Callysthentics", obvs.'

'She could start giving penmanship lessons and call it "Callygraphy",' said Anna, attempting to join in the office banter.

Lysette and Sandi looked blank, while Janey gave her a disapproving raise of her eyebrow. They were interrupted by Priya carrying a sheaf of papers. 'Janey, can I have a word?' she said. 'I was going over some old accounts and I've got a few questions. It's not quite adding up.'

Janey sighed as if her life was continually burdened by the problems of the idiots that surrounded her. 'If you must.'

'Yeah, I must,' said Priya. She was not, Anna felt, the sort of person to take well to being patronised, and had on the sulky look of a schoolgirl wrongly accused of having cheated in an exam. As Janey turned, Priya flicked her a V-sign behind her back, entirely for Anna's benefit.

Later, Anna walked into the kitchen with Antigone to get her after-school snack when she saw him, talking in fluent-sounding Spanish to Bea. She thought people you only saw in photographs were supposed to be disappointingly small in real life, but Sholto Carpenter was the opposite – looming over Bea so that their silhouettes could have formed the models for the sign for parent-and-child parking spot. It wasn't his height or that head of unruly thick hair that was so striking, but the fact that he was so involved in his conversation with Bea that he hadn't noticed them arrive through the front door. He was kind, Anna realised, on top of everything else.

'Daddy!' shouted Antigone, and she ran, this time shrieking with excitement, to his arms, where for once she allowed herself to be enveloped. 'I've missed you. As though I didn't have an arm.'

Sholto laughed. 'I've missed you like a missing heart.'

'You said I was your heart. Which means I must always be with you, inside here.' She touched his chest.

'You are always with me, wherever I am. And not just because we're always Skyping.' He turned to her. 'And you must be Anna. We're so pleased that you've joined us.'

'No, thank you for choosing me.' She blushed.

'An Oxford classicist, I gather. We'll have to swap names at some point. Some of my mates are dons now.' He smiled. 'When I say that, Cally always thinks I'm talking about the mafia. I really need your help too.'

'I'm sorry?' said Anna.

'I've been given a script to develop about Edward Gibbon. You might have some wisdom to impart.'

'Gibbon who wrote *The Decline and Fall of the Roman Empire*?'

'Do you know any others? I'm not sure it's really working at the moment. It's done as a story of his life interwoven with scenes from Rome – you know, to provide a contrast. There's not a lot of sex in his life after all.' Anna glanced nervously at Antigone.

'Don't worry, I know what sex is,' she said. 'It's when a man puts his penis into a woman's vagina and his sperm meets her eggs to fertilise them.'

'Of course, good. Well, at least that's something I don't have to teach you.' She laughed in an attempt to show how completely and utterly relaxed she was about the whole sex thing in front of this man and his small child. 'Nor could Gibbon, really, what with the hydrocele testes and all.'

'Hydro meaning water,' said Antigone. 'What are testes?'

'Balls, he had swollen balls,' said Sholto. 'This man was a writer in the olden days when they used to wear really quite tight trousers, so this was a real problem for him.'

'Mummy wears tight trousers, except they're called skinnies.'

'That's right, clever you. That's because you have to be skinny to wear them.'

'But Bea's not and she wears them. Very tight trousers. She should call them fatties rather than skinnies.' She looked over to Bea innocently.

'Indeed.' He turned to Anna. 'Listen, I know you're supposed to be doing something educational with her tonight, but I'd really love some time to muck around with my daughter.' He ruffled Antigone's hair, or at least the tiny tendrils that were not restrained by the perfect ribbons.

'Of course.' Lucky Antigone, thought Anna. 'She's supposed to complete her reading journal by tomorrow and there're a couple of worksheets . . .'

'I'm sure we can deal with her teacher tomorrow on that score.' He winked. Anna felt her legs buckle. 'They get too much homework, don't you think?'

'I don't know. My friend who's a teacher says that all parents say that there's too much homework while at the same time badgering them for more.'

He laughed.

'I didn't mean that's what you do, I'm sure you're right and don't say that not meaning it. If you see what I mean.'

'I'm sure that will be all, Anna,' said Janey's voice from the kitchen door. How did she do that: arrive so silently? She moved as though on castors rather than those high heels.

Anna retreated, watching as she did so Janey greeting Sholto with all the physical intimacy that she had shown with Cally the day before. She stared at them for a second, watching Janey whisper something into Sholto's ear. Anna was transfixed by what seemed to her to be a shocking intimacy. Beneath his salt-and-pepper stubble, Anna was sure she'd seen a blush at whatever words had been dripped to him.

She realised that she was not the only one watching them.

'Quite the picture, aren't they?' said Priya, who had appeared next to her.

'What do you mean?'

'Just that; they're quite a picture those two.' She laughed. 'This whole house is a proper picture, innit?'

'I suppose.' Anna longed to ask her for specifics. 'Have you worked here long?'

'Nah, just six months. I get paid shit, but it all helps with my uni fees.'

'You're a student?'

'Yeah, accountancy. I'm going to be an accountant, a really rich one. It's supposed to be good experience too, working here, that's why I get paid so little. I'm not sure it is; Janey's got the craziest bookkeeping systems I've ever seen. "Unorthodox", she likes to call it. Still,' she said, giving Wadim a lascivious look as he passed them in the hall, 'there are other perks. Know what I mean?'

'Not really. Aren't you engaged?' said Anna, having noticed the ring she wore. Maybe it was to be an arranged marriage or something.

'Yeah, I am, and my man's gorgeous. And before you ask, it's not an arranged marriage. You lot have all seen too many bad TV programmes.'

'No, no,' blushed Anna. 'I never thought that. I've friends from lots of different backgrounds.' She was making it worse.

'But you know, a lifetime's a long time, isn't it? Don't look at me like that, girl. The men in this house are bare hench, know what I'm saying?'

Not really. 'Yes, right,' said Anna.

'Don't say you weren't mooning after Sholto.'

'I admire his work.'

'Work? So that's what they're calling it these days,' scoffed Priya. 'Listen, if you're going to survive around here, you'll need some advice from Auntie Priya.'

'What do you mean?'

'I know what you're thinking: it's all so perfect, Cally's so perfect, la-di-da, it's like a copy of *Vogue* come to life.'

'Maybe.'

'Well, you're wrong. Nothing is right at all. Everyone's on the take, so you should be too – or at the very least be aware of it. That Lysette and Sandi, what a pair of parasites. I've seen them nicking designer clothes off Cally like they're on a shoplifting spree at Harvey Nicks.'

'Really?'

'Yes, really. But they're just amateurs. Don't get me started on the rest of them. I could tell you some stories.'

'Will you?' said Anna, hating herself for longing for the secrets to spill.

'Totally. You and I, we'll go out for a drink next week and I'll proper sing.' Wadim passed them once more. Priya raised her voice. 'Wadim, wait – can I have a word with you? It's about my leaking tap.' A quick wink to Anna and she was off.

'Gentle reminder' was the title of the email from Janey, and Anna supposed it was, in a passive-aggressive-anything-but way. She and Antigone were to go swimming in the basement pool after school – 'a good 25–30 minutes of vigorous exercise'. She now regretted her boasts about Personal Bests at Butterfly and second in the Freestyle at her secondary's swimming gala. She regretted more her quick-dry cossie with the baggy elastic. More shameful still was the body beneath it, a sturdy, hockey-playing schoolgirl's that lacked the hair-less, plasticised sheen of the alpha females of Lorston Gardens.

As Anna stood in the hall, steeling herself for revealing her swimsuited body down in the pool, Janey appeared, unbidden as ever. 'Let me demonstrate how everything works downstairs.' She looked at Anna. 'It's probably a little different to the pools you're used to.'

'Did you – I mean Cally and Sholto – build the pool, or was it here when they bought the place?'

'Good god no. There's not a single shred of wallpaper or floor tile that has survived from then. The pool was part of the work that was done when we dug down to the basement.'

'What was there before?'

'Chalk,' Janey said. 'Anything beneath the hallway level didn't exist until we excavated.' Anna imagined archaeologists scraping away at buried ancient treasures. Or a grave-digger piling in. 'Twenty-five feet down. It's one of the deepest basement excavations in this area, though I do believe there are multistorey versions in parts of Knightsbridge. They call them iceberg houses because you can only see a small part of what lies beneath.'

'Wasn't there enough room in the house before?'

'Hardly. We added well over five thousand square feet down there by extending underneath the garden.' She gestured outside as they passed the window out onto the garden. 'There's a gym, pool, spa, home cinema, and other bits and pieces down there.'

'Wow,' said Anna, as they entered the lower level.

'Oh it's really very modest – other people build internal climbing walls and dance floors and car lifts beneath their houses. And that would be ridiculous. This was a lot of work even for something so discreet, but it was worth it.' She smiled. 'Just about.'

'You lived here while it was going on?' Anna asked.

'No, of course not,' said Janey. 'That would have been impossible. No, a house was rented nearby and the family took a six-month hiatus in LA. But it was hard – you know builders. It was upsetting to see our beloved home floating on joists above the slurry.'

Their beloved home, you mean. 'I can see that,' agreed Anna.

'I oversaw the whole thing. It's my vision, really. The rest of the family were barely here. The gym is through there. You are, of course, welcome to use it.' Another flick of a glance up and down Anna's body. 'But you will need to check the online timetable on which I mark all Cally's appointments. And if you should go there and find it already in use, you will of course desist.' Anna looked through the windowed door to see a room that was mirrored on all sides and housed myriad strange contraptions. There were some that she recognised as running machines or cross trainers, but the others seemed either space-age or as if from a medieval circus, with nothing in between. 'This is the spa room.' Music that Anna could only describe as plinky-plonky dolphin sounds wafted out, even though there was no one being treated within.

They travelled down yet more steps, passing various unmarked doors along the way. 'And here's the pool,' said Janey.

'Wow,' said Anna. The stone door revolved to reveal a swimming pool not far off the size of a municipal one, but unlike it in every other way. There were no red and white plastic spirals to divide the fast lane from the slow one, or bored-looking teenage lifeguards sitting on high plastic chairs amid the stained concrete, or windows with fire-resistant wire running through them. There were no floating verruca plasters or posters exhorting users to refrain from dive-bombing or heavy petting. No stately old-age pensioners waiting to launch themselves from the side just as you approached your length's end. The ceiling was pitted with tiny lights that lit the water as the stars do the sea somewhere far away and paradisiacal, while from the bottom of the pool further lights threw up their glow.

It was quiet. Anna had never been to a swimming pool lacking the soundtrack of screeching voices amplified by the acoustics of water. It made her think of late nights or early mornings at the pool, but even then there would be some dogged swimmers doing their lengths. It unnerved her, as if one side of the pool might slide open, in order for an evil genius to let sharks into the water to attack her.

Anna sniffed the air and could at last place the whiff of chemicals that seeped into Antigone's playroom.

'The water's ozonated,' said Janey. 'Much kinder to the skin and hair than nasty chlorine. And it doesn't smell.'

'It does a bit,' said Anna.

'But it's the smell of fresh earth, don't you think?'

No, thought Anna, it's the smell of ammonia or chlorine, just like any other pool but marginally milder. 'Yes,' she said, inhaling deeply. 'Fresh earth.'

They were ushered to a corridor flanked with changing rooms, where Wadim was fixing a piece of flaking plaster in the ceiling. He retreated, scowling, at the sight of Janey.

'If that's all,' said Janey, 'I'll be off. I've some unfinished business to take care of.'

Antigone was a strong swimmer for her age, ploughing up and down the pool with a perfect every-third-stroke breath. But that's all she did – plough, like a middle-aged woman determined to swim a kilometre before breakfast. When Anna had splashed her, she reacted with puzzlement before putting her goggles on and doing her lengths. Anna realised that she was not there for aquatic-based larking, so concentrated on throwing down the weights for Antigone to recover and getting her to calculate her total swim based on the length of the 18-metre pool and then to convert this into fractions of a kilometre and then into yards and miles.

Once they'd done sufficient aerobic exercise, Antigone and Anna sat on the wide steps at one corner of the pool, kicking the water with their feet.

'You're good at swimming,' said Anna.

'Yes, I am.'

'You're good at most things, aren't you?'

'Yes, I am,' she repeated.

'Is there anything you're not good at?'

Antigone thought for a second. 'I'm not very good at being silly.'

Anna laughed, before realising that she wasn't joking.

'People at school are always being not very sensible and I really don't like it.'

Anna wondered whether the family fortune wouldn't have been better spent on someone who could come and be silly with Antigone, instead of a grown-up who too shared this inability. 'I like that you're sensible.'

'And, of course, I'm not very good at being thin.' She grabbed one of her thighs. 'See? Mummy's brilliant at not eating, but I'm rubbish at it. I get hungry, you see, and I know I shouldn't.'

'Now you are being silly,' said Anna. 'You're perfect.' In truth Antigone was quite thick around the waist, with broad shoulders that powered her impressive swimming. Fat was the wrong word, but solid would do. She was so different from her mother, no doubt due to the stout English genes from Sholto's side.

'Thank you, but I'm fat. Everyone knows that.' This was a fact, her voice suggested, like the earth spinning around the sun.

'Daddy!' she squealed, and leapt up to greet Sholto, who'd arrived wearing the sort of second-skin knee-length swim shorts that Olympians sport to confer speed advantages. But where a swimmer's body would be sleek, his had an old-fashioned bulk to it, with incongruously hairy calves like a rugby player's.

He grabbed his daughter and dunked her into the water. Now she splashes, thought Anna, with a double dose of envy. Dan followed Sholto, having replaced the dark suit he wore for driving and security purposes with a pair of retro short trunks – a small piece of material yet somehow well tailored. Or maybe it was the body beneath that was well constructed. She remembered he'd told her he'd trialled for Arsenal, and she could see that his body was one of a professional footballer slash underwear model. She tried to drag her gaze away from the near-naked men, but there was nowhere else to look in the twinkling lights of the underground swimming pool. The air temperature was heated to an oppressive 27 degrees, which combined with the chemicals and the bodies made Anna feel as though she needed to be anywhere but here. She looked over at the opaque skylights that burrowed into the garden at the far end of the underground lair and wished she could crawl through them, coming up for air on the outside like an escapee in an old-fashioned prisoner-of-war film.

'All right?' said Dan.

'Fine, yes. Great, thank you.' She lifted her legs slightly so that her thighs no longer splayed on the side. As Dan turned away, she examined his body from behind. She had never thought herself to be one of those women, the sort who talk of 'tight butts' and 'ripped abs' with exaggerated lustiness, but then she realised that this was in part because she'd never actually seen such bodies in real life. The boys she'd slept with – and there weren't very many since, as with jobs, she was always yearning romantically after unknown perfection – usually got undressed beneath the duvet, pulling off their pants at the last minute. It always seemed to be cold when she'd had sex and the men stoned or drunk. Her longest relationship had been with Dominic, who used to refer to himself as a 'scholar', and whose crippling asthma made him a latter-day Keats, all wheezy and allowed off games. Since they'd been together from October to April, he'd never removed his favourite merino wool top, so her view of his chest had always been when she'd made half-hearted attempts to go beneath it. Sex for Anna was now associated with the stale smell of a much worn but infrequently washed wool jumper and she would have flashbacks when hit by the similar odour in a charity shop.

Faced with the reality of Dan's back laced with muscles and the perfect symmetrical loops that they made with each other, like a Rorschach inkblot, she realised that, actually, they did move her at an instinctive level. Or was her interest more scholastic? She had, after all, studied ancient Greece. Either way, Dan was, to use an appropriately idiotic and vapid word, *hot*. This place was a hierarchy of hotness, and she only just above Martina and Bea.

Dan dived in and swam a couple of perfect lengths before getting out with a surely self-conscious push and whoosh, so that water flayed from his pumped muscles. He grabbed a towel and flicked it at Sholto with the words, 'Oi, granddad, you going to take me on?' Sholto responded by grabbing him, whereupon they tussled manfully before falling into the deep end. You didn't need to be a Classics scholar, thought Anna, to come over all Ancient Greek at this display.

'Antigone, we'd better get going.' If I can just make it to the pile of fluffy white towels that were rolled and piled in a neat pyramid and cover myself before they finish their race, she thought to herself, then no one will be able to see my body in swimwear.

'No, Daddy's going to race Dan. A hundred metres. Well, that's what they call it, but it's obviously not since they're doing six lengths which makes it one hundred and eight metres.'

'OK, we can watch, then we need to have supper and do some learning.'

Anna grabbed a couple of towels, surprised at the small spores of mould that had formed on the walls of the diagonally placed shelves. She watched as Sholto carefully rolled on a swim cap and goggles and then launched himself into a complicated warming-up process of squats and stretches. Finally the two men got into their dive poses at the far end of the pool, where light from the circular skylights fell upon them as if they were entering *Star Trek* teletransporters. Antigone set them off and they both did impressive crawls. Dan's style was effortless and he was clearly a natural sportsman. As he got to the last turn, Anna saw him glance round to see how far ahead he was of Sholto. He went for the tumble turn, but then stayed underwater so long and so motionless that she worried he'd been overcome with a bout of cramp. At last he surfaced, as Sholto pulled ahead of him to finish the length in pole position.

They emerged from the water, Sholto red-faced from exertion, staggering towards the changing rooms to recover, Dan standing there as fresh as he had begun, daring Anna to stare. He looked at her as if he knew that she had seen his tactics. He nodded in acknowledgement, then grinned.

At that moment, Janey clipped her way over to Dan, still managing to retain her elegance despite the elasticated blue plastic bags she was wearing as overshoes to protect the precious marble of the swimming pool surrounds. His face became serious as she spoke to him, and more so as a loud voice echoed across the pool.

'Where's Wadim?' Priya was stomping in without the protective foot covers.

'I told you to leave immediately,' said Janey.

'But why is it just me that has to go?' said Priya. 'Why not Wadim? Where is he?'

'You know you broke the terms of your contract. Let alone the one you may have with your fiancé. Or shall I ask him what he thinks of what I can show him?' Janey said.

'What's it to you?' said Priya. 'This has got nothing to do with that and you know it. That's why you're getting rid of me and not him.'

Dan, still in nothing more than his swimming shorts, took Priya's arm.

She angrily shook him off. 'Get your hands off me. I bet you're getting off on it – likes it rough, does she? I'm going, all right. I'm better off out of here anyway. I can get paid more making coffee.' She scowled at Dan and Janey, before turning to Anna. 'Bye then. Good luck with these shitheads. Don't ask any questions and you'll get told no lies. That's your motto, isn't it, Janey?'

With that she walked away, deliberately heavy-footed, and Anna felt as though she was taking with her any chance of a friendship within the house.

4

Amo Amas Amat

'Well, hello there, Mary Poppins,' said the only remaining pap on the street to Anna as she came back from the school run. The shuffling and shouting of the ranked mass of men was the chorus to her morning departure from the house, but only on the days when Cally was at home.

'I'm not a nanny.'

'Yeah, and you don't have a magic umbrella and bag neither,' he said.

'I'm really not Antigone's nanny, I'm her . . . oh, never mind.' What was she, really? Could she honestly say that her job was not remarkably similar to that of a nanny? If there were a Venn diagram with nanny in one circle and 'mentor slash tutor to an eight-year-old' in the other, wouldn't there be an overlap almost as big as the circles themselves? Bea did all the domestic parts of the role, the cooking of homemade fishcakes and the bathing, but Anna did the rest. Together they were a Frankenstein's nanny, with Anna providing the head and Bea the heart and ample bosom. 'What are you still doing here anyway?' she asked the photographer. 'I'm presuming it's not to take my picture.'

'I don't know,' he said, looking her up and down with appreciation. Anna stiffened in objection to being so objectified, while noticing that he wasn't bad looking himself with a wholesome glow that differentiated him from his greasy-skinned co-workers. 'Apparently Cally and the trainer will be going for a run later. Got to love a workout picture, especially if I can snap some embarrassing sweat stains.'

'How do you know that's going to happen? The run, I mean.'

He tapped his nose. 'That's for me to know . . . What's your name, anyway?'

She looked around, conscious of the security cameras and the feeling that she was fraternising with the enemy. 'Anna.'

'Nice name. Mine's Jack.'

'Why do you do this?' she asked. 'Why do you stand around outside somebody else's house and wait to take pictures of them doing something totally unremarkable like going to get a cup of coffee?'

'I'm actually researching for a novel I'm writing. It's a thriller called *Shooting Stars*, about a paparazzi vigilante.' He grinned in a self-conscious way that suggested he'd been told it was appealing. Like everyone else in the world of Lorston Gardens, he was just slightly more handsome than you'd expect, as if this was real life as recreated by actors.

'Really?'

'Nah, but I thought a posh girl like you would be more impressed with that explanation than the truth.'

'Which is?'

'It's a living. Just about, though hardly that any more with the rates plummeting. Sometimes I only get a tenner for a photo to be put online. Stupid camera-phones; everyone reckons they're a pap these days. Giving away photos, they are.'

'You think it's bad everyone having a camera on their phone? Imagine what it's like for the people on the other side of the lens.' Anna was still not inured to the tiny flashes that accompanied her walks with Antigone. Some people did it brazenly, as if their subjects weren't truly human and so wouldn't notice. Others would pretend to be speaking on their phones and then swing them round to snap quickly, knowing that what they were doing was wrong. She didn't know which was worse. She tried not to think of these people scrolling through their pictures later, showing them to friends, narrated by judgements on Antigone's looks and her companion, 'just the nanny'.

'Oh, don't look at me like that,' he said. 'Like you've got a bad smell under your nose. Someone's got to do it.'

'But they don't, nobody *has* to do it,' said Anna. 'Don't you see how weird it is for you to be stalking an eight-year-old girl?'

'I don't stalk Antigone. Only her mother. I don't think she's exactly innocent in all this. We need her, but she needs us even more. We're all part of the game, love. Celebrities, publicists, editors, the police. The ordinary public who demand these pictures.'

'Not me.'

'You're earning a living off them, aren't you?' He nodded his head towards the house. 'And they owe their living to people like me. We're no different, you and me; we're both working for them. Except I reckon you'll be doing better out of it than me. I keep thinking I'll give it up but, you know, one big photo and I could get five figures, even six for a really good one.'

'What sort of picture would you need to get to be paid that much?' asked Anna, by this time sitting on the low wall next to Jack, close enough to see that his eyes were slate grey like a newborn baby's. She knew that what he did was not exactly a normal job, but he still seemed a lot closer to being an ordinary worker than the rest of them. I'm lonely, she realised with surprise. I had no idea. She had arrived in London and yet was failing to see any of her friends, as if the capital only consisted of this tiny village, with the house as the local church around which everything else revolved.

He looked wistful, as if describing a romantic dream of his. 'Exclusive, obviously. Eye contact, that helps. A picture's worth much more if their eyes meet the camera lens rather than looking down or away. Off duty – none of this red-carpet stuff with them all gussied up and doing the old one-leg forward pose or the head looking backwards over their shoulder. Obvious baby bump before a pregnancy announcement, that's not bad; it will get more if mum's got her hand protectively across it. What else? The baby itself, clearly visible for the first time – but not breastfeeding, as that freaks people out. Fat, not having lost her baby weight, or thin, having snapped back in record time. Your Cally was a genius at that after Ant was born: don't think I've ever seen someone look so good so quick. Said it was all in the Spanx, but she must have been doing some serious juicing and training postnatal. What else? Obviously some sort of extramarital relation caught on camera is dynamite; Cally snogging a co-star or even holding hands with him walking down the street, but only if she's been caught inadvertently, not if it's posed to drum up publicity for a film. Public can sniff them out a mile off. But do you know what, I'd happily just have a snap of her with her skirt tucked into her pants.'

'How charming. But I still don't know why you want to do it, or,' she wrinkled her nose, 'why people are interested in seeing these sort of pictures, of stars doing really quite boring things.'

'Don't tell me you never look at a celebrity mag or website.'

'I really don't. I prefer to read a proper book.'

'A proper book,' he mocked.

'Yes. Now, if you'll excuse me . . .'

'Nice talking to you,' he said.

It had been nice for her too, for the most part. 'See you.'

'Remember, if you ever have any information that would be useful to me, I can make it worth your while. Thirty per cent cut on all sales.'

Anna shook her head, feeling sullied.

Anna was having a stilted conversation with Antigone in French in the kitchen as supper was being prepared by

Bea. Antigone had sophisticated tastes, liking any manner of raw fish, be it sushi or ceviche, which was a caprice that Bea happily indulged, always making enough for Anna too.

Anna watched as Bea gently helped Antigone peel a papaya to go into the fruit salad.

'How long have you worked for Cally?' Anna asked her, glad to end the conversation she had been having with Antigone about what vegetables to buy *en vacances*.

'And Sholto,' Bea corrected. It still surprised Anna to hear her use their first names, since Bea's air of subjugation and deference made her think that she would call them 'Mr Sholto' and 'Miss Cally', or some other such title, like a maid in a film about the Deep South. 'I work nine years. More or less.'

'And before that you were back home in Mexico?'

'No, I live in Los Angeles.' Anna liked the way she did that Spanish thing with the 'g' in the word. 'I meet Cally there and I work for her.' Anna noticed a flash of distaste in Bea's face as she said the word Cally, as if it were a swearword in Spanish.

'You must miss Mexico very much,' Anna said, looking out of the window at the drizzle that seemed to have started when she'd arrived at Lorston Gardens. 'Are you planning to go home?'

Bea frowned. 'Home? It is difficult to say. Home . . .' Her voice drifted off.

'Presumably you don't want to work for them for ever?'

'It's different for you,' said Bea. 'This just a job for you. For me, it is my life.'

But someone else's life, thought Anna. 'You're so good with children. Would you like them yourself?'

'I have child.'

Anna didn't know whether this statement was born of an error in the use of verb tenses, since Bea's English was erratic, or if it was true, that Bea had a child or children left behind in Mexico. Anna had read about women from the developing world who gave up their children to be brought up by their grandmothers while they transferred all that love and kindness to the children of first-world parents. It must be so hard for them; no wonder she was so maternal with Antigone. She was about to ask more when they were interrupted.

'Bea,' said Cally sharply. Bea flushed and began manically chopping a peeled kiwi. 'Janey told you not to put full-fat yoghurt with the fruit salad.' Anna's recent close study on the pronouncements of Cally Steward meant that this exhortation came as a surprise to her – wasn't she always saying that fat in food wasn't the enemy and that she 'slathered' her salmon in all sorts of creamy sauces? 'Why don't you go and sort out the clothes now? Ask Janey to get Martina to finish up in here.' Cally turned to Anna. 'So lovely to see you. I feel that we haven't really had a chance to get to know each other yet.' Anna's arm was squeezed conspiratorially.

'No, I suppose not.' This woman was both her boss and a global celebrity. This made her a little intimidating. *Anna, snap out of it, it's not as if she's Germaine Greer.* 'I've got to know Antigone pretty well.' She looked at the little girl perched on a stool and realised that she hadn't really, since she was so unknowable, but that she did like the little she knew so far.

'I know you very well too,' said Antigone. Anna smiled at her and got a grin in return that displayed those outsized adult teeth that Antigone had so recently grown to replace the tiny white pearls of her baby ones.

'That's lovely. We're so grateful to you, Anna. Her teachers say she is pulling even further ahead than before. They don't use words like genius lightly, but there is talk of moving her up the school since she's already spending so much time in the grade above.'

'Maybe.' Anna's own adolescence had been blighted by being a year younger than the rest of the girls in her class at secondary, who seemed to arrive aged eleven wearing bras, cherry-glossed lips and a knowing air.

'Antigone, honey, let's you and me have some special time together,' said Cally. 'Do you want to go to our café to grab a mocktail? You can tell me all about what you're up to at school.'

'I've had supper, thank you. After I've eaten this fruit salad I'd like to go and finish the maths that Anna and I were doing.'

'Math,' said Cally, almost inaudibly. 'The word is math.' She walked out of the room with all the poise of an award-winner on the red carpet.

Anna picked up the cartoon book that was supposed to make Latin fun.

'*Amo amas amat*,' she said to Antigone. 'That's the only Latin anybody knows.'

'*Amamus, amatis, amant,*'Antigone continued.

'Get you, already exceeding the vast majority of adults.'

'Obviously. What does it mean?'

Anna was surprised at this rare display of ignorance. 'Love. I love, you love, he loves . . .'

'I know that, silly,' said Antigone. 'But what does love mean?'

'Gosh Antigone, that's a very interesting question. You want to know what love is. Love is a many, er, splendoured thing.' Oh dear, the whole conversation sounded like a series of banal song titles strung together. 'What do you think love is?'

'The girls at school say they love everything, like hair clips and stickers. One of them will say, "I love your shoes," and then someone else will say, "Why don't you marry them?" And then they all laugh. Every time.'

'How wearisome.'

'But it's not the same, saying I love your Lelli Kellys, and the love that makes you get married to someone or the love you can feel for a painting. It really shouldn't be the same word, should it?'

'No, you're absolutely right. It causes lots of confusion. When I was younger, people would say "love love" instead of just love when they wanted to talk about the thing that makes people get married or whatever. Your Mum and Dad, for example, love love one another.'

Antigone shook her head. 'No, Daddy doesn't love love Mummy. He love loves someone else.'

Anna glanced at the camera that occasionally blinked

at them from above the playroom desk at which they were sitting. She opened her mouth and then decided to remain silent.

Anna always checked the street for paps as she went out towards the school to pick up Antigone. That way she knew when she returned with one of their targets. There had been no one on the way out, so she was surprised that they were not alone by the time she came back with Antigone under an hour later.

'All right, Antigone?' yelled Jack-the-pap as they approached the house.

'You,' said Anna. 'Just leave her alone.'

Antigone frowned. 'Anna, don't be silly. It's Jack.'

'You know him?' said Anna.

'Have you got any more of your magic tricks to show me?' Antigone asked Jack. 'Though you do know I know that it's not real magic but just sleight-of-hand?'

'Of course I know that, Antigone. Harry Potter could come by on his Nimbus Two Thousand and you'd still be unimpressed.'

'Well he won't, because he's a fictional character, Jack,' said Antigone.

'Really? It's an education talking to you, sweetheart. Here, watch this. Pick a card, any card.' He did some complicated shuffling that Anna tried hard not to admire, followed by some comedy pratfalls and faux-ineptitude that couldn't hide his unexpected physical grace. Anna thought that Antigone would be far too sophisticated to find it funny, but she did that rat-a-tat laughter of children that sounds almost forced. 'Now you need to blow on the cards.'

Anna watched as Antigone looked tentative and then reassured by the way that Jack carefully moved his hand so that it was out of the way and the girl could lean forward without fear of her chin touching it. He glanced up at Anna and they shared a smile. He then knocked the deck against his thigh and one flew out into his other hand.

He revealed it to Antigone with a flourish. 'Was it the three of clubs?'

'No,' said Antigone. 'You got it wrong.'

'Oh no, I'm an idiot.' Antigone giggled at him, a rare sound. 'Can I look in your pocket?' Jack noticed Antigone blanching as he approached. 'Can you look in your pocket for me, sweetheart?'

She took out a card, the five of clubs this time. He looked at her and she shook her head. 'Am I the world's worst magician? Oh well, better get back to taking photos. Can you help me?'

Of course, thought Anna, all this is some preamble to getting a really good close-up of Antigone.

'But what's this?' he said, showing Antigone the back of the camera. In place of the screen was a playing card, face up and lodged firmly.

'Jack of hearts! My card.' Antigone frowned at him.

'My card, too. Jack of hearts, get it?'

Anna groaned.

'I just don't know how you did it. Tell me how you did it, please, Jack,' said Antigone.

'We'd better get inside, Antigone,' said Anna.

'OK,' sighed Antigone. 'It was nice to see you, Jack.'

'Likewise,' said Jack, looking from one to the other and smiling. 'See you soon.'

'Does he often do tricks for you?' asked Anna, when they were safely inside the house.

'Yes, he's nice. He never calls me names either and he tells the others off if they do. I think maybe he's a bit bored. It must be quite boring standing out there waiting for Mummy to come out in her PE kit.'

'Indeed. Antigone, can I ask you something? Why don't you like being touched?' Even Jack had known that she wasn't to have skin-to-skin contact. The only people allowed to touch her were Sholto and Bea. Even other children, or especially other children, were kept away by Antigone's force field.

She shuddered. 'I just don't like the way that skin rubs skin up the wrong way.'

'I don't understand.'

Antigone sighed. 'Let me try to explain it. Do you like velvet?' Anna demurred. 'Doesn't it make you feel sick to rub the velvet the wrong way so that it changes its colour?'

'No, it doesn't. I quite like that about velvet, though I've not really thought about it before.'

Antigone searched for another way of describing her feelings. 'OK. What about when you're eating sushi and your teeth go along the chopsticks and you can feel their fibres?'

'I know that feeling. You get it on an ice lolly stick

too.' A bad analogy, Anna realised, since the only lollies Antigone was allowed were homemade fruit freezes made by Bea in dinky plastic moulds.

'That's how I feel when other people touch me. It makes me feel like I'm going to be sick, like they're rubbing my skin the wrong way. Aldous at school gave me a Chinese burn.'

'I'm so sorry, we must tell your parents—'

'I didn't mind. I don't mind when people touch me hard. It's stroking stuff that makes me feel bad.'

'Like if you hold a stinging nettle tightly, it doesn't sting, but it does if it brushes against you?' asked Anna.

Antigone beamed. 'Exactly. Well done.'

Sholto could do anything with Antigone though, and the ice-lolly stick sick feeling never appeared. He tickled her and stroked her and covered her in kisses, while Cally could only look stiffly on, trying to distract her daughter with offers of special girly treats.

While Cally observed Sholto and Antigone's affection from her position as gooseberry, Anna would allow herself to admire the film-star good looks of her film star of a boss. They were such that it surprised Anna every time she caught sight of her. Her beauty almost appeared to be something so extraordinary as to be a separate entity to its owner; a person in its own right, so perfect that it made her curiously unrecognisable. Every time Anna saw her, she'd be forced into identifying her once again since she had none of the wonkiness or imperfection that make most people so themselves.

By living at Lorston Gardens, Anna was allowed to see the reality of Cally's beauty tips. The exhausting demands that she made of her acolytes were nothing to the actual routines that she followed. Jude, the personal trainer, shouted, 'Who makes it happen you make it happen', and the like, for two hours a day, while a nutritionist delivered strict recipe instructions for Martina to follow. A whole week would go by without her putting anything solid past her lips. She claimed to be intolerant of dairy, wheat and gluten which, as far as Anna could see, left nothing to eat. She swam or did yoga in addition to the morning workout. Her skin would be flayed by acid and high-tech sandpaperers, before being massaged with serums and potions by a woman in a white coat, a physician of physical beauty. It seemed as if she was always working out or being worked on. She was like a bride, called upon to raise herself up to the best that she could look to be worthy of all those gathered to stare at her and cluck, but she was a woman who had to do this every single day rather than once in a lifetime.

Anna wasn't the only one aware that Cally was on a permanently restricted diet.

'You have absolutely no idea,' Cally was saying to Antigone one day in the kitchen, 'how lucky you are.'

'But I don't want to be lucky. I want to go to the normal swimming pool that everyone else goes to with the floating slide and the wave machine.'

'When I was growing up I didn't even have a house, let alone a swimming pool.'

'Is that why you have to have three houses now?'

said Antigone. 'I don't understand why one isn't enough for us.'

Cally sighed. 'You want to live like I did? Being poor isn't fun. It's awful, it's exhausting; it doesn't leave you any room to think or to create because all you can think about is the next meal. My mom had to do terrible things just to keep us alive, let alone get me to school. It was all so different for your Dad. His parents were rich and now we're rich and he's never known any different, just like you. You know that bit in *Gone With The Wind* when Scarlett says,' and at this point Cally put on a hammy Southern accent, '"As God is my witness, I'll never be hungry again." I never want to go back to being poor and hungry.'

'But Mummy, you *are* hungry. You're hungry all the time. You never eat.'

Sholto had come into the kitchen by this point and laughed at Antigone's remark.

'Yeah, real funny,' said Cally. 'As if you'd love me if I got fat.'

Bea clattered the tray she was holding down onto the sideboard and walked out into the back kitchen. Anna, too, found herself pulling in her stomach in response to Cally's words.

Sholto shook his head, 'I don't love you because you're thin.'

'No,' said Cally. 'You . . .' She glanced at Antigone and her voice trailed off.

'Only me,' said Anna to Jack-the-pap as she came back to the house after her run. This was a new habit of hers since she'd read Cally's pronouncement that running really 'whittles your waist'. No, that's not right, it wasn't a new habit; she had run in the past to maintain her fitness when she'd played a lot of tennis. Now she ran for different reasons. It was no longer about what her body could do, but about how it was viewed.

'That's a blow,' he said, 'what with you all sweaty and everything. Would have been a great circle-of-shame photo.'

'Sorry to disappoint.' She knew she should get back inside and away from the enemy but she couldn't help but admire the way that the outdoor life had tanned his face and arms. She found herself doing her stretches in front of him. He looked appreciative as she pulled one arm across her chest, which boosted her breasts, flattened as they were in the binding of her sports bra. She found she liked his gaze, which was saved from sleaziness or lechery by the boyishness of his ever-present grin and the sun-kissed freckles across his nose.

'Absolutely not a disappointment,' he said, his eyes focused on her. 'No disappointment at all.' He shook his head with an exaggerated 'snap-out-of-it' gesture. 'Tell me, how's life in the lap of luxury?'

'Fine thanks.'

'Any news you'd care to share?'

'No. Obviously. Why, what news do you think I might have?'

'I don't know, what news do you think that I might think you have?'

'What news do you think . . . oh, this could go on a

long time,' said Anna. 'You probably know more than me. I don't see a lot from where I am, anyway. In fact, you must know all the comings and goings of Cally and Sholto far better than I do.'

'Him, not so much – no one's really interested in pictures of men unless they're seriously buff and running in short shorts along Malibu beach with a cute dog in tow. But her, yes, I've a pretty good idea of her schedule. It's very feminist really, my world, as women are worth so much more than their blokes.'

'Only the young and the beautiful women.'

'And the mad ones. Those more than anyone. Young, flaky girls who shave their heads or shag married men. They're my holy grail. But men like Sholto are pretty useless. Unless I can catch him snogging the make-up artist in the park, *in flagrante delicto*, if you know what I mean.'

'Yes I know what that means. Obviously. But you never have, have you?' She saw Jack's eyes slightly narrow at the question. 'Caught him on camera with someone else?'

'Not on camera, no.'

'Which means?'

'That I've never seen him with anyone else. But, you know, there are rumours.'

'Really? But Cally's so beautiful.'

Jack snorted in derision. 'Because being beautiful keeps your man from straying?'

'Doesn't it?'

'You're very young.'

'I'm twenty-three.'

'Only a couple of years younger than me,' he said. 'Who'd have thought it?'

They looked at each other for a couple of seconds and Anna felt that they were doing so as people, or, worse, as a man and a woman, instead of merely employees, informal and formal, of the empire of Cally and Sholto. She wasn't sure that she liked this feeling, but then she knew she didn't dislike it. 'You were saying, about a woman's beauty being no –' she paused, looking to regain her superiority the only way she knew how – 'prophylactic against infidelity.'

'Prophylactic. Interesting choice of word.' Anna blushed, cursing herself. 'Look, I'm just saying that, in my experience, the more beautiful a wife is, the more likely a man is to stray. And with birds who aren't a patch on his missus in the looks department. Especially if he's no oil painting himself.'

'That's rubbish. Don't they always say what man would have a burger out if he could have steak at home?'

Jack snorted. 'Bollocks to that. How can you tell who's steak between the sheets?' He frowned, aware that the analogy wasn't working. 'And, anyway, nobody wants to eat steak every day. Sometimes, there's nothing better than a Maccy D.'

She glanced at the discarded polystyrene at his feet. 'So I see.'

'You never know, maybe one day I'll get to try some steak. Oh no,' he said, 'that didn't come out how I wanted it.'

'See you, Jack,' said Anna.

Jack began to fiddle with his lens. 'Yeah, see you around, Mary P. Say hello to Antigone.'

There were photos of Cally and Sholto all over the house and in magazines and on the internet, often captioned with an 'expert view' as to what their body language at that precise moment said about their relationship. There was one much-analysed red-carpet photo where Sholto's hands were in his pockets, which one body-language expert said was indicative of how relaxed they were in each other's company, while another saw this as a sign that he was pulling away from her, while 'her eyes are turned towards his face, indicating a neediness that he finds unattractive'.

Anna and Antigone came into the kitchen on their arrival home from school. Martina was, as usual, wiping down the vast kitchen unit, which she seemed to have invested with a talismanic quality. No man was an island, but Martina seemed to identify with this one. Bea had prepared a batch of bran muffins, which she was decanting from their tray. They smelled as good as something that had as their main ingredients unrefined bran and grated carrots could ever smell.

Anna felt the room's atmosphere charge up as both the other women stood up straighter and stopped what they were doing momentarily. Antigone must have felt it too, because she swung her stool round towards the door.

'Daddy!' she shrieked, and ran towards his open arms. She never normally ran unless it was specifically required of her in some sporting arena. 'Hello, Mummy,' she said to Cally, who was behind him. Anna felt the room change again as Bea retreated to the laundry room and Martina scrubbed the island even more vigorously.

'Hello, sweetie. Daddy and I thought it was time for some family time.'

Anna never knew what to do at these moments. Was she required or not? She felt that the family should be left alone, but at the same time was learning that servants weren't necessarily seen as existing in a way that would impinge on their privacy. Her bosses could see themselves as being on their own even while in the presence of their staff, who didn't count.

'We're just having a muffin and then Anna and I were going to carry on with our project on Pompeii,' said Antigone. 'We're making models of people copied from the remains of people preserved in the lava and Anna is teaching me all the verbs in Latin for what they're doing. Some of them were playing dice, did you know that?'

'Is this a school project, honey?' asked Cally.

'No,' said Antigone, as if this were a question both inane and insane.

'Well, why are you doing it then?' This question was directed at Anna.

'*Ars gratia artis*, I'm sure,' said Sholto, catching Anna's eye. 'It's Latin,' he said to his wife.

'I know that,' she snapped.

'Really, what does it mean then? *Ars gratia artis*?'

'*Ars gratia artis*? It means you're an ass, Sholto, or should that be arse?' she said in a faux British accent.

He turned to Anna. 'Cally thinks Latin is what they speak in Latin America. Don't you, my dear?'

'Fuck you!'

'No, that's Anglo-Saxon, my darling.'

Cally walked out, their special family time having lasted all of three minutes. Martina visibly relaxed on her departure, while Bea immediately returned to the kitchen.

'I'm sorry about that,' Sholto said. All three women fluttered in response. '*Mea culpa.*' He scooped up Antigone, who clasped him hard back. 'Now then, Anna, will you come with us? Let's go have a look at this wonderful-sounding Pompeii project.' He put her hand on her back. Anna felt herself slightly lean into it, blushing.

As they emerged into the hall, Anna saw Janey and Dan talking with their heads close together. Janey looked up and stared, very directly and without embarrassment, at Sholto. He nodded and they continued to make their way down to the playroom.

5

Nocturnal Ramblings

Janey had suggested that their meeting to discuss Anna's first month's work should take place in the nearest pub. Granted, it was a posh pub, one of the first in the country to serve seared scallops instead of pork scratchings, but even so it seemed a bit déclassé for the elegant Janey.

'I thought we could be more open if we got away from the house,' said Janey as they sat down with their shared bottle of Chablis.

It was odd, reflected Anna, how infrequently she left Lorston Gardens, or the strict path between it and Antigone's school and the various extracurricular activities that she took her to. She lived in one of the world's great cities, but rarely enjoyed its delights. She vowed to start living life in London rather than just reading about its fashionable restaurants and red-carpet events through the prism of the internet and the way it reflected the lives of her bosses.

She gulped down her wine with nerves.

Janey watched her with amusement. 'You're doing fine, don't worry. By every measure, you're making quite the difference. Antigone's marks have gone up and she seems to be stimulated once again. Some of her more unusual behaviour was, her parents are convinced, a result of her being bored at school. All the evidence suggests that you've not only improved her academic work but, either as a result of this or your own example, you've also made her behaviour fit into a more conventional view of what is good. I for one was very impressed by the certificate she got for being a helpful and considerate member of the class.'

'I think I was more excited about that than she was.'

'It was very nice news indeed. Something of a first. It won't come as any surprise to you to learn that Sholto and Cally have decided to extend your contract for a further three months. Congratulations.' She raised her glass.

'Thank you.' Anna was so flattered to have passed her one-month trial with such flying colours that it didn't occur to her to question whether the job had passed its test for her.

'And how's it been for you?' asked Janey, as if mind-reading was another of her otherworldly skills, to add to being able to float invisibly into rooms.

'Good, thanks. I think. Sorry, I don't really have much to compare it to. I love Antigone.' Did she? She certainly felt very fond of her. 'And everyone seems very nice. Bea's great.'

'There's far more to Bea than some people might give her credit for. Don't underestimate her just because her English isn't perfect.'

'Right, I won't. I don't. She must be very strong,

emotionally, to have made the sacrifice to live so far away from her child.'

'What are you talking about?' said Janey. 'She doesn't have a child.'

'I must have misunderstood, I thought she told me that she did.'

'What exactly did she say?' snapped Janey.

'Nothing really, I'm being silly. You know, sometimes her English can be a bit, well, you know. My mistake.' Janey was leaning towards her with an interest that she found unnerving. 'And Cally and Sholto, they're so nice, aren't they?' Anna continued. 'Very down to earth.'

'You think?' said Janey, who still seemed distracted by Anna's previous remark. 'Yes, of course they are. It's amazing isn't it, that they should remain so with all their achievement and talents.' Anna had by now learnt that Antigone didn't really get sarcasm. She was wondering whether she herself struggled to recognise irony when in conversation with Janey.

'I've read that they give lots to charity,' said Anna.

'Yes, they do a lot for charity. Those parties and fund-raisers can be such hard work.'

'How long have you worked for them?'

'Me? Long enough. I started a year or so after Antigone was born, when they moved into Lorston Gardens. I was working as an executive PA in the City and this seemed to be a bit more fun than those super-nerds that I was hooked up with before. And it's certainly been that.'

'How long do you think you'll do it?'

'As long as I'm needed, I suppose.'

'You're a sort of wife, aren't you?'

Janey put down her drink abruptly. 'Whose wife?'

'Cally's I suppose,' said Anna. 'My mother worked but she had to do everything else – you know, the sorting out holidays and name tapes and getting the washing machine fixed. She always used to say she needed a wife.'

'Everybody needs a me.'

'And you enjoy it?'

'Yes, I do. I'm good at it.'

Anna felt emboldened by the wine and the temporary escape from the house. 'Do you ever think that it's strange? Our jobs? That one family should need such a lot of staff around them just to keep going when most families don't have that and seem to manage just fine?'

'It helps if you don't think of them as one family but as an industry. Cally alone is big business, so like any business she needs employees. I'm no feminist, but I do think there can be double standards about outsourcing women's work when there isn't about doing the same for more traditional male ones.'

'What do you mean?'

'Nobody judges a man if he takes the car to the garage to be fixed, but somehow women are supposed to be able to do all the traditional things – the cooking, the organisation, the mothering – and be successful in their careers.'

'But doesn't Cally promote that view by making out in interviews that she doesn't have any help? That she does it all with just a little support on the side from some friends dropping by?'

Janey pursed her lips. Anna wondered whether she'd gone too far. 'You may say that, Anna.'

'Sorry,' said Anna. 'I didn't mean to criticise.' She had thought they were having a discussion. It had been such a long time since she'd had one of those.

'As I say, Cally and Sholto's life is a business with employees. And it's very important that they can trust those employees. Trust, Anna, trust is the key.'

'Yes,' said Anna. 'I understand that. They can trust me.'

Anna tried to sleep, but realised that she'd drunk more with Janey than she'd intended and hadn't eaten anything since a solitary courgette fritter cooked by Bea at teatime. The bed was undulating as she lay upon it. She imagined Sholto's hand on her back and then pictured him in those swim shorts. Then drunken thoughts of Dan began to invade her head, then Sholto and Dan together. This felt like a sort of infidelity to Sholto and she suppressed those muscular distractions.

She got up to try to walk it off in the unusually warm air of the late spring night, thinking that if she stayed on Lorston Gardens itself, she'd be safe from the scariness that lay beyond that one street.

'You're here late,' she said to Jack, who was packing up his camera outside in his usual spot. He was wearing a T-shirt and she noticed how strong those camera-wielding arms were and she found herself yearning to touch him. Or touch anyone. It had been so long since she had felt the skin of another.

'Got a tip-off from my mate outside The Ivy that Sholto

and Cally had come out of there looking pretty frosty with each other, so I thought maybe I'd catch a good tiff shot of them coming back here.'

'And did you?'

'Nah, couldn't see anything through the car windows. Do you want a drink?'

'I think I've had enough actually. Oh all right, actually, I should get out more.'

The late-night bar was very different from the pub she had visited with Janey. Where that had been heritage colours and organic vegetable chips, this was painted red, black and white like an Eighties pizzeria but without any food to eat. She dithered between a glass of water and a vodka, before settling on the latter, a double as it turned out, which was not what she'd requested.

'So Jack, tell me, what do you do when you're not stalking strangers?' she asked.

'Play a bit of football, hang around with mates. Take photographs of kids.' She was alarmed. 'Not like *that*. Portraits of families, nice shots of children playing outdoors; you know, the sort of photographs that their parents never get round to taking but are nice to put in mismatched frames and have on the wall. And those baby shots,' he cringed. 'You know, the ones of babies asleep in flower pots and stuff.'

'No, I don't know,' said Anna.

He got out his phone and scrolled through pictures of sleeping babies propped on their elbows, wearing knitted hats, pearls and pairs of glasses, or curled up inside Easter baskets. They were utterly absurd, but undeniably cute.

'I'm more of a cat person myself,' said Anna. 'But you're clearly good with children. Antigone was much more relaxed with you than she is with most people.'

He shrugged. 'I like her. Even admire her, in a way. It can't be easy being who she is.'

'You're right. Which is why it's so weird that in a few years' time, you'll be trying to get photos of her pants.'

'We call them up-skirt shots.'

'Ugh, please.' Anna shook her head.

'Another?' he nodded towards her drink.

'Why not?'

'I've been thinking,' she said as he returned with another double, 'about what you were saying about beautiful women being cheated on. I think that if you're right, it's because those men are punishing these perfect creatures for making them feel unworthy.'

'All men feel unworthy, whether or not we've hooked up with a looker or not. We know how filthy we really are. If you had any idea of what went on in our heads, you'd never come near us.'

'What is going on in your head then? Now?' Was that a flirtatious comment? Gosh, it was, she thought, and wanted to high-five herself in surprise.

Jack looked down. 'I think you know.'

Anna had been told she was clever for so long that it always surprised her that anybody might think of her in any other way than as a brilliant brain. Other girls said that men were only after one thing, but all her experience had shown her that the one thing was long, earnest conversations about who was your favourite character in Tolstoy, or can we prove that we really exist or do we just imagine that we do. 'Trust me,' she said. 'I really don't.'

They looked at each other. For once, his grin had disappeared and nervousness flitted across that boyband-handsome face of his. Emboldened by drink, she leant forward. She'd never done this before, initiated something; she'd always been passive and, given the passivity of the boys she had been involved with, this process could go on for quite some time, waiting interminably for the arrival of the lunge bus. She suddenly felt as though she wanted to act as though she were in a bad erotic movie, to put her legs around his waist and to be taken right outside against the wall and to yelp and say 'yes, yes' and all those other things that other people apparently wanted to shout, but that she'd never felt like doing herself, or at least not with anyone else in the room. Jack blurred into Sholto and Dan, into the one great synthesis of man. They kissed and he roughly put his hand between her legs. She liked it. An image of her bending down with her skirt hiked up, right there, right then, flashed through her mind, but she was neither drunk nor uninhibited enough to see it through.

'Let's go,' she whispered. 'Where do you live?'

'Not as near as you do.' His voice was hoarse. I'm going to do this, she said to herself, I'm going to fuck him. Even in the confines of her mind, she felt a surge of shame and excitement at using the word as a verb.

Make love, oh no, have sex, urgh, do it. We're going to have sex, yes we are. They stumbled out of the bar and she grabbed his hand and started to run, but his rucksack of heavy equipment held him back. She thought for a second about that hardware and all that it represented, but quickly suppressed the foreboding.

'Shhh,' she whispered, theatrically putting a finger to her lips when they got to the gate at Lorston Gardens. She punched in the code for the door. She saw him glance up at the Cyclops of the security camera. Ah, *quis custodiet ipsos custodes*, she thought to herself, and then of Sholto, who'd be able to tell Cally that it meant: who watches the watchmen? This, as she was later to reflect, was the moment when she could have stopped it, when she could have thought of the wisdom of bringing this man into their midst.

Jack took his time coming up the stairs to her rooms above the garage, pausing at the door that led from the bottom of the stairs into the main house. She was impatient to get on with it before she thought better of the idea, so she chivvied him along, sounding more like a hockey teacher than the wanton woman she had felt like moments before.

'Nice gaff,' he said, looking around her small kitchen area when he finally got there.

'You haven't seen the bedroom.' Yes, she thought, you can do this. You can be someone who says such facile things and laces them with lust. You can be a body not a brain. You're not a brain at all. My brain feels funny. I feel very odd. I'm going to be sick. Oh no, I'm not going to be sick, just so long as I go to sleep. That's the choice: sick or sleep. 'Sick or sleep?' she said out loud. 'Hey, that sounds like trick or treat? Trick or treat, trick or treat? Sick or sleep? Sick or sleep?' If she kept the words coming out of her mouth then maybe there would be no room for the vomit.

She lay on the bed, trying to position her legs in a come-hither way. Then she realised how much more comfortable it was to lie down properly, and she began to count alcoholic units. Two large glasses of wine at the pub, that would be four units, then the two doubles, that makes eight. All those even numbers, Antigone wouldn't like them. How much had she had to eat? Nothing. But it's only eight units. One, two, three, four . . .

Something had died in her mouth, a small bird. She hovered over the toilet, wondering whether she should try to expel it or hope that brushing her teeth would be enough. She put her toothbrush into her mouth, gagged, and realised that she'd never be able to get Antigone to school if she didn't try to rid herself of some of the poison that coursed through her body, the one she had thought of as so sexy and wild last night. She stuck her fingers down her throat, but being unskilled it took a horrifying amount of intervention. And, afterwards, she felt as though she had rid herself of the danger that she would be sick, but not of the way her whole body had been rubbed to a nauseating state of fuzziness. *It's only an hour, get through the next hour.*

She hoped that Antigone would allow them to walk to school in silence.

'What are we doing this morning?' she immediately asked. 'Would you like me to sing the sonata? I can, you know.'

Anna's voice was hoarse and sounded unfamiliar to her. 'I thought we could have a competition to see if we could be silent the whole way to school.'

'But I don't want to.'

'Please.'

'No. No. No. There, I've already broken the silence.'

'OK,' Anna said. 'Twelves gold level. Seventy-two?'

'Easy. Six times twelve, twelve times six. This is just too easy for me. Do some division. With numbers that don't go into each other so I have to express them as fractions. No, I'll do them as decimal points.'

'All right, let me have a good think first.'

'Come on, Anna, I'm waiting,' said the little human calculator beside her.

'OK,' she said slowly. 'One hundred and fifty-six divided by thirteen.'

'That's too easy, it's twelve. I told you to give me numbers that weren't exactly divisible.'

She'd woken at four, taken some painkillers, and then noticed that Jack had gone. At the time, she'd felt only relief that there was no body against her clammy skin, but now she wondered how he'd known the code to get out of the door.

'Come on, Anna. Do a more difficult number,' Antigone said.

'Three hundred and three divided by nine?'

'Thirty-three and two-thirds. Or thirty-three point six recurring. Six six six six six six.'

'OK, Antigone, we get the picture.'

'Point six six six six six six six six six . . . I can go on for ever . . . six six six six six.' Her voice rose as the sixes poured out. 'Six, six, six . . .'

'Stop it!' Anna baulked at the shock on Antigone's face at her raised voice. 'I mean, sorry, please can we just not talk this morning?'

'You are paid to talk to me,' Antigone narrowed her eyes. 'You have to do everything I tell you to do.'

'No, I don't. You do what I say because I'm the grown-up.'

'No,' Antigone hissed back. 'You do everything *I* say because you have no point otherwise. I am the boss, I am your boss.'

'Please do not talk to me like that, Antigone.'

'I'll talk to you however I like. You're not my real nanny, anyway.' With that she scooted off so rapidly that Anna had to crank up her tired and hungover body into a run to stop her darting out into the road.

As Anna walked back from the school, she tried to revert back to the disjointed film that ran through her head, but realised that she could no longer force the projector to screen it. Instead she thought about Antigone and how all her hard work seemed to have evaporated in a moment of stupidity. It's true she wasn't her real nanny, or even her real mother, but she had thought that they had reached a happy accord. It felt as though she would have to begin again. What if Antigone complained about her to Bea, who then passed on these complaints to Janey? It wasn't as if she enjoyed the job, particularly, but she had become almost agoraphobic in her need to stay cocooned within Lorston Gardens.

Her thoughts were interrupted by the sound of a can being kicked along the pavement behind her. She turned around to see Dan, who was now doing some impressive keepy-uppy with it as he walked.

'Hello, what are you doing here?' Damn it, had he seen Antigone running off like that?

'Same as I do every day.'

'Which is?'

'Walking ten paces behind you and Antigone. They may trust you with her intellectual development,' he spat out the last two words mockingly, 'but you're hardly going to protect her from stalkers or kidnappers, are you?'

'So you're there, all the time?' Anna wondered if she'd ever picked her nose or pulled her pants out of her bum with him walking behind her. It was one thing to feel you were starring in the movie of your life, it was another to realise that your imaginary audience was a real one, if only made up of a solitary person. 'I thought you were just accompanying me at the beginning, for the first couple of weeks, that's what I was told, not walking –' *stalking*, she thought – 'a few paces behind me without my know-ledge after that.'

'Just on the regular routes. You know, the ones that

someone else could work out for themselves and so provide a threat to her little ladyship.' He walked beside her now. He laughed. 'Aren't you supposed to be clever?'

'I am clever,' she said with indignation. 'I mean, I'm academically bright. If that's what you mean?' Which it clearly isn't, she thought.

'Well, for someone so clever, you act pretty stupid, don't you?'

They had arrived back at the house. He glanced up at the security camera and then back towards her and grinned. 'Take care,' he said.

Anna looked around the kitchen table. In her interviews, Cally always described its vastness as necessary, 'because we love everyone piling in for Sunday lunch – we often end up with twenty people lining up to try my famous Yorkshire puddings. I can eat five at one sitting.' But now Anna realised that it was probably to accommodate the vast number of staff who were now convened for a meeting. If Cally was a business, so was Lorston Gardens; one with a changing cast of employees.

There were Bea and Martina, of course, for once sitting rather than busying themselves with the infernal wiping and shining, chopping and cooking. Wadim looked out of the window as if wanting to be anywhere but there, perhaps with the unceremoniously deposed Priy. Lysette, the stylist, had joined them, though Anna had never realised she was a permanent member of staff, especially since it had always been maintained publicly that Cally had her own strong sense of unique style. Like everyone

Anna had come across who worked in fashion, she dressed really badly. Today she was wearing a long, shapeless beach dress that hung from her wizened frame. Sandi sat beside her looking at some photos that Lysette was showing her on her phone. There was Jude, whose hard body was matched by the hardness in her face. She appeared to be condemned to wear her gym clothes at all times, which consisted of a pair of skintight capris and a cropped bra top, whatever the weather. Her body so revealed was a thing of wonder, like a Da Vinci drawing of tendons and sinews, but the one time Anna had seen it in normal clothes, it had been a disappointment, looking incongruous and the wrong shape for anything other than Lycra, like those pictures of gleaming Olympic swimmers who are ungainly and broad-shouldered in their celebratory frocks and heels. Dan was next along, looking relaxed. There were another three people she'd never seen before and, of course, Janey, presiding at the top of the table with two empty seats beside her. She cleared her throat as if to silence the room, but no one was talking anyway. At that exact moment, Cally and Sholto walked in towards their waiting chairs. Jude leapt up with the quickness of someone who bench-presses before breakfast, Cally graciously gesturing for her to sit down again.

Sholto's face was stern. He had a reputation for being a rigorous director, and Anna could see that the laid-back persona he had cultivated around the house was just that, a persona. Cally was wearing beige and melancholia. Her face was cocked to one side, à la Princess Diana in the three-people-in-the-marriage period. She looked as though a perfect tear might roll cinematically from her eye at any moment.

'I'm sure you're wondering why we've got you all here together,' said Janey. Her face, too, was in grim repose.

The only sound was of Martina picking at the table, unable to resist cleaning even then.

'Some of you may have seen certain newspapers earlier this morning,' she continued. 'Or, possibly, though I hope not, seen various blind items on the internet over the previous week on some of the sites less grounded in reality.' Cally's face cocked so far to one side, her ear almost met her beautifully buffed shoulder. Sholto frowned – which, Anna decided, actually made him look more handsome than the goofy cheerfulness he usually sported.

'Obviously this is nothing unusual for a couple as celebrated as Sholto and Cally.' She looked towards them and Sholto gave a weak smile. 'And tabloid untruths and rumours are to be expected and dealt with by myself and the publicists.' She paused to allow them to reflect.

Even Anna, with her scant knowledge of Sholto and Cally's schedules, knew that most of what she read in the papers was untrue. There had been a story not long after she had begun working for them about how Cally was busy house-hunting in Los Angeles, when only that morning Anna had seen her doing one-armed press-ups in the garden. These stories were usually so innocuous that Anna wondered why they bothered to make them up. The only thing harmful about them was their lack of veracity.

'Normally I wouldn't be gathering you here to discuss it,' Janey continued. 'But for the fact that these particular items suggest a leak from within this very house. A leak that can only have come from a member of staff.' She again stopped to let this sink in.

'As you are all aware, you have signed confidentiality agreements that mean that if you are spreading such untruths, you are not only putting your job at risk, but that you can be sued for breach of contract, putting your whole financial future in jeopardy. For the rest of your lives. We take such matters extremely seriously. We are also extremely vigilant about maintaining the privacy of this house, to the extent that sometimes we may have promoted falsehoods so that we can pinpoint with certainty where the leak is coming from.'

While Anna had realised that the papers and websites published untruths, now it seemed things were even more complicated than she had realised. There were truths, both promoted and denied, and falsehoods, whose sources were similar. How could she tell the difference between a good lie and a bad one? How could Cally and Sholto? This was collusion and delusion.

'Listen guys,' said Sholto. 'This isn't Salem, we're not going to start a witch-hunt. We just don't want anything like this to happen again. And to stress that whatever you've read is absolutely untrue. Isn't it, darling?'

'Of course,' said Cally. 'It's all bullshit.'

'We have our suspicions,' added Janey. Anna watched her gaze to see if it gave any indication of where these might lie, but she stared carefully at the large clock on the wall. 'If anyone has any information that they would like to share, we will receive it in confidence.'

Anna dared to look around the room. Martina was still picking at some imaginary stain on the table, which could indicate some sort of Lady Macbeth-like admission of guilt, she supposed. Wadim was staring out of the window. Surely it wouldn't be him? He was the guy to fix the leaks, of which there seemed to be a growing number by the swimming pool, rather than cause them. Bea had on her usual expression of bovine, or beatific, calm. Jude, Anna was convinced, had nothing more in her head than a running tally of squat thrusts and static lunges, but she'd never trusted Lysette, in a way that she'd never trust a woman who wore a 'Hello Kitty' necklace into her thirties.

'Please go away and think about anything you might have said, even if inadvertently, or seen,' said Janey, and with that they were dismissed.

Anna ran as fast as she could to her room, fired up her laptop and began to search for stories that might have prompted the meeting.

The first thing she found was a gossip site that was considered to be reliable in its way, in which the original blind item was republished:

'Which gorgeous import's husband deals with her higher fame quotient and inability to eat (despite her protestations to the contrary) with a habit of nocturnal ramblings? It's not that he's a sleepwalker either.'

She found a tabloid website that went on to fill in the blanks, with Cally and Sholto's names and a few more details. Anna would never have made the connection to them had it not done so for her, nor did she know what it meant by 'nocturnal ramblings'. The piece ended with the question: 'Sholto, haven't you ever heard of the expression about not doing things that need clearing up on your own doorstep?'

She sought further clarification from a more upmarket (relatively) website – one that relied heavily on the words of 'sources close to the couple' or things that a 'friend' might have said. 'Cally,' said this unnamed friend, 'has been so busy with her film career and skincare range that she sometimes forgets she's a wife too. It's not really surprising that Sholto might feel the need to seek support elsewhere.'

It fleshed out the piece with far more detail about the night when these supposed ramblings had taken place. '"Cally and Sholto are trying to work things out," said the friend, "and so they went for a romantic meal to spend some quality time together." Observers say that the couple spent the meal exchanging few words and many stern looks.'

Anna looked at the photo that illustrated the piece. There they were, looking undeniably hatchet-faced, emerging from a restaurant, ignoring the flashbulbs ahead of them. She read the caption: 'Cally and Sholto leaving The Ivy.'

The Ivy, Anna thought, with mounting panic. The night they went to the Ivy. Jack's words echoed in her head:

'Got a tip-off from my mate outside The Ivy that Sholto and Cally had come out of there looking pretty frosty with each other.' Of course, they were talking about four days ago. It was that night; the night where she'd tried to be a new sort of Anna.

Dan was right. For someone so clever, she could act pretty stupid.

6

Saying Sorry

Anna felt breathless as she entered the pub. It was as though Lorston Gardens exerted a force field around it, so that it had become Anna's only planet and if she were to leave she'd shrivel up or pass out. But she couldn't risk meeting Jack within its orbit, and so found herself fiddling with a beer mat in an unfamiliar bar in an unfamiliar area.

'All right, beautiful,' he said as he came in, and she couldn't supress the vision of her grappling with him on a street corner and dragging him back to her rooms. The cheerful good looks that she'd found so appealing now seemed smug and self-regarding. 'I thought you were avoiding me.'

This was odd considering he'd been absent from his post outside the house for the week since that night. She must have shown surprise.

'I know I've not been around,' he said. 'But you know, I couldn't. I thought it would look like I was stalking you if I hung around outside your gaff.'

'A courtesy that you don't extend to Cally and her family,' she said, stiffly.

He laughed. 'You know they don't count.' He leant

over to clasp her hand, which she swiped away quickly. At his touch, she felt something of what Antigone always said about the revulsion at other people's skin.

'Do you know why I wanted to see you?' she asked.

'Not for the reason I'd hoped, clearly,' he said, leaning away from her.

'That night, you know, the night we . . .' She blushed.

'We what? As far as I could tell, we didn't actually do anything, what with you passing out and all.'

She pulled out of her bag the dossier she'd prepared. She slapped the printouts from the website that detailed his betrayal.

He read them with a look of puzzlement. 'Yeah, I saw this last week. What's it to do with me?'

She felt fury rise at his shamelessness. 'Jack, you can drop the innocent act.'

'What act?'

'Come on.'

'I don't know what you're talking about.'

'You used me to get into the house. And you must have sneaked out. I'm not sure how you knew the key code from my bit to the main house, but you must have done somehow and then you saw something that you sold to these gossip-mongers.'

'I woke you up out of your stupor, don't you remember? Just after you passed out muttering something about one and two and three. I asked you for the code of the gate and you wrote it down for me.'

'I didn't. I would remember.'

He got out his wallet and pulled out a scrap of lined

paper with the number scribbled across it in a sprawling version of her usually schoolgirl-neat handwriting.

'OK,' she said. 'But why have you kept it? This proves you were using me to get access to the house!'

'The rest of the house is alarmed, surely?'

'So you've thought about it.'

'Yes . . . No!' He pointed at the piece of paper. 'But this is the exit code,' he said. 'The entry one's different.'

'Aha, so you know that. How do you know that? You've tried to break in?'

'No, you told me that's what it was, and look,' he pointed to the paper, 'you've written "exit".'

'That doesn't explain why you kept it though, does it?' He looked embarrassed. 'No smart answer for that, is there?'

'I kept it because I wanted to have something . . . oh, never mind.' He read the printouts again. 'Really, I had nothing to do with this crap.'

'You must have done. I don't know how but you got into the main house and you must have seen something, something to do with Sholto and his, you know, nocturnal wanderings or whatever. You must have seen him with someone. It's too much of a coincidence that this stuff came out about the one night when we . . . when I did something stupid.' She thought of Priya and whatever she had done with Wadim. 'It's in my contract that I'm not to engage in any inappropriate sexual relations.'

'We didn't do anything at all, remember?'

'Please don't insult my intelligence any further.' Anna could hear her voice become strangulated with posh vowels. 'You must never see me or be seen near the house ever again.'

'What? But it's my livelihood.'

She felt an irrational hurt that this should be his first response. 'Mine too. One that you've now completely screwed.' She blushed again.

'But I didn't, I really didn't. I don't care about not taking pictures there any more; I realised that gig was over when we, you know. But I really like you. Why wouldn't I? You're absolutely gorgeous and clever and not at all like anybody else I meet.'

She felt a painful accord. Jack too had been so unlike the other men, and she had liked this otherness. She had loved it.

'I thought we had a good time,' he continued.

'I did too,' she conceded. 'But then after that we seem to be remembering two completely different nights.'

'You really think I'm responsible for this leak? It doesn't even say anything anyway. What does it mean, "nocturnal ramblings"? It's just meaningless crap they fill websites and papers with. Who are they saying Sholto's shagging anyway? "Closer to home", that's pretty obvious code for someone who lives there too, but who?'

Not me, thought Anna. Sadly, it's not me. It's OK that he's with Cally, she's beautiful and famous, but if he's going to be with someone other than his wife, then it really ought to be with me, surely? 'You never give up, do you?'

'Jesus, you are just not going to believe me whatever I say. I promise you I had nothing to do with this story!'

She shook her head and stood up to leave, feeling a mixture of sadness, anger and, damn it, desire for him, as she couldn't help but remember the last time they had met.

He frowned. 'Anna, you've really got to start looking closer to home.'

'What do you mean?'

'For the leaks.'

'Don't patronise me. I know that Cally or Cally's publicists talk to you lot about when she's coming out. I know half those pap shots are a set-up. I'm not stupid.'

'That's not what I'm talking about.'

She paused, desperate to ask him what he meant. Then she lifted her chin and drew herself up tall, inadvertently sticking out her chest. 'Goodbye, Jack,' she said, and then walked out of the pub towards the bus stop that would take her back home. Not *her* home, she realised with a start. If she had begun thinking of it as home, then she was in danger of losing it.

She half hoped that Antigone would be replaced that day by the vile, spoilt child that she had witnessed the day after her night with Jack; the one she had nicknamed 'Antagonistic' in her head. That might have made her meeting with Janey and its surely inevitable outcome easier to bear.

But neither the old Antigone nor the one who had spoken to her so imperiously seemed to be in attendance that day. Instead there appeared a new one, who seemed to know that she was socially ill at ease, instead of the one who seemed quite immune to the pressures the rest of us feel. Anna and she spent the hours after school in agonising politeness, addressing each other with the formality of a Victorian governess and her well-bred charge. At bedtime, they read another chapter of *Treasure Island* together and Antigone sighed.

'What's wrong?' asked Anna.

'I want to say something but I don't know how. Not because I can't pronounce the words or anything. Obviously.'

'Obviously. What is it?'

'I've been thinking a lot about why I've not been feeling right. I think it might be that I'm sorry.' Antigone frowned with puzzlement.

'For what?'

'For the way I spoke to you last week.' She shrugged. 'When I told you I was your boss.'

Anna was touched and reached out instinctively, before pulling her hand away quickly. 'Thank you, Antigone, I really appreciate it. Why did you find that hard to say?'

'I don't think I've ever said sorry before. Perhaps I've never done anything I've had to be sorry about.'

'Perhaps. For such a short word, it can be really hard to say.' Anna cringed at the thought of how much she would need the word when it came to her meeting with Janey.

'It's not hard to say,' said Antigone. 'But it's quite hard to feel, isn't it?'

Anna laughed. 'I love you sometimes, Antigone.'

Antigone frowned. 'Don't say that.'

Was saying the word 'love' the oral equivalent of touching her? 'Sorry,' she laughed again, nervously this time. 'But I do. You're so funny and clever.' She found her eyes welling up.

'But you mustn't. Because you'll just leave me. People always do, especially those who say they love me. Only those who hate me get to stay. Even Bea went, did you know that? Just left and didn't even say goodbye. Nobody told me where she'd gone.'

'I'm so sorry. See? I can say it too.'

'I'm right, aren't I? You are going to leave me.' She wasn't plaintive, she didn't cry. She just looked burdened by the permanent pressure of being right. 'Please don't leave me,' she said.

'Good night, Antigone. Sleep well.'

Anna closed the door and stood there on the top floor, leaden with misery. She walked down the winding staircase that bored through the full height of the house and paused on the first-floor landing. She passed through it each day as she did the bedtime reading, but had never been allowed behind any of the doors that led from it. She knew the master bedroom suite was here. She'd seen photos of it in an article about Cally's decorating taste, and 'master' had seemed an inappropriate qualifier given its extreme femininity.

Across the hallway from the marital bedroom, a door was ajar and she dared to look through to the room beyond, wondering if this was where the servants slept. She saw a space that was almost a parody of masculinity, all dark wood panelling and tartan rugs, like the smoking room of a gentleman's club. She edged nearer, wondering which man in the house would get his own room, for surely Sholto shared the cushioned whiteness of the bedroom she'd seen in the magazine.

She thought back to her parents' bedroom – the double bed that she and her brother and sister had jumped into every morning, the make-up on the dressing table that she'd snaffled, the sneaking in to try to guess what was inside the wrapped packages on Christmas Eve. She wondered whether Antigone ever bounced on the bed in either of these two bedrooms, the male one and the female one. She'd never seen any evidence that she did.

She jumped as Martina emerged from the male domain, nodded her acknowledgement and sprang down the stairs as quickly as she could.

Janey's promised tour of the whole house had never happened. Now it probably never would.

'Come in,' said Janey, from beyond the panelled door.

Anna had never been to her office before, which was on the other side of the house, far away from the kitchens. Janey's administrative HQ was clearly deemed to require the same amount of square metres as Anna's whole living space.

Which, upon seeing the room, seemed fair enough. A whole wall was covered with shelves on which sat row upon row of box files, all pristine white, as if a normal office had been buried beneath a ghostly dust. They were labelled 'Architect's plans', 'Wages #11', and other marks of complex activity. On another wall hung a cluster of framed photos, most of which seemed to be of the house in various stages of dishevelment, as if performing an architectural striptease. A starkly beautiful photograph showed a view through the centre of a building where all the floors and internal walls had been removed, leaving a clear vista through the roofless canopy to clouds above. There were a few of Janey with her celebrated employers, dressed up as if for an award ceremony or charity fundraiser. She looked relaxed and quite their equal. Anna knew that if that had been her with Cally and Sholto, she'd have either looked awkward or overexcited, like one of those pictures that fans have taken of themselves standing next to their gracious idols, unable to resist doing a thumbs-up sign.

But the photos of people were outnumbered by endless shots of roofs, joists, close-ups of wallpaper, brocade swatches of fabric, artistic reflections upon the glass-topped tunnels of the basement – black and white, fetished, like Robert Mapplethorpes of shining male anatomy.

Anna was reminded once again that the whole world around Cally was a multimillion-pound business, one that stretched beyond this room to publicists' offices, distribution companies, agents and all those other people taking their percentage from her beauty and persona. Janey was the home-front CEO; she was both executive and operator and here was her high command. Her desk formed a huge L with views over the garden. At either end of it was a sleek computer. Anna could imagine that at the touch of a finger on a keyboard, Janey could animate the staff in the various wings of the house.

Janey swung her chair round to face Anna. She gestured at a sofa and Anna sat down, disconcerted that she should be at a lower level than Janey. She tried to read Janey's face, but she was giving nothing away.

Anna gulped and then began. 'There's something I need to share with you.' She paused. 'The leak, the thing about the, you know, "nocturnal ramblings" on that website . . . I think it was my fault.'

She had expected shock or anger, but instead a look of faint amusement flickered across Janey's face. Anna had that feeling again: that she was unable to discern irony when deployed by Janey. There was a pause as she waited for her to express something, anything, but she remained silently smirking, prompting Anna to gabble.

'I need to tell you about something that may explain how that got out.' She was going to spill it all, like a criminal faced with a taciturn interrogator. 'I would hate someone else to get the blame, when the blame is mine, or at least due to my actions. I didn't tell anyone about anything, I really didn't, I promise.' She looked at Janey's gleam – of healthy hair and toned skin, never of sweat or nerves – which seemed to match the unstained silk of the sofa's upholstery and the symmetry of those endless box files. Anna realised how quickly she'd become accustomed to luxury and physical beauty. The world that she'd be returning to seemed suddenly so tawdry, like a boarded-up row of high-street shops in comparison to a scented department store.

Anna blurted it out as quickly as possible, wishing she could up and run as soon as she'd said it. 'I invited a friend round to mine – his name's Jack and he's a photographer, you might know him – and he spent some time, not much really, in my room and I think I'm pretty certain that when he left he might have seen something, or not seen anything, but anyway it was that night, the one you were talking about in the staff meeting.'

Another excruciating pause before Janey said, 'Don't you think "photographer" is a little too grand a title for what he does? I mean, he's hardly Annie Leibovitz, is he?'

'You do know him?'

'We all know Jack.'

Janey swivelled back towards her desk, picked up a sleek tablet computer and handed it to Anna, before tapping it so that the screen lit up.

An image opened. It was black and white, grainy, like the images the police reveal from CCTV cameras.

'Do scroll through them,' said Janey, 'there are plenty.' She was as cheerful as if they were sharing holiday snaps.

As Anna scrolled through the dozens of images, she realised that they were indeed stills from a security camera. The first was taken just outside the front gate of Lorston Gardens and showed her and Jack locked in a vigorous kiss, her skirt rucked up to show her unglamorous underwear. The next was of her pushed up against the gate by him, their mouths wide open. This was how real people looked when they kiss: they are ungainly; their mouths gape; their heads don't lock together like a perfect puzzle. The others were more of the same as cameras tracked their progress all the way to the door by the garage. Anna, in particular, looked dishevelled, so different from the images of Cally that she had become used to seeing captured and pinned onto a computer screen. Jack, on the other hand, she thought sadly, actually managed to maintain his allure in the pictures, his face at such an angle as to showcase his cheekbones, as if he could be the sort of man that other paparazzi might chase.

Anna prickled with embarrassment. She'd been the child who was mortified when anybody kissed on television while she was watching with her parents. And here she was, practically having sex in public, watched all the while by the Cyclops eyes that studded this kingdom to digitally preserve her humiliation. 'I-I . . .' she muttered. How could there be such a gulf between how something had felt and how it looked? She had been so sexy and cool, so abandoned and appealingly reckless when she'd embraced Jack – she'd felt as though she'd been in some arty French film. But the photos looked like those pictures that appear in newspapers to illustrate 'Britain's booze shame', of grotty town centres where drunken women sprawl with their bare legs in the air and men urinate on war memorials.

'You knew about me and Jack?' she said to Janey, at last. 'You called that staff meeting and yet you knew?'

'I know everything, Anna.'

'We didn't do anything, I mean, we didn't have sex, honestly.'

Janey laughed. 'I don't think that's of any relevance.'

'Has Sholto seen these?'

'Not yet.'

'Please don't show them to him. I'll leave. I know I've been an idiot. I've jeopardised everyone's privacy. I'm so sorry. I'll resign; please don't sack me. At least let me resign.'

She didn't want to be sacked. It had been just a year since she'd graduated with her uselessly brilliant degree and now she was to be sacked from the only near decent job she'd managed to get. Oh god, Toby would have to know and he'd hate her. He'd tell everyone what she'd done and the pretty girls with the flicky hair would laugh at her. Her parents – she'd have to go back to them; her poor parents, bewildered by her misery at not finding a job, befuddled by the world that contradicted all that they had told her about the importance of a good education. The money they'd spent on music lessons and French conversation. Her moaning at them about how she was a failure, their reassurances that they loved her, her fear that they did not since she was no longer the accomplished girl who had filled them with such pride.

Janey said nothing, still looking at her with something like a smile.

'Please don't say anything to Antigone.' Anna had held herself together until that point, but then she thought of the girl's pinched face, with her assumption that all who love her leave her, and she began to cry. She looked up to the ceiling, desperate to stem the tears or to hide them from Janey. She, Anna was sure, never cried. She certainly would never have done anything so silly in her life as to have caused such tears. The effort of trying to hide them from Janey caused Anna's skin to tighten across her nose and a migrainous headache to begin to fizz around her skull. She was leaving clammy prints on the tablet's screen.

Janey continued to stare coolly at her, in no hurry to end her discomfort.

'Please, I'm so sorry.' Unlike Antigone, she didn't find it hard to feel sorry. The thought of Antigone's tight little apology made the tears pool inside her and she tried to huff her breath out in an effort to stop them from falling. It was no good. She began to sob in the ugly noisy way she always did.

'You won't be resigning,' Janey said at last.

'Please, I know I was stupid, but technically I don't know that there's anything in the contract to stop me from –' she struggled to find the right word – 'entertaining friends in my rooms.' Entertaining? The word made her sound like a Victorian prostitute. 'Is it a sackable offence?' Toby could help her; he knew employment lawyers. Cally and Sholto wouldn't want her to cause a fuss, so would pay her off and give her a good reference, wouldn't they? 'Please don't sack me.'

'We won't be sacking you, either,' said Janey. She stood up and took back the tablet computer.

'You won't? I don't understand . . .' She looked at the computer that Janey had put back onto her desk, with a mad hope that she had suddenly developed the super-power to set objects on fire just by staring at them.

'I shall be keeping these photos on my hard drive, but I see no reason to show them to anybody else. You can stay and carry on the good work.' Janey laughed.

Anna slumped with relief. 'Thank you. Thank you so

much, Janey, I really appreciate this. You're so kind. How can I make it up to you? I want to prove myself again, I really do. Please tell me what I can do.'

'As I think I've said before, your loyalty is key. We value loyalty above all else.' She looked very directly at her. 'You won't see your friend Jack any more.'

'No, I won't. I've told him that already. Is that all?'

'And if you see anything unusual in the house, anything that strikes you as strange, you will tell me all about it.'

'Like what?'

'You're a clever girl, or so I'm told – you'll know when you see it. You are my second pair of eyes and ears, and you will report to me regularly. Do you understand me, Anna?'

'Yes,' Anna nodded, while at the same time not understanding very well at all.

7

Changing Rooms

Anna's phone buzzed in her pocket. She checked it, wondering if it were Jack again, but it was her parents. It seemed as though they and Jack were the only people who called her these days. She'd tried to revive her college friendships with those who'd also ended up in London, but they might as well have not been in the same city for all their lives resembled hers. The ones that didn't live with their parents rented grotty flats in gritty neighbourhoods, not going out until ten at night, expecting her to take the terrifying night bus home (St John's Wood not being the sort of area they were likely to go drinking in). She couldn't even suggest they came to pre-load in her rooms, since the business with Jack had put paid to her inviting anyone round.

Somehow weeks and months had drifted by since she'd first moved to London and they no longer texted her. It was as if they'd never been part of the present, only the past.

She didn't feel like talking to her parents much, either. They asked irritating questions about how long she intended to stay there and was she looking for a 'real job' and to remember that they'd kept her bedroom just as

she'd left it. She felt their sticky concern invade her mani-
cured existence like Japanese knotweed. She tried to kill
it with neglect.

But the fact that her exile from her previous life was
self-imposed did not stop her feeling isolated. She spent
long hours writing lesson plans for Antigone, and prac-
tising chess and backgammon so that she could share
these edifying games with her, but also to fill the hole
in the day when Antigone was at school.

How she wished Priya were still here, or that she
hadn't blown things with Jack. They had offered a bridge
to the outside world, being both of and not of Lorston
Gardens.

'Bea,' asked Anna one day as Bea busied herself
preparing food just before Antigone's pick-up time,
'what do you do, when you're not here?' She wasn't sure
that Bea was ever off duty. She seemed to spend all day
in the kitchen and all night down by the swimming pool,
picking up the discarded towels; two used by every visitor
and then thrown aside to be washed after only one
outing, along with the endless towelling robes to be kept
fluffy.

'Why do you want to know?' Bea answered.

'Just curious. I mean, I don't quite know what to do
with myself when I'm not working. It's funny, there's
something about living here that makes you not want to
leave.'

'But also to want to leave,' said Bea. 'Need to leave.'

'Exactly,' said Anna, thrilled to have hit upon such
empathy. She realised that she had been confusing poor

English with a lack of perception. Maybe Bea could be her work friend. 'It's so lovely and perfect, of course. And you cook me such delicious food that it's like a mixture between a luxury hotel and a . . .' She couldn't finish the sentence.

'*Cárcel*,' said Bea. 'A prison.'

'Yes, albeit a five-star prison. And one that nobody is stopping me from leaving.'

'And still you do not go.'

'I don't, do I? There are all these amazing things in London I could be doing, but I mooch around here instead. That's why I was wondering what you do when you're free.'

'Free?' said Bea. 'I would not say I'm free. Not like you, Anna. You are free to go. Maybe you should. Soon. Before too late.' She turned away from Anna and began to concentrate very hard on what was cooking on the stove.

One thing that Anna did enjoy was swimming. Endless lengths, accompanied by the audiobooks of Proust that she'd downloaded onto her player. Listening to *À la recherche du temps perdu* as she ploughed the glittering waters that lay beneath the house had the benefit of quelling the questions about Janey and what she was asking of Anna.

While Proust improved her mind, she worked hard on her body, making it what magazines would call 'bikini ready'. Not that she wore a two-piece, but she felt she ought to look good for those that she might meet down there.

Today was one such day.

'Hello there,' said Sholto. He said it in such a way that it sounded as though he was there as much to see her as to have a swim, as if this feeling of Anna's was mutual.

'Hello back.' It truth it was no surprise to her that he should be there, because she'd begun to recognise his schedule.

'And how's old Swann and his madeleines?' he asked, gesturing at her ear buds. In his eagerness to engage her in conversation, he too seemed rather lonely.

'Oh, you know, melancholic as usual.'

'You know, it is so wonderful to have a woman in the house with whom I could talk about Proust. If I ever got round to reading him, that is.'

They laughed. He was so modest; it was one of the things she liked most about him. She watched him dive in and she admired the way that his body, unlike Dan's, did not have that off-putting perfection about it, but a slight paunch that suggested good times. Yes, his modesty was only one of the things she found attractive.

Here she was, in a house worth millions, in one of the world's greatest cities, swimming and talking about Proust to a great filmmaker, nay, an *auteur*.

She felt sorry for him. He must have so little in common with his wife. When they had married, the papers had been full of comment about what a lucky man he was, as if he were the school geek hooking up with the prom queen. But, Anna thought, Cally was the one who had been punching above her weight.

Anna was glowing from exercise, and a few in-jokes at the end of each length, when she returned to the changing room. Her good mood was broken by a text from Jack, its very existence reminding her of the fragility of her position in the house.

'Please call. We need to talk.'

She pressed delete. If only it were so easy to eliminate all memories of that night.

Anna doubled her lengths one evening and sat afterwards hugging her knees in her favoured changing room, zonked as she listened to the classic literature that she piped into her brain through the ear buds, putting off the moment when she'd return to the loneliness of her rooms. She felt as if she was suffering from both claustrophobia and agoraphobia: scared to leave Lorston Gardens, yet oppressed by the living quarters that appeared to shrink the more time she spent in them.

Even the changing rooms seemed to be bigger than her room. They were whole rooms, not the partitioned cubicles that she had been used to. The combination of Proust and the thousands of tiny mosaic tiles made her feel trippy. She stared upwards to the ceiling, fascinated by the crack that ripped diagonally across its width. She followed its path as it crept to the corner and then noticed, with surprise, that the wall had come away from the ceiling to leave a hole of at least a centimetre, like the gape of a midriff between crop top and trousers.

It was with a start that she noticed her changing room

door swinging slightly. How had she forgotten to lock it? She turned off her audiobook and pulled out her headphones, wondering what it was that had caused the door to whoosh. The combination of the ear buds and the water in her ears made her feel as though she was coming down from high altitude, and she yawned and masticated her jaw so that her ears popped and sound flooded into them. She quickly realised that her door had not swung on a whim, but because someone had gone past her, into the changing room next door. They wouldn't have known she was there because the door would have appeared unlocked and her body had been balled up on the bench in the far corner, enjoying the peace of the empty basement. She knew she should make herself known to whoever it was, it would be odd if she didn't; but as the minutes past it became more and more awkward. She tried to clear her throat to announce her presence but no sound emerged.

She could hear sounds from the changing room next door, surprisingly clear through the fissure at the top of the ceiling. A zip was pulled down or up; someone must be about to go swimming. As soon as she heard the splash of the person entering the pool, she'd make her move or show herself, a jaunty 'hey' was all that was needed.

She listened, trying to stop her own breathing. Still no sound of anybody emerging from the changing room. *Come on, come on, what were they doing in there?*

Then a groan rang out, causing her to start. She froze once more, sure that her sudden movement would have alerted whoever was on the other side of the wall.

But instead the moans continued, along with the low creaking of the cedar wood bench that ran along one wall of each of the rooms. Rhythmic, almost soothing, the moans and creaks were synchronised into some obscure piece of sound art. It was, she realised, the sound of pleasure, but it also seemed to be expressing some deep sadness.

She tried to gauge how near to release those moans were. Were they quickening? Any minute now, surely. She didn't have enough experience of either porn or real life to be able to work out the timing with any accuracy. Think, Anna, it's got to finish, whatever it is, and then there will be some business with towels or Kleenex and a moment to reconvene. The moans were male, of that she was sure, but she couldn't tell if the pleasure was self-administered or if someone else was there too. She gathered her kit together as silently and as quickly as she could and then eased herself out of her changing room and into the wide corridor that would lead her to privacy.

'Uh!' The voice from the next changing room shouted out with relief. Then, much quieter, but still just audible: 'thank you'. Anna thought the voice sounded familiar, but it was too quiet and there was not enough to place it.

She stopped in the hallway, shocked for a few seconds, her fear of exposure outweighed by her surprise and fascination. The door to the adjacent changing room opened quickly and she realised that she'd left it too late to run. A comfortable shoe, followed by a thick ankle clad in skinny jeans, emerged from it.

Bea was dabbing her mouth delicately when she caught sight of Anna, who was rooted to the spot. They stood looking at one another for a second. Anna waited for her to say something, but Bea just nodded as though they were bumping into each other in the kitchen. Anna acknowledged her back in an almost comically polite way, and then turned to escape as quietly as she could, not daring to look back.

Anna maintained this exaggerated courtesy the next day as Bea served Antigone her tea.

'This tofu is amazing,' Anna said to her, 'how do you do it?'

'I soak in miso overnight.'

'I see,' said Anna. Either Bea was much better at hiding her embarrassment than she was or she wasn't feeling the same mortification. Or Anna had misconstrued the whole situation and there was an innocent explanation, like some silly comedy sketch, and Bea had actually been blowing up a pair of armbands in that changing room. 'What did you eat at school today, Antigone?'

'Cottage pie. It was disgusting. I'm going to have packed lunches next term, aren't I, Bea? Mummy says they'll be much healthier than that Brit crap they serve at school.'

'Antigone,' admonished Anna.

'"Brit crap", that's what she said. I'm quoting directly so I can't be wrong.'

Anna tried to concentrate on what Antigone was saying, but was distracted by Bea. Even the sight of her using a spoon and then wiping her mouth with a napkin made Anna blush. Bea looked up and caught her eye.

'Six o'clock already?' Anna gabbled. 'I suppose I had better let you get on with bath time. I'll be back to do our reading, Antigone. I'll make sure I have your vocabulary book with me too. What was that word we wanted to put in it from yesterday?'

'Frond,' said Antigone. 'Do you remember, it said, "All around him, fronds overhung into his eyes like a fringe that needed trimming."'

'Yes that was it, "fronds". All right then, see you later.'

As soon as she got to her room, she realised that in her haste she'd left her phone behind, so returned to the kitchen to retrieve it. Antigone was still sitting on one of the high stools by the island, but she now had her hand inside a tall glass jar of unidentifiable brown stuff. She was licking it off her fingers with the glee of Winnie the Pooh with a pot of honey. She looked up and at once seemed much younger than Anna had ever seen her. She giggled – she actually giggled – and Anna felt a burst of affection towards her, but also envious of Bea and her ability to turn Antigone into a normal little girl instead of the self-possessed prodigy everyone else saw.

'You seem to be enjoying that, what is it?'

Through a mouthful, Antigone said an unfamiliar foreign-sounding word that she couldn't quite catch.

'*Carhetar*?' repeated Anna. 'What's that?'

'Milk of goats,' said Bea, firmly.

'Oh, right.' It looked too brown and sticky to be that.

'Is it Cally's? She's dairy intolerant, isn't she?, but I think she's allowed goat's milk yoghurt.'

Antigone giggled again. 'I don't think Mummy would like it.' She and Bea shared a conspiratorial look.

'Can I try some?'

'No,' said Bea quickly, and removed the jar from Antigone, putting the stoppered lid back on and disappearing off into the larder.

'It's just for Bea and me,' said Antigone. 'And sometimes Daddy too.'

'Anna,' said Bea, who had returned from the larder. 'You do not need to say anything to Janey.' Her voice rose at the end of the sentence questioningly.

'About what?'

'About this.' She gestured towards Antigone, whose face was still messy with the brown stuff.

Or that, thought Anna, reminded of Bea's own sticky-mouthed emergence from the changing room by the swimming pool.

When Anna got back to her room, she turned on her laptop. She googled the word '*carhetar*' which responded with results for the search 'car heater' or 'catheter'. That wasn't right. The 'h' in the word had been raspy when Antigone said it, so maybe it was Spanish. She tried '*carjeta*' and the search engine, in its bossy, patronising way, suggested that actually she might have meant '*cajeta*' and unveiled another set of results about a Mexican sweet treat. She clicked on an image that showed the toffee-like mixture being poured into a row of glass jars exactly like the one she had seen in the kitchen.

She read the definition. A caramelised substance made by boiling goats' milk, or a mix of goats' and cows' milk, together with large amounts of sugar until the liquid evaporates to leave a stiff, sweet goo, like toffee or the product of boiling up a can of condensed milk. Known in other parts of Latin America as *dulce de leche*, *doce de leite* and *manjar blanco*. Anna could almost taste the sweetness on her lips as she read descriptions of children eating baguettes spread with the glorious goo and the recipes for brownies sandwiched with a salted caramel mix.

No wonder Antigone had looked so childishly delighted. Even grown-ups would have the same expression if caught with their hand inside a jar like that.

It was no surprise either, that Bea should have looked so shifty on having been caught. If she was prepared to flout one of Cally's central commandments, that 'there shalt be no refined sugar in Lorston Gardens', which other ones was she breaking?

Anna continued to delete Jack's texts, often without even deigning to read them. She did the same with his emails and his voicemails. There were so many ways to be contacted, but all of them had ways to be negated.

In the end he used the most unusual, the craziest, the zaniest, most original form of communication of all. He wrote her a letter. It had a stamp on it and everything, imagine, and he posted it in a letterbox.

Anna returned from the school run one day to find an official-looking brown envelope waiting for her. Her address was typewritten and visible through the window. It was one of those letters that begged you to ignore it, but Anna being Anna meant that she opened it promptly in expectation of it requiring action, be it from the tax office, bank or student loans company.

She scanned the pages quickly to see Jack's name at the bottom, below the typed text. She was so surprised that she didn't immediately throw the letter aside, but found herself reading it. She admired the subterfuge he'd used in disguising it to her, though she later found out that it was not in order to fool her that he had presented it as a letter from a more official source.

'Anna,' it began. 'I know you don't want to hear from me and that's fine if you're not interested, but not if it's because you think I've done something wrong. Betrayed you. That's probably the word you'd use, isn't it?' Yes, thought Anna, that's exactly the word I'd use. 'I know what you think I did, but it wasn't me and I'm sorry that I couldn't convince you by just telling you the truth.

'However much I denied it, you wouldn't believe me,' the letter continued. 'So I realised that I'd have to find out who really was responsible, so that you'd know it wasn't me. I started off by doing some digging to try to find out who it was that told that story to the press. I didn't get much – protecting sources and all that (a strange sense of honour us lot have). I've got my suspicions, it's been done before, but I'm not going to say anything until I've got proof. You won't believe me otherwise, you'll just say I'm making it up to protect myself.

'So, I thought, what's my other way of proving that I didn't use you? (Well, use you to get a story, I mean. I did fully intend to use you and your gorgeous body for other purposes, but that was surely mutual? I hope so.)'

Anna smiled at the memory and then forced herself to concentrate on the letter again.

'You've seen a story in the papers that I didn't spread and you assume it's from me. So, I turned that on its head and thought, what if Anna sees some photos that I really have taken and haven't sold, if you see what I mean. Then maybe she'll believe me.

'Trouble was, I didn't have any good photos, obviously, or I'd have sold them before I met you. So I had to go and get some. Took a different route. Didn't try to follow Cally, but went after other people from your gaff. I don't trust any of them, which is why I had to send you this letter in an envelope so it looks like it's coming from a bailiff, as otherwise it would get intercepted or something.

'Please take a look at the photos I've put in the smaller envelope and get in touch with me if you think you've seen enough to know you can trust me. They might also make you think about the people you're living with.

'Breaks my heart not to try to sell these, but I tell myself you're worth it.

'And you are.

'Love, Jack.'

Inside the bigger envelope was another smaller one with 'pix' written across it.

For all of a second, Anna contemplated not opening it, and then dived in. Out fell a handful of photos, in an uneasy echo of Janey revealing the CCTV images of her and Jack.

In them, Janey was clear, sitting at a table at the very pub where she had held Anna's one-month review. That seemed so long ago. The photos had been taken through a window, presumably at some distance since they were grainy and the artificial lights of the pub had dissipated to create an orangey glow. Next to Janey on the banquette, with his head near to hers as if deep in conversation, was a man in a tweed cap and thick-rimmed glasses. Anna could imagine how Jack would describe him: 'Tosser'. She squinted at the man and saw – and it seemed obvious once she knew – that it was Sholto. She quickly shuffled through the other photos and they were more of the same, but by now she could see Sholto more clearly. Sholto leaning in to hear what Janey was saying; Sholto looking into his drink thoughtfully; Sholto looking down as Janey touched his arm; Sholto sitting alone as Janey made a discreet exit.

Anna wasn't sure what reaction Jack had hoped to inspire in her, but she surprised herself at feeling relief. There was something about the possibility of Sholto with Janey, sad as she was that he hadn't chosen her, which seemed to confirm her view of the world. They were alpha people belonging to superior species and it made sense. Anna could finally admit to herself that she had hoped that were Sholto to stray from Cally then it would be with her, with a woman who liked to discuss literature and art. But if it wasn't to be her, then Janey was a logical choice. Anna had, she now realised, begun to wonder whether there was another candidate in the house for the role of Sholto's mistress, and even the idea of him with someone like *that* had made her feel unnerved. She had always thought that she believed that inner beauty trumped superficial good looks, but when faced with something to confirm this wisdom she realised she was just as shallow as anyone else.

That had not been Jack's intention, though, in sending her these pictures. No, that wasn't it; the key was in going to all the effort of taking these pictures and then showing them to no one but her. It was as though he had undertaken a modern and twisted chivalric quest, some sort of grail that he had followed to prove his love for her was pure.

She lay back on her bed, trying to understand it all: her and Jack, Sholto and Janey, Sholto and Cally, Bea and . . . well, that was where the card game of pairs was derailed.

It was a week after the strange incident in the adjacent changing room before Anna dared go back to the basement, and this time she made very sure to lock the door. When she was safely plugged into her audiobook, she went out to the glittering pool area and found that, once again, she was not alone. Cally sat on the shallow steps at one end, scissoring her legs in an unenthusiastic way.

'I'm sorry,' Anna said, and turned to leave.

'No, stay, stay, sit.' She patted the water beside her.

'OK.' Anna felt both too exposed and too covered up. Her costume was a burka in comparison to Cally's minuscule bikini.

'We haven't really had a chance to get to know each other.'

'No.' That's because I'm employed to teach your daughter, not to hang out with you like the rest of them – Lysette, Sandi and Jude. 'I suppose not.' And if we are to get to know one another, couldn't it be when we're wearing something more than what is effectively underwear?

'I expect you know my daughter better than I do.' Anna thought Cally's voice was slightly slurred.

'I wouldn't say that. She's too clever and unusual for any of us. She's not a book that's easy to read.'

'No, she's a book with like, really, really small letters and lots and lots of pages. The sort of book Sholto reads, but I don't. I only read lists of beauty treatments and articles about myself, he says.' She paused.

'What're you listening to on that?' She pointed at Anna's ear buds.

'Oh, you know . . . music to swim by.'

'So tell me about Antigone then.'

'Your daughter? She's lovely.' She is, she really is. Anna felt that core of love for her, which had been growing since she thought she might have to leave the job, blossom just a little more.

'She's unusual though, right?'

'Yes, she is. In a good way. I think she's adapting to school more now. She's got a new friend, a proper one. He's a footballer's son. A famous one, or so I'm told, but I don't know much about it. He's sweet, the boy: Miras.'

'So he's a jock?'

'No, that's the funny thing. Miras is hopeless at sport; he much prefers sketching clothes and shoes, and he's really good at talking to Antigone about all those things that she likes talking about. Plus, he's teaching her some Kazakh, so that's good. I suppose.'

'I'd like to be Antigone's friend,' said Cally, still doing her underwater exercises.

'You're her mother, though, that's so much better,' said Anna.

'I guess. Have you ever really wanted something? So much that you think about getting it every minute of every day?'

I want to get out of this pool, thought Anna. I wanted Jack and look where that got me. I want Sholto, too, to notice me, to let me feel the sunshine of his attention. 'Yes,' said Anna.

'I really wanted kids. With Sholto. Jeez, I wanted them *so badly*. My life was divided into two-week chunks, endlessly: two weeks of hope, two weeks of disappointment. For years, you know? Can you imagine? It was so crazy to get so many goodie bags and gorgeous dresses from designers when all I wanted was to wear one of those weird Lycra belts that pregnant women wear.'

'You must be very proud of Antigone.'

'There's the thing. You want something so much and you think it's the one thing that's stopping you from feeling happy, but it never is. You know, like getting bigger tits or something. I remember when I got mine,' she looked down and Anna was surprised, since they were so small yet beautifully formed that she had assumed them to be real, 'and you know, I was just me with better tits. And then later, you know – it's always something else.'

'I'm sure.' I'm not, I really am not.

'And when you really want something, you'll do anything to get it. Doesn't matter if what you do is a bit – how would you guys say it? – dodgy. Especially when what you want is so innocent and natural. A baby! I mean, it's not bad to want a baby, is it? I kept on saying that I was ready to be unselfish, that I wanted to think about someone other than me.'

Anna nodded and said nothing. Her job was to remain silent on the other side of the invisible confessional box.

'But do you know something? That's bullshit.'

'OK . . .'

'No, it is,' Cally continued. 'You don't become less selfish when you have a kid. You just find a way to double your selfishness. Antigone's all about me – well, she was supposed to be, and she's just not, is she?'

'She's very much her own person.'

'She's somebody's person, all right. I'm not stupid.' She looked at Anna. 'Sholto thinks I am, but I'm not.'

'They're not allowed to use the word stupid at

Antigone's school,' Anna said, in an attempt to change the subject. 'It's considered a swearword.'

'I think maybe we should introduce that rule here. Are they allowed to say "patronising bastard" at Antigone's fancy school?'

'No, definitely not.'

'I'm not stupid, I'm really not. I know Antigone's going to hate me anyway. They all do. I've read the books. She'll probably write one of them or, like, get one of those legal divorce things that kids can get from their parents. I don't know why I was so desperate to have a child when we all have children who hate us.'

'I don't hate my parents.' Anna felt a shard of pain at her neglect of them. She would ring them tomorrow, she promised herself.

Cally laughed, her eyes becoming ever more glazed. 'I'm not talking about you people. Us, we, people like me. Our children all grow up to hate us and become stand-ups who make us the centre of their routine or write books about how Mommy wouldn't let them use wire hangers or try to become actors themselves and blame the fact that they never get anywhere on us and the fact that nobody would judge them on their own merits. Boohoo, poor me.'

Anna was by now completely befuddled. 'I think I'd better get back to my room.'

'Stay,' said Cally, grabbing her arm with surprising force. 'You haven't had your swim.'

So Anna did a couple of self-conscious lengths before returning to Cally, who was now doing impressive plank exercises by the side of the pool. When she caught sight of Anna, she toppled over and into the water, only to emerge giggling. With her hair wet, she looked astonishingly beautiful and much younger than her years (which were anything between 38 and 47, depending on your source). Anna couldn't help but think of how much Jack would love to capture this uncharacteristic loss of control from the red-carpet queen. She felt a strange sense of regret on his behalf. He would kill for pictures like this and here she was, just letting the moment go to waste, disappearing into the ether of the unrecorded.

'I think I'd better go,' said Anna again. 'But I'm not sure . . . Well, are you all right if I leave you here?'

'You think I'm drunk?' Cally's laugh had a descant of hysteria. 'Have you any idea how many calories there are in alcohol? It's like drinking sugar, I tell you. Like pouring sugar into a glass and slugging it back.'

'No, I wasn't suggesting . . . I thought you might be tired or something.' Anna noticed how Cally's pupils had dilated so much there was almost none of the greeny-yellow of iris left.

'I do love Antigone though, I really do.' She seemed desperate to convince Anna.

'I'm sure you do.' Well, stop telling her she's fat then, Anna said to herself.

'It's kind of a shame she doesn't love me back.' With that she lowered her head back into the water and floated in a star shape. Then she plunged down into a ball and came up once again, before getting out and staggering off to lie on one of the loungers that surrounded the pool, tapping her feet to the metronomic drip that came from some corner of this underworld.

All that remained of Cally in the pool was a large hank of hair extension, floating on the surface like a dead animal that had been washed up after an oil spill.

8

Eyes and Ears

'Jack,' Anna recorded onto his voicemail. 'I got your letter. Thanks. I think. We should talk. I'll actually pick up the phone if you call. So call.'

She immediately regretted the message. Yet another footprint she had no ability to erase herself. It was out there, permanently scorched onto an indestructible hard drive. Whenever there were those reconstructions of the last steps of murder victims, Anna would wonder whether they were looking down on themselves, regretting the choices that they had made that day now that they had been so scrutinised. Would they have bought that pizza or cheap bottle of wine in the supermarket if they'd known that it would be their public legacy? Would they have worn those nondescript clothes that the police would source and dress an actor in for the reconstruction?

She thought about the way her life would be pieced together from the mosaics of electronic records she was leaving. She glimpsed up at the security camera as she left Lorston Gardens with Antigone, trying to work the runway as Cally would do, conscious of her angles.

On the way back from school, her phone rang with the call she was expecting.

'Hello, Jack,' she said stiffly, stopping suddenly to concentrate.

She felt a bump that almost knocked her off her feet and turned around to see Dan, who had been following her so closely and yet so invisibly.

'Got to go,' she barked into the phone. 'Hello, Dan, how are you?' Her body felt soft and vulnerable beside his steel bulk. 'You gave me a shock.'

'Why?'

'Because you just bumped into me, that's all. I didn't realise you were following, I mean, behind me.'

He nodded towards the phone. 'Did I interrupt your little conversation?'

Anna was distracted for a second with the thought that almost no one ever uses the word 'little' without sarcastic inflection. 'No, not at all.'

'Friend of yours, was it?'

Anna was beginning to wonder whether Dan hadn't seen too many geezerish gangster films. She found herself responding to his cliché in similar fashion. 'You could say that.'

'Could you now?'

Anna, on the other hand, hadn't seen very many of the genre, and so her script had quickly run out. 'It was nothing. It was no one.'

'Good. Because I would hate to think that it was something to someone.'

'Sorry? No. I don't think it was. Something to someone, or whatever it was you said?'

'Because doing something with someone got you into a bit of trouble, didn't it, Anna?'

She blushed, the images of her wrapped around Jack with her skirt rucked up flashing into her head with mortifying clarity. 'I suppose.'

'And you wouldn't want someone else to know that you were still in contact with somebody, would you?'

'No.' The someone being Janey and the somebody being Jack? The advantage, Anna realised, of this opaque cops-and-robbers talk was that it could mean anything to anybody.

Dan raised his hand slowly. For a moment, Anna thought he was going to hit her. Fear raced through her body and, to her horror, a shocking spasm of something else, something that felt like desire. He patted her lightly on the shoulder. 'Go home, now, girl. Be careful.'

Anna had spent her whole life following rules, but then she'd always understood them. Here at Lorston Gardens they were cloudy, so it was unclear why she had to obey them. Her teenage self had never smoked, nor stolen anything from the newsagent's. But at last, ten years on and clutching her phone in readiness, she felt the joyful rush of petty rebellion.

'My letter worked, then,' said Jack as they met in a messy garden square far from the house.

'I suppose so.' She couldn't even look at Jack as she

said hello. He, for his part, hugged her. Not in a particularly sexual way, more like a man-hug or one you'd give a child. Ever since she'd seen the photos of her and him, she'd not been able to shake off the feeling of being under surveillance and so glanced nervously into the sky.

'Here,' he said, giving her a coffee that he'd bought from the vegetarian café in the square's centre. He took a gulp of his. 'Fuck, this tastes like it's made of mung beans, not coffee beans. Bloody disgusting. Sorry.'

'Thanks. And thanks for the letter and the photos . . . I think.' She frowned. 'I'm not sure I really understand that it proves anything, but somehow you going to so much trouble shows something.'

'That was the plan . . . I think.'

They laughed. Among all those who worked within and surrounding Lorston Gardens, and she included Jack in this, he was the nearest thing she had to a friend, the nearest thing to normality. He touched her arm to guide her to a park bench. She flinched, as Antigone would, for a second, and then allowed herself to press into it. She felt his warmth spread through her as though she could see it, like an orange glow on a thermodynamic image. They sat so close to one another that their shoulders touched.

'It's been odd not to see you outside the house. I'd got used to you there.' She could say she'd missed him, not out loud, but she had.

'It's been odd for me too. Not to mention, financially inconvenient. My most reliable source of income, they were.'

'Sorry about that.'

'Still, I suppose I can come back to my usual spot now, if you don't have a problem with it?'

'No. I mean, I wouldn't mind, but other people might. You know, Janey.'

'Her? Bitch. What's she got to do with it?'

'She showed me some photos. Of us. Taken off the security cameras. I don't know how we could have been so stupid. Well, me, yes, I can see why I didn't think of it, but you're more savvy, aren't you? Why didn't you make sure we weren't seen? If you weren't trying to get some dirt from the house, what madness was it that made you think it would be possible to sneak in without being seen?'

Jack shrugged. 'Yes, I know. It was madness. I find having a gorgeous unobtainable woman with her legs wrapped round me does tend to distract me from my usual caution.'

Me, gorgeous? thought Anna. Brilliant, clever, quirky, yes. But gorgeous? The orange glow was now pulsating within her. She was the one getting distracted now. 'Well, we both should have thought. You coming to my room coincided with the story about Sholto getting leaked. They put two and two together.'

'And got five. It doesn't prove anything against you.'

'It doesn't really matter what they think and what's actually true,' Anna said. 'I don't think Sholto and Cally would be impressed with me fraternising with the enemy anyway.'

'Fraternising? Is that what they call it these days?'

'You know what I mean,' she snapped.

'Not really. I don't think of myself as the enemy. Neither would Cally, nor Janey. To carry on with your Second World War lingo, they're definitely collaborators.'

'What do you think Janey is up to with Sholto in those photos you took?'

Jack shrugged. 'God knows. She's a piece of work, that one.'

'You don't think they're having an affair?'

'Having an affair? What a nicely old-fashioned phrase that is. But no, I don't. Why, do you?'

'Well, I assumed that's why you'd sent the photos. You once said Sholto was only interesting if you caught him with another woman, and so I just thought that you had, and by not selling them you were proving to me that you wouldn't in fact sell your own grandmother's kidney for a good story.'

'If I had caught Sholto groping some other woman, well . . .'

'I can actually see the pound signs in your eyes. For real,' said Anna.

'Hang on a minute, I was going to say I'd have passed any information or photos on to you to prove my innocence against the other accusation. But anyway, Sholto and Janey, I don't think they're doing it. These men, your Sholtos, they usually do it with employees or people working under them, so to speak. Make-up artists, they're always doing them; assistants, that type. It's never people who work in supermarkets or teachers or something. So you're right, Janey being an employee means she's exactly the sort of person he might be doing but that wasn't the vibe I was getting from them in the pub. Not at all.'

'So what were they doing cosied up like that? Sorting out the staff rota? Just a friendly drink?'

'No, no. It was more like a business meeting they weren't supposed to have. She was in control; he looked anxious.'

Anna tried to recalibrate her understanding of the byzantine dynamics of Lorston Gardens. She felt as though she were seeing its world like a child looking at her parents' dinner party through the spindles on a staircase. Small glimpses, snatched half-conversations, never quite knowing which halves made up which couples.

'Anyway, I don't want to talk about them,' Jack said, pushing a lock of her hair away from her face, brushing it lightly with his fingers as he did so. She felt sure he'd got the move off a film, but it worked, it definitely worked.

'But Jack, you must see we can't . . .'

He put his finger on her lips. She shocked herself by taking it into her mouth. She crossed her legs with longing as she sucked it, her eyes locked to his. He took out his moistened finger and ran it down her neck to her clavicle, leaving a small trail of her own saliva. She longed for him to take that finger and run it over her nipples, then to stick it inside her. He leant forward and kissed her gently, then more forcefully. She wanted something to calm the bubbling she felt inside; she needed to feel him against her, so almost involuntarily moved so that her crotch pressed against his knee, her leg against him, feeling that he wanted it too.

Suddenly she saw herself from the outside. Not as the mother with her children in the playground across the way would have done, though god knows that was bad enough. No, she saw her manoeuvred body as in a photograph shown to her on a computer: sordid, shameless, tawdry. She thought of Sholto shaking his head over the images, or of Antigone's face falling as she was told that yet another person in her life was to be dismissed.

She pulled herself away, looking around with panicky self-consciousness. 'Jack, we can't do this.'

'Why not?'

'I'm sorry. I came here to talk to you, to apologise, to ask you about those photos you sent me, but not to do this. I can't.'

'Why not? You're a tutor, not a nun.' He reached out to the back of her neck. She shook him off.

'Janey said I should never see you again.'

'Or else?'

'I'll lose my job.'

'She can't sack you without a good reason. That's illegal.'

'I think she can, my contract says so. It definitely says I'm never allowed to talk to the press either during or after my employment. I agreed never to talk to the press and never to take Cally and Sholto to a tribunal. She can do what she likes.'

'Figures,' said Jack. 'Their type are always getting sued

by the staff. That's why they call those that work in the kitchen sous chefs.' He looked at her stricken face. 'It's a joke.'

'I know, I know. I like your jokes.' She never seemed to laugh any more. 'I'm sorry, I don't know what I was thinking coming here. It was silly. I do like you, Jack, but I can't lose my job. It's the first one I've had, so it would look bad on my CV. And Antigone; she needs me. I need to look after her for a while. She needs someone to stay there who understands her and I can't let her down.'

'When you're done here,' Janey said to Anna as she read with Antigone, 'come to my office, won't you? I'd like a word.'

As they traversed the house, Anna craned to look at the newly decorated adult sitting room. There was an invisible Berlin Wall that divided Lorston Gardens, and there were huge swathes of it into which she rarely ventured. These rooms were for the adults, of which she was not one, who would gather for small parties, where the number of guests would be exceeded by the additional catering staff brought in for the occasion, while the guests raved over the food 'made to recipes Cally had inherited from her beloved Southern grand-mother', or so the stories went. Cally, or more accurately her interior decorator in protracted consultation with Janey, was moving away from the previously favoured pale greys and towards a more 'rock-and-roll palette'. A purple and black zebra-print rug vied for domination of the room with a huge portrait of a naked Cally. The style of the artwork would be most accurately described as a Photoshopped Lucian Freud – thick oil-painted flesh, but with none of the lumps and misshapes that characterised his work, the texture of the paint smoothed out as if with a plasterer's lathe.

'And here we are once again,' smiled Janey, ushering her into the office.

Yes, yes, thought Anna, I was already thinking about *those* photos you showed me here, you didn't need to remind me. Then she thought about the other ones, of Janey with Sholto. If only she knew their meaning, she'd be able to sit all straight-backed and smug, just like Janey. 'Yes, so we are.'

'I'll cut straight to it. I gather you've been in contact with our not-so-tame photographer again.'

'Sorry?'

'I think you know who I'm talking about.'

'No. I mean yes, I know who you're talking about. But no, I've not been seeing him much. At all.'

'You're a terrible liar. Believe me, I know all about how to lie well. You said you wouldn't see him any more. And now it seems as if you are. There will be consequences if you should persist. You know what we discussed previously, don't you, Anna?'

'Yes of course, but I don't actually think you're right about him having leaked all that nocturnal ramblings stuff.'

'Oh?' said Janey, raising her eyebrows, her forehead remaining miraculously unfurrowed.

'No, I don't.'

'And you can prove this?'

Anna thought of the sweet but ultimately weak evidence that had swayed her. 'No, not exactly. But I am utterly sure.'

'Explain.'

'I can't.'

'I see. And who do you think might be responsible then, if not Jack?' She said his name as though it were the brand name of a budget toilet bleach.

'I don't know,' muttered Anna.

'Well, shall we show Cally and Sholto the photos of you and him together that night and ask them to make up their own minds? Or have you some other evidence that they could weigh that up against?'

Anna shook her head.

'Well then,' said Janey. 'We need you not to see him any more. The fact that you still want to, suggests that you're not as loyal an employee of this house as we would like. I'm sure Cally and Sholto would agree with me. Do you wish to stay in employment, or did you think that fluorescent tabard you wore in your last job was so flattering that you can't wait to get back into it?'

How did she know about that? 'No, of course I don't. Please, I want to stay here. I like it now. And Antigone's important to me.' Don't throw me out into the real world: you've ruined me for it.

'If you are to remain here, then you will be working for me as much as for Cally and Antigone, do you understand?'

'Yes.' No, not really, what did she mean?

'You will be my eyes and ears among the staff. You will tell me if you see or hear anything that strikes you as unusual.'

'Like what?'

'You'll know. Were you to see Bea behaving in a way that you think inappropriate, for example. Doing something she shouldn't do, being somewhere she shouldn't be.'

'Bea?'

'Just an example by way of illustration. I'm as interested in Jude, Lysette, Wadim, Martina . . . everyone. Once a week I'd like you to tell me of anything you might hear or see. And remember that I also hear and see a lot, so any omissions will likely be noted. After the way you've behaved, you're under more scrutiny than any of them.'

'Ooooh-Kaaay . . .' said Anna, drawing out the letters in her uncertainty.

'And another thing. Just a little one.' Janey laughed. 'Actually, that's an inappropriate use of the word "little". You'll no doubt be aware that poor Cally is being made to feel most uncomfortable about the way Antigone is, how can I put this . . . growing.'

'Sorry?'

'You know, growing. Not up. But out.' Janey looked at Anna's blank face and her control was momentarily suspended. 'Oh for god's sake, aren't you supposed to be clever? Her weight, Antigone's weight.'

'I don't think there's anything wrong with Antigone's weight. Lots of girls go through a phase where they're not skinny, almost as if they're laying down the reserves to shoot up and grow. I know I did.'

Janey did an exaggerated look up and down Anna's body by way of judgement. 'It's really very embarrassing for a person in Cally's position. Do you know,' she leant forward, 'there was one well-known personality who used to make her daughter wear a corset for photo calls.'

'That's terrible. You're not saying we should do that to Antigone?'

'Not yet. We want to ensure that there's no need. Cally would like you to help. Just keep an eye on what she's eating. Write a little food diary for us. Make sure all the milk is skinny, no sweet treats, that sort of thing. Occasionally point out to her that what she puts in her mouth may have consequences. Make her mindful of calories. Do you understand?'

'I think so. You're asking me to tell Antigone that she's fat.'

Janey laughed again. Sometimes Anna felt as though Janey, for all her social grace, had some spectrum disorder that made her laugh at very random points in a conversation, as though she'd been told that it was important to do so at regular intervals. 'No, of course not. Not fat, exactly. That's not a nice word. I'm sure someone of your intelligence can find a better way of putting it.' She stood up to usher Anna out. 'And remember. I do so look forward to all that you will have to tell me.'

Anna hated herself for even looking at the stories that came out on the web. She knew it was tawdry. She knew it was odd, that she should be reliant on these unknown sources, probably sitting in a darkened room in Florida, for information about the people who lived in the same building as she did. She visualised a spinning globe, with the stories pinging their way from London to some server in the Far East and then all the way back to her computer.

The worst, she knew, were the blind items, those where the names of the protagonists were hidden or suppressed, but were usually quite easily detectable. Anna was becoming wise to the tricks that they used. Celebrities with the surname Green were described as colourful; if the stories involved a footballer, their team or their position would be tenuously mentioned, something along the lines of 'International scandal could appear' or 'which sportsman is Right Back where he started by banging his sister-in-law?'

She read the latest one and frowned.

Which Cautious Superstar complains of press intrusion in her adopted city of London, but makes quite sure that her photo opportunities are well exploited through some not-infrequent tip-offs to the press? Paps joke that photos of her are selling so cheap she should instead tip them off about when she's NOT going to be coming out of her house. Funnily enough, she's treating the privacy of her offspring as a matter of weighty importance, threatening to sue if anyone comments on the growing issue.

Of course, it could be that it wasn't about Cally, but the clues were all there, what with the 'Cautious Superstar' ungrammatically capitalised to spell out the initials of Cally Steward, the 'adopted city' and that horrible dig about Antigone's weight. She was quite the expert now. And hadn't both Janey and Jack at different times suggested to her that the circus outside of Lorston Gardens was one being managed, even encouraged, by Cally? Part of her found it incomprehensible that anyone should invite such intrusion. But, at the same time, she knew the strangely seductive nature of the attention. Even she, in whom nobody was interested, felt a frisson when she was greeted by the paps outside. Even she was fascinated to see herself photographed on a site devoted to celebrity offspring and, more shamefully, thrilled that she was described as Antigone's 'attractive nanny'.

They had been snapped on their way home from school that day too, of course. There's only one thing better than a celebrity child, and that's a celebrity child hanging out with another one. 'Antigone's got a boyfriend!' they'd say, completely ignoring the yukkiness of talking about eight year olds in such terms.

Antigone got asked on many play-dates. She had hosted numerous ones too. But she had never once expressed any interest in inviting anyone back, until the day she asked if it would be all right if Miras came round some time. Cue much excitement at Lorston Gardens. Bea even cried, while Dan immediately volunteered to drop the boy back at his parents' in the hope of meeting his famous footballing father. As soon as he heard the news, Sholto stood a little bit taller and puffed out his chest, like something from an anthropological study of primates, talking of how maybe they could have a dads' kickabout one of these days. Cally insisted on ringing Miras's parents, as though she were just a regular mother and Antigone were just a regular daughter, when they were both so strange in their different ways. The conversation wasn't entirely successful, since Mrs Aronov's English was hampered by the fact that she had brought her mother and three sisters over to London to live with them, and so far her vocabulary was restricted to the international language of designer names.

Everyone said well done to Anna and she glowed with pleasure before wondering what had happened to her world that this was its greatest achievement.

When the day came, she wondered what they were all so frenzied about, since it was in fact a Tuesday like any other. She had crammed in three hours of tuition the night before so that Antigone wouldn't fall behind schedule, and prepared a variety of improving activities for her and Miras to do should they so wish: a collage inspired by the works of Matisse, a recreation of scenes from the legend of King Arthur and a general knowledge quiz.

In the end, Miras and Antigone wanted to go to the bottom of the garden to bounce on the trampoline, which would count towards the half an hour of daily physical exercise that Anna was now exhorted to fit in to Antigone's timetable alongside the Latin, music practice and fine art.

The extensive play area was hidden from the house by the row of trees that hemmed the edge of the lawn. It was not clear why it needed to be so camouflaged from view, since it was far more tasteful than the primary- and rust-coloured, potentially fatally dangerous metal frames of the playgrounds of Anna's youth. A wooden-framed swing, rope and bridge area extended out above the grey-brown of the chippings that would break Antigone's fall (except, of course, for the member of staff who would probably get there first). The trampoline, too, was not the mesh-encircled eyesore of a million back gardens, since it was sunken to below ground level.

The trees had an ancient loveliness that suggested they had been planted in days of yore to create an enchanted woodland grotto for a climbing wall and ball park. 'Don't you think these trees are beautiful?' she asked Antigone as they walked down, she and Miras solemnly marching in time with one another, their equivalent bonding process to normal children holding hands.

'We've got much bigger trees in Kazakhstan,' said Miras. Somehow he managed to make this bald statement sound camp. He gave a flapping hand gesture towards Antigone every time he spoke, as if there were a silent 'girlfriend' or 'get her' glued to the end of each sentence.

'I'm sure you do. Do you want to pop your shoes off before going on the trampoline?'

Anna watched as he removed his exquisite leather boots. He was a tiny emaciated boy who looked more as though he should be appealing to prospective parents in an international adoption catalogue than amid the well-fed and -bred children of an oversubscribed London private school. His father's neck must be wider than the boy's torso, Anna thought. The difference in size between the two children made for some rather lopsided bouncing, as every time Antigone landed, Miras was flung high in the air, to much merriment. Laughter was not a familiar sound here and Anna would have luxuriated in it, were it not for the fact that she was too busy running around the trampoline nervously, fearing that someone might be propelled outwards and she would then be held accountable for Miras's lack of sporting prowess in later years.

As they bounced, the children chatted, the volume of their voices distorted by their contortions.

'My dad's more famous than your dad,' said Miras.

'Oh definitely,' said Antigone, 'but my mother is more famous than all of them.'

'Do you think so? She's so beautiful and I love her style, but footballers are very famous, you know. We can go anywhere in the world and people ask my dad if they can take a picture of themselves with him. It was madness in Thailand.'

'That's funny, people usually just take a picture of Mummy without them being in it and without asking. I wonder why that is?'

'Maybe they don't want to be in a photo with her because she's so beautiful.' Miras sighed.

'She is, isn't she? I don't look like her.' Antigone's white-blonde hair rose above her to make a halo of tendrils as she bounced.

'No, you don't. You're really white, aren't you? My mother's an orange colour.'

'Mummy sometimes paints that stuff on too,' said Antigone, 'especially on her legs.' They stopped to put their arms next to each other, but not touching, to compare colours. 'I think I should probably put some on too. Then maybe I'd look more like her.'

'Yes,' said Miras. 'And dark colours are very slimming too.'

'That's why Mummy often wears white. Because she can.'

It was then that Anna noticed Janey had materialised by her side. They looked at each other for a second, before Janey turned to look at Antigone and then back to Anna, her eyebrows raised in expectation.

'Antigone,' said Anna, as if pre-programmed, 'jump higher, why don't you? It's such good exercise.'

Her self-loathing was not ameliorated by Janey's small nod of approval.

'All right, Miras?' said Dan, who had joined as if it were important that the number of adults should always exceed the number of children.

'Fine, thank you.'

'Fancy a game?'

'Of what?' Miras kept on bouncing with determination.

'Of what?' Dan laughed. '"Of what?" he says. Football, of course.'

'Urgh, no thanks. I thought you were going to say chess or mah jong. I hate football,' he said with vehemence.

'Detests it,' added Antigone.

'Loathes it,' said Miras.

'Despises it.' Antigone waited for his rejoinder but he looked blank. 'Disparages it, abhors it, scorns it . . .'

'Hark at Antigone,' said Dan. 'Swallowed a dictionary, have you?'

'I think you mean a thesaurus,' said Antigone, as she bounced ever higher.

'Antigone, your playroom is really stinky,' said Miras as they walked down to the basement.

'Isn't it? I can hardly breathe.' She clutched her throat dramatically, having at least inherited her mother's thespian tendencies.

'It's not so bad,' said Anna. She would have thought she'd be used to the strange chemical smell by now, but if anything it was getting worse.

'I have a very sensitive sense of smell. In fact, all my senses are extraordinary,' said Antigone.

'Me too,' said Miras. 'My optometrist says I've got the best vision she's ever seen.'

'I've got an ophthalmologist. I think that means he's an actual doctor.'

'I'm sure you're both amazing,' said Anna. 'Now shall I get the art stuff out?'

Miras and Antigone huddled near one another on the sofa, hunched over the phone that Miras had produced from his pocket.

'Three million, eight hundred and forty thousand,' he shouted. 'And fourteen million, one hundred thousand.'

'Approximately three and a half times greater, no, three point six times greater. Busted,' said Antigone. 'Next.'

This game carried on for a while, with Miras typing into his phone and then shouting out ever-increasing numbers, which Antigone, in human calculator mode, compared to one another, then expressed as percentages, then as quotients.

'What game is that?' Anna asked. 'Is it a maths programme?'

'No.' Miras looked at her as if she were stupid. 'It's how many Google hits people from school get. And their parents. Look at her,' he held out the phone, which showed a picture of the child of a singer and model. 'I mean, clearly nobody's interested at all. And yet she thinks she rules the school. Loser.' He did an L shape with his index finger and thumb, except it was back to front so looked more like a J.

'Ask me another,' said Antigone, giddy with the way that an awareness of others was intersecting with maths for possibly the first time in her life. 'We could make Top Trumps cards of everyone we know, with different sections and points given. Shall we do that, Anna? Like those ones you got me of Greek myths. Google hits, statistical increase in babies being given their name . . .'

'Style levels . . . I mean,' said Miras, flashing the phone, 'look at her cropped jeans. Hello?'

'I'm not sure it's a good idea. Why don't I get the Greek myths out?' said Anna.

'I'll say it again. Greek myths? Hello?'

'Fine, Miras,' said Anna. 'I'll see if supper's ready, but

Antigone, always remember you're more than just the sum of your parents, won't you?'

Antigone looked up at her and smiled.

Anna took some satisfaction from Antigone's increasing confidence with friends – well, the fact that she actually had a friend. She took pleasure from the fact that her charge's reading age now exceeded that which could be measured by such tests. Her IQ, once thought to be immutable, had also increased a few points. She could now serve overarm in tennis and had recently taken, and passed with distinction, Grade 4 on the piano.

Yes, she took professional pride in all these things, but she wondered if she wasn't like one of those high-powered women who'd given up work to home-school their child and took all their self-worth from their prodigy's achievements. It felt like getting the leftovers from someone else's plate and, however delicious they tasted, there was something cold and unsalted about them.

Anna needed another project. She should write a book, find an orchestra or chamber group to join, learn another language. All the things that people tell themselves they'll do when they retire, take a sabbatical or go on maternity leave. Like most people in such situations, she instead watched more television and faffed around on the internet.

Self-knowledge was being replaced by self-loathing, as she watched her intellect squelch into a mess of celebrity websites and reality TV shows.

But now Janey had provided her with a project. One

that used all her powers of observation, her ways with the written word and her perception. Janey was already impressed and had written her an email: 'Very pleased to see such improvement in your attitude. I will be conveying this to Cally and I'm sure it will make your position more secure. Re. other part of our agreement, to be my eyes in the house, please come to me on Friday to discuss.'

So Anna had been taking notes. Ah, the joy of notes, of annotations, of memos-to-self scribbled in pencil on scraps of paper and transcribed. If she treated this new duty as a project of observation and interpretation, then it felt almost like an intellectual exercise rather than some borderline immoral espionage on those whom she should consider her peers.

The day before her meeting with Janey, she updated her document. She was trying to think of ways of including some impressive long words, to make it what Toby would call 'polysyllable-tastic' (this being his recommended style for any progress report to parents).

Document 1:
1. Bea: gives blow jobs to unidentified men in the swimming-pool changing rooms. Has the temerity to look as though she enjoyed it even though we all know that overweight people shouldn't be allowed to have sex, let alone take any pleasure from it.
2. Also gives Antigone fattening sugary foods. Ditto: too much enjoyment is displayed in this process.

3. Dan: makes me feel uncomfortable, both scared and a little bit (the shame) aroused when he threatens me while all the while looking me up and down as if he wants to take me right there, right then. Could be construed as non-verbal, non-contact low-level sexual harassment?

4. When I'm walking back from school, I sometimes hear Dan on the phone saying things like, 'yeah, yeah, sorted, don't worry' and then looking shifty if I make it clear I can hear what he's saying.

5. Lysette: pulls snarky 'as if?' faces behind Cally's back, which doesn't seem like the behaviour of a bestest friend.

6. Jude: sometimes vomits into the downstairs toilet and isn't very good at cleaning underneath the rim. Afterwards she has a protein shake into which she adds stuff in funny unmarked bottles. Sometimes her chin shows definite signs of having been shaved, especially in the early evening.

7. Sholto: having an affair. That's what everyone says. I don't know who with. But it's definitely not me, more's the pity.

8. Sholto: has secret assignations in the pub with a member of staff in which he looks still handsome but concerned. But you know that one don't you, Janey?

9. Martina: I can't think of anything to say about her. She really is very dull. Which is unacceptable, surely?

10. Wadim: doesn't wear pants under his boiler suit. I know this as he also pees in the garden when

he thinks that nobody's looking. You could see his cock from space. It's enormous. Perhaps you know one that already? Or is it only Priya who was privy to that little, or should I say big, secret?

Anna giggled at the daringness of using such language in a 12-point font. She liked the author of this document. She was funny and snarky and scabrous. She was a bit afraid of her, too, but mostly in awe. She wanted to be her. Well, she was her, but only in written form. One day, she hoped to be her in real life too.

9

Cracks and Leaks

Janey made her wait outside her office for over ten minutes, having to stand in the absence of a chair. Anna recognised this tactic of intimidation from her school days and the headmistress's office. Not that she'd ever been sent there, obviously, but she'd seen the girls who had, loitering sulkily for half an hour or so until Mrs Henderson finally deigned to tell them that, most of all, they were letting themselves down.

'Come in,' Janey said finally. 'How is it going?'

'Fine. Really well. I think the play-date with Miras went well and her Latin is coming along by leaps and bounds, *mirabile dictu*.' And that, thought Anna, is for making me wait outside for so long.

Janey frowned. 'Absolutely, yes, fantastic news. Long may it continue.'

'*Deo volente*,' said Anna with a smile.

'Yes, yes. And what about the other thing that we discussed? The part of the job that's just as essential you carry out to the best of your abilities. Have you anything to report to me?'

Anna picked up her bag slowly and pulled out a document, one sheet of A4 with a list printed on it. She glanced at it just to check it one last time before handing it over to Janey.

Janey looked impressed by the efficiency. Wait until she reads it, Anna thought.

'Will that be all?' she said, standing up to go.

'No, no, I'd like you to stay while I look at this.' Janey began to read it. 'In fact, we can discuss each item and its significance as we go through it. Number one . . .'

Anna flinched momentarily. She knew she had been careful, but had that fear she sometimes had when holding her passport, that she might be overcome with some mad impulse to throw it out of the car window into the road – that there might be some suppressed self-sabotaging urge that she had been unable to control. What if she had become possessed by some evil sprite and had printed out the wrong list? She waited to hear Janey reveal the first of her observations.

'"Wadim left his phone charging, even when it was full, thus wasting valuable electricity". Well, yes, that is bad,' said Janey, frowning.

'It is, isn't it? And number two, Jude filling up Cally's water bottle with water from the non-filtered tap. We can't have that happening again, can we?'

Janey's eyes narrowed as she looked at Anna and then the list. Using an innocent tone of voice to hide one's sarcasm – Anna had learnt that skill from the mistress.

'Number three,' continued Janey. '"Lysette gave Cally a scarf that was made of man-made fibres". I'm not sure that's so bad. Micromodal's man-made and it's really very desirable.'

'I'm sorry,' said Anna. 'Perhaps you should cross that one out.'

'I shall.' Janey did so with quite unnecessary violence.

'The next one's about Dan,' said Anna.

'Dan? How interesting. "Dan sometimes leaves the engine running when he's waiting to take us home from school when it's raining". Hmm, quite the environmental emphasis you've chosen, haven't you?'

'It is our children's future,' said Anna. 'I know it's something Cally feels strongly about.' As she boards the private jet. 'And I know she really wouldn't be happy if she knew that Martina sometimes uses the wood cleaner on the ceramic tiles. That's the next one, by the way.'

'And the last,' said Janey. 'Thank you for this.'

'My pleasure. I expect you want me to keep up the good work?'

'Yes, of course. The good work. Except, maybe, you could perhaps concentrate on less domestic matters. See if you notice anything unusual in relations between staff and with Antigone. Anything you might overhear them saying about Cally or Sholto. Or me.'

'Like what?' asked Anna.

'I don't know,' said Janey, 'that's why I'm asking you for any information you can give.'

'OK . . . Like if Wadim doesn't say thank you when Martina makes him a cup of coffee?'

'No,' snapped Janey. 'I mean, yes, but perhaps things of a more significant nature. Say, should Wadim appear as if he is too close to a member of staff or member of the household. Or, if not him, someone else. Say, Bea.

Evidence too would be useful. Your phone has a camera on it, doesn't it?'

'I think that may be illegal. Taking photos of someone without their permission.'

'Well, you'd know all about that, what with your close relations with paparazzi.' Anna blushed, feeling at last outmanoeuvred. 'Remember, Anna, there are plenty of unemployed graduates out there who'd be happy to have your job. Antigone's getting quite attached to you, but I'm sure it wouldn't do her any harm to have a new mentor. One who might encourage her to exercise a little more. And I believe there are always people needed to solicit for charitable donations on the street. Do I make myself clear?'

'Yes,' said Anna. Damn it, she had been winning until injury time, when Janey just tipped in that last-minute victorious goal. Janey was good, too good, but Anna was getting better.

Janey thought she was so clever. But cleverness was Anna's domain.

'So, to what do I owe this pleasure?' said Jack. He was less confident than usual, burned too many times by Anna's vacillations.

Anna was not only meeting Jack, another step in her evolution from mouse to manipulator, but she had also travelled once more from the safety of her exclusive zone of London into a rather scabby bit of town, to a pub where velvet curtains vied with stuffed animals to create, according to the reviews she'd read on the internet, an atmosphere of Victorian intrigue. It made her feel kind of asthmatic and she didn't even have asthma.

'I need your help.'

'Ah, so you're just using me.' Jack sighed. 'I so want to be used, but not like this.'

'I know, I'm sorry. I'll make it up to you, I promise, but things are weird in the house and I can't risk anything at the moment.' She looked around the room, as if for a camera concealed in the mangy face of the badger beneath its glass case.

'Go on, spill then.'

'It's about Janey. She's up to something and I don't know what.'

Jack snorted in derision.

'What's that for?'

'Of course she's up to something. She's always up to something.'

'What do you mean?' Anna felt as though after years of short-sightedness, she was just putting on glasses for the first time but they weren't quite the right prescription. Things were clearer but not yet exactly how they were meant to be.

'She's a player. She controls everything in that place.'

'Like what? I know she's Cally's gatekeeper and she's in charge of the diary and all the employees and household accounts, but what are you talking about?'

'She's not just in charge of what goes on in the house,' Jack said, moving closer to Anna, 'she's in charge of what comes out. She tells us lot, paps and press, what's happening when, what Cally's moves are, when we should get round there, what sort of lenses we need, what we can't get sued for.'

'But I thought it was Cally who was always leaking her moves? She's the one who craves the attention.'

'What makes you think that?'

'I read one of those stories, you know the ones without names in them but you know who they're talking about, and it implied that Cally was desperate for the attention.'

'I'm sure she's not averse to it, but I'm not sure she's that desperate. You really mustn't believe everything you read on the internet, you know.'

'Yes, I know that. I'm not stupid.' She punched him on the arm, vaguely aware that was what teenage girls do to boys they fancied.

'Especially when many of the stories are put there by Janey.'

'Janey is the source of all those stories?'

'Yeah, well her and that driver bloke, what's his name? Dodgy looking.'

'Dan? The good-looking kind of muscular man?'

'If you say so. He gets paid for them, she tends to do it for free. It really wouldn't surprise me if she spread that story about Cally tipping us lot off.'

'Janey spreading a story about Cally spreading stories? I'm getting confused now.'

'Welcome to my world.'

'I wish you'd told me this earlier. Do you have any proof of Janey tipping you off?'

Jack frowned. 'I don't think so. She uses a phone with

a blocked number and doesn't usually identify herself. We just know it's her. What does it matter anyway?'

'She's threatening me with the sack unless I do what she says, so if I had some information on her to use in my defence in order to protect myself, it would be useful.'

'Of course,' said Jack. 'That stupid thing about nocturnal ramblings, the one that got you into trouble in the first place.'

'What about it?'

'Well, I bet it was Janey who put it there.'

'But why?' asked Anna, the picture becoming blurred once more.

'Look, she knew I'd been in your room that night – she saw the security pictures. So if she could make you think there were consequences to that, which she was protecting you from, well, then you're in her service, aren't you?'

'Have you got any evidence?' said Anna.

'I doubt she'd be so stupid as to leave a mark. And Cally and Sholto aren't going to be looking to get rid of her. From what I gather, she's very highly thought of by them, isn't she? They need her as much as the other way round. More so, probably.'

Anna thought back to her first meeting with Janey, when someone – whom she now presumed had been Cally – had rung her from a foreign city, pleading for an omelette. That amount of dependence must be so empowering for the strong one and so infantilising for the supplicant.

'Can you ask around for me, though? See if you can get any information that might be useful if she turns on me again? I don't want to lose my job. Not just for me, but for Antigone.'

'Antigone's all right, isn't she? I thought she was weird, but she kind of grew on me the time I was standing outside.'

'You make her sound like mould. But yes, she is all right. She's more than all right. She's really special. And I love her.' I do, Anna thought, I really do. 'Jack, she's made so much progress since I've been there. She was pretty unusual and she had no friends. And now she's doing so much better and I think I might even be quite good at this.' She frowned in shock. 'I might want to be a teacher when I grow up.'

'Would Miss Thomas like me to stay behind for detention?' Jack said.

Anna punched him again. 'Give it a rest. I can't leave Antigone unprotected from Janey. Janey hates her. I think she actually hates her.' Another piece of fuzziness seemed to be becoming clearer. If Cally wasn't responsible for the press tip-offs, then why on earth should she be the one generating the obsession with Antigone's size? 'I think Janey might be playing us all off against each other. Me against Antigone, even.'

'Can't you just tell Cally and Sholto this?'

'They won't believe me. Like you say, she never leaves a mark. It would be my word against hers and they'd never believe me. She's got some sort of hold over them, more than just being this goddess of efficiency who organises their lives so perfectly. If I could just work out what it is, then I'd be able to protect myself. And Antigone.'

'I think she's good at messing with people's heads. She messes with ours the whole time,' he said. 'One day telling us every last detail of their plans, the next telling us she's going to have us arrested. Changing like that all the time really keeps people on their toes. You should know that, Anna.'

'What do you mean?'

'You've not exactly been the soul of consistency with me, have you? I think the phrase is blowing hot and cold. And there's a worse phrase too.'

'I know, I'm so sorry, it's just that with all this going on, I'm a bit distracted. If I could just sort it out, then maybe I'd be a bit more normal. Please keep an eye out and ask around your contacts?'

'All right.'

'I'd really appreciate it. You managed to get those photos of Sholto with Janey, I'm sure there's something else that would help me to work it out.' Anna paused. 'Sholto with Janey. That must have something to do with her power. Could you not hear what they were talking about?'

'Don't be daft, I was outside the pub. He looked serious, she looked calm, that's all I can say.'

'How are you, anyway?' asked Anna, aware that it had been all about her. It was rare that she was the one making demands of others. Firing out questions was the language of her middle-class background, to the extent that afterwards people could walk away from her bruised by an interrogation, instead of impressed by her well-brought-up interest in others.

He shrugged. 'Business isn't great. I think I need to do something else. But I don't know what. This is all I know how to do.'

'Go back to college and get yourself some sort of additional qualification?' She groaned. 'Actually, ignore that, I don't believe in education as a solution any more.' She frowned, feeling like a bishop announcing his atheism. 'I'm sure you'll work something out.' She wasn't even sure she believed that either; there were plenty of people her age for whom it would never work out. 'Thanks for having a drink with me. I know I'm being annoying, but I just want to sort out my job and feel a bit more secure before I do anything else.'

He raised his eyebrows at her. She wished he wouldn't do that. It made her feel a bit dizzy.

'I've got something for you,' he said, drawing an envelope out of his bag of equipment. 'Is it weird of me to take a picture of someone asleep? Yeah, it probably is, but taking pictures is what I do; it's just the way I talk to people, really. I don't have your way with words. And it's just gorgeous, I think; it's one of the best photos I've ever taken.'

The photo showed her asleep on the night that they'd spent together, exactly when she had suspected he was off prowling the rest of the house. 'It is a bit weird,' she said. A still image of a sleeping person could, in theory, look like a photo of a corpse, and yet she saw more life in this shot than she ever saw in the mirror. Even though it was black and white, there seemed to be colour in her cheeks. A flush of pleasure in them that made her remember how he had made her feel, like someone else, someone who loved life. It made her look beautiful, both desired and cherished, even if at the time she'd been passed out drunk. 'But I like it.'

Anna swam up and down the pool trying to process what she had been told. If Janey was the source of the stories and tip-offs that came out of the house, then why wouldn't she be the source of every dodgy story that had appeared on the web and in the tabloids? And there were plenty.

She decided to see if she could swim a whole length underwater, having never lost that childish desire to set herself goals and overcome them. She pushed off as hard as she could, enjoying the way her body had become more streamlined since arriving at the house, and then checking herself against the attitudes that allowed her to think, even momentarily, that it was acceptable to goad an eight year old into losing weight.

She wanted to return to childhood, where life was simple and where you got picked for the first team if you were good, not if you were pretty or well connected or slept with someone at the top. The lights at the bottom of the pool glittered, beckoning her down to them, making her feel like some noble pearl diver.

The sub-aqua illumination at first appeared a random scattering of lights, like seeds thrown into a field, but by the end of the length, Anna could see through her goggles that they were evenly spaced to create the perfect shimmer. She took a deep breath and decided to go for a second length, just to challenge herself. At the far end, where she had begun, she saw that there the lights were not quite symmetrical, since there was a slither of something of a different colour and consistency at the bottom of the pool. She took another breath and plunged down to the bottom, just as a child does when their father throws coins in at the deep end.

As she swam near, she saw that it was a crack in the bottom corner of the pool, widening to the size of a football at one end. Strange, since the pool was only two years old. She came up for air and then looped down again to put her hand into the rip in the marble floor. She prodded and her hand just kept going until her arm went as far as her elbow. She pushed against it and found the sides of the fissure yielded like chalk, rather than the stone she had been expecting; it clouded up towards her face.

Just as she began to remove her arm to come up for air, she found herself being sucked downwards as if swimming above a riptide in the sea. Her shortness of breath was exacerbated by panic into near suffocation as she fought to rise the short distance she needed to travel back up to the surface. The more she tried to push herself upwards, the more she was being pulled down by some unseen force. She could see nothing but water, feel nothing but panic. Must get up, must get up. The cloudiness of the water disorientated her further, so that she didn't even know if she was pulling in the right direction.

She saw the chalk and the water and the sides of the pool and the air above it, then she saw images of Lorston

Gardens that seemed real but could not be. The last of them was of Bea in an old-fashioned nylon nightie that clung with static and damp to all the wrong places. She had her arms around Antigone, who was wearing the very pyjamas – sweet, old-fashioned gingham ones – she'd worn when Anna had read *Great Expectations* to her that night.

She thought it was air in front of her, but it seemed to ripple and bend like the horizon at the end of a hot road. It became as alien to life as the water had been and she felt herself unable to breathe. She was the opposite of amphibian; she could neither breathe in water or on land; she belonged nowhere. She remembered nothing else.

10

White Lies

Anna felt a mouth upon hers and a sickness welling up inside. Sick, she felt sick, and she realised that it had nothing to do with the body above hers. She escaped the disembodied mouth and tipped her body across the cold of the tiles, which she then splattered with a very dilute vomit.

She heard a voice shout something in a language not English. '*Ayúdame*,' she thought, that's help in Spanish, isn't it? Help, I need help, yes I do. She tried to call the word but nothing came out except more water. And then she heard something about '*mia*' and then an '*ay dios*' that she understood without having to understand. The flapping of small feet running on the stone. As consciousness returned to her, so did self-consciousness, leading to a brief shame at having been sick in public.

'I'm so sorry,' she groaned, trying to raise her head. She'd got properly drunk only once at university and remembered not remembering and the humiliation of the taste of the vile banana and brandy cocktails both on the way down and on the way up her throat. She tried to lift her head but it wouldn't move.

'Shhh,' said the voice, which she now recognised to be Bea's.

'You're here,' Anna said, seeing the image made reality and feeling the electricity bounce off the nylon nightdress that Bea was wearing in the flesh and not just in her head.

Bea helped her to sit up and then held her head, stroking the wetness of her hair and murmuring comforting words of Spanish. Anna felt safe both in her escape from the whirlpool that had engulfed her and in those stout arms. She didn't know that she had ever been held by any woman but her mother, but it felt good, so different to the wiry energy of Jack or of the wilting boy-men from before. She desperately wanted to go to sleep, if not in her bed, then here on the damp slipperiness that could not be further from a comfortable resting place.

I'm alive, she realised only then, and was surprised to feel a fleeting disappointment, frustrated to have been denied the knowledge of what happens after you die. For a few moments she had felt that she was about to be let into life's biggest secret, death, but now she was just like everyone else once more.

Wadim arrived, holding a phone that he waved at Bea. 'They're on their way.'

Who? Oh, not Sholto, please not him. Or Janey and Cally and all the rest of them. She tried to remember how she had got there. Her hand in the crack in the pool – yes, that was it. Why had she done that? She had been like a child that cannot see railings without sticking their head through them. And why had just pushing her feeble hand into the crack caused some greater fissure to open up? She racked her schoolgirl geography and thought about fault lines and plate tectonics and shifting sands and, no, she did not know how she had turned a small crack into a vortex. She looked towards the pool and saw the water was now draining off rapidly and noisily into large plugholes that had been opened up, presumably by Wadim.

Antigone had come back and she too was wearing the exact gingham pyjamas that Anna had imagined she had seen as she tried to escape being hoovered down by the transparent jelly of the pool.

She sat up properly. 'I don't understand.'

'There was water coming into Bea's room, it was dripping through the walls. Actually then it came pouring in,' said Antigone. 'So we had to escape, but when we came round the stairs we heard a splashing so Bea came to check and I followed her. We found you trying to get out. We pulled you out and then you collapsed. You were talking such nonsense, Anna, it was actually very funny.'

This did not make things any clearer for her. 'Bea's room?'

'It's there,' said Bea, gesturing vaguely beside her.

'There are more rooms and levels down here?' said Anna. 'Beyond the pool? I never knew that.'

'Where do you think the servants sleep?' said Bea, a little testily. They really were below stairs, thought Anna; far, far below stairs. 'There is a big house under here.' She pointed downwards.

'Was a big house, it will all be wet now,' said Wadim. 'We will have to live somewhere else. Janey can make us a new house.'

Bea's face was stricken. 'All my things, my photographs,

my clothes, everything I have here. We must . . .' Wadim nodded and rushed away.

'Don't worry, Bea, there's lots of room upstairs,' said Antigone. 'We've got seven bedrooms. Nine if you include Mummy's two dressing rooms. Ten if you count where Daddy sleeps, which is quite far away from Mummy's bedroom. You can sleep with me up there instead,' she said to Bea, who responded by putting a trembling finger to her lips.

Anna heard a siren cutting through the echoing space, shortly followed by the arrival of a couple of paramedics, who began to examine her and direct questions to Bea.

'Is she confused?'

'Yes,' said Bea.

'She's really confused,' said Antigone. 'She doesn't seem to understand anything we're saying.'

I don't understand, thought Anna, I don't, but that's not to do with the water, it's to do with how murky everything is becoming. 'Please can I get a robe?' she asked.

'Are you cold?' said the female paramedic. 'Is she cold? Her skin is bit bluish around the lips.' She put her hand to Anna's forehead.

'I'm fine. A bit cold, not particularly,' said Anna. 'I'd just like, you know, to be wearing a bit more.'

The male paramedic started wrapping her in a hospital blanket, making her feel like a crash victim.

'I'd really prefer a towelling robe. There's a whole cupboard full of them over there. Or my clothes, please just let me get my clothes on.' She tried to stand up, but was prevented by the grip the man held on those blankets.

'I get it for you,' said Bea.

'Thank you so much. And my clothes too, please. They're in the changing room.'

'The one you always use,' said Bea.

'Yes, that one. Thank you. I'm sure I'm fine, really,' she said to the paramedics.

'You have to come into hospital,' the woman said firmly. 'According to this very brave little lady, you passed out.'

'Who? Antigone?'

She could see a flash of recognition across the woman's face without a flicker echoed in the man's. 'She's Antigone, is she? Yes, this girl was the one who dialled nine-nine-nine. You're a clever little monkey,' she said to Antigone in an adult-to-child singsong voice. 'Would you like a lolly? And Dave here can blow up a rubber glove and make it look like Nemo the fish.'

'No, thank you,' said Antigone.

'But I feel OK,' said Anna. 'Really I do. Please let me stay here.'

'Anyone who suffers a near-drowning incident has to see a doctor. You could have lung complications, electrolyte imbalances, any number of ailments. Would you like someone to come with you?' the woman asked. 'Perhaps Antigone's mother?' She couldn't hide the hope in her voice.

'God, no. I'll come on my own.'

Anna was taken, now with towelling robe and a bag full of clothes, to the ambulance parked in the driveway.

The sensor-activated lights of the house's forecourt shone upon a group of people who stood with all the tetchy faux patience of those evacuated from an office during what they assume to be a routine fire drill. They were dressed and accessorised as though in one of those Renaissance paintings where the subjects are surrounded by visual clues as to their lives and occupations. Martina was holding a J-cloth. Dan was leaning on the car that had just returned with his bosses, who sported a very tiny dress for the chill of a late spring night (Cally) and a worried expression (Sholto). They were huddled in conversation with Janey, who wielded a tablet computer in much the same way Martina did her cleaning wipe, as a blatant status indicator.

Anna paused for a moment before getting into the ambulance, waiting for the trio to leap upon her to express their concern for her health, but they barely glanced in her direction.

She sat in the ambulance in her flip-flops, swimming costume and bright white towelling robe, trying to digest the strange events of the evening, letting the conversation of the paramedics waft over her.

'She looks so tiny in the flesh, doesn't she?' said the woman.

'Unlike the house,' said her male colleague. 'Flipping huge, isn't it, though it looks almost normal on the outside. It's like a Tardis.'

'A very expensive Tardis,' she said. 'House prices around here.'

'Who were all the people?'

'Staff, I suppose.' They spoke as if Anna was not there. 'And the little girl is the daughter. Antigone, that's her name.' She pronounced it carefully. 'I've read all about her. She has very expensive handbags and goes to posh restaurants, but she seemed quite sweet really.'

'Have you called anyone?' he asked, lowering his voice. 'You know, who might be interested?'

'Nah, I don't do that stuff. Jennifer in admissions is the one with all the contacts. Makes a bundle on the drunk tank after the awards ceremonies and all those heart attacks.' The woman tapped her nose. 'Know what I mean?'

Anna returned to find much activity, with builders' vans and unfamiliar cars blocking the driveway. She dumped her bags in her room, where there was a large bunch of flowers with a printed message reading, 'Hope you are fully recovered. Best wishes, all at Lorston Gardens'. She went to the main house, keen to discuss the repercussions of the rent in the swimming-pool floor. There was no one in the kitchen, so she went down the stairs to the base-ment and then to the spa area.

Anna thought there was something so poignant about empty swimming pools. They were like all seaside towns in winter, clowns removing their make-up, or a play-ground swing rocking forwards and backwards with no child in it. The small puddles of water that remained at the bottom seemed to be telling Anna that summer was over, although it had not yet even begun. The crack that she had opened had been covered with tarpaulin, so that it was now hidden like a scrubbed bloodstain. There were unfamiliar men measuring, sucking in their breath and shaking their heads. Janey was in the middle of them, looking mildly concerned. This was as worried as Anna had ever seen her.

'Hello, Anna, how are you?' This was asked perfunctorily, as if merely a polite greeting rather than a genuine enquiry to someone who'd just been rushed to hospital in dramatic circumstances.

'Fine, I was fine yesterday really.' Was it only yesterday? It was as if whole seasons had passed. She had the sense, even then, that everything was now going to change forever, the way you do sometimes when school friends gather to celebrate the end of exams. 'Just a bit of a shock. Do you know what happened to the pool?'

'I was rather hoping you would tell me. There was a small fracture in the casement that got aggravated in some way.'

'I touched the crack down there. But I don't think I aggravated it. I just touched it for a few seconds. And it wasn't a small fracture, it was really quite deep.' She gestured to the length of her forearm.

'That must have been what set off the problem. The weight of thousands of gallons of water onto the walls of Bea's room just meant that it began pouring through.'

'But I really didn't do much,' said Anna. 'I was trying to help, you know, like the Dutch boy who put his finger into a dyke to stop it leaking and saved his whole country?'

'Except you did the very opposite.'

'But even if I did, which I didn't, then surely the whole

thing shouldn't cave in. It's really dangerous. What if it had been Antigone diving down instead of me?'

'Indeed. That would have been dreadful. Still, I daresay she wouldn't have been mucking around like that in the first place. That tiny crack is causing big problems.' She gestured to the men around the pool area. 'All the staff have had to be found temporary accommodation, while poor Cally can't use her gym until we're sure it's all safe down here.'

'I could have been killed.'

'Come now, it was just a little drip. It's probably much worse for Bea. All her possessions are waterlogged.'

'Yes, I know, that's terrible for her, but it could have been so much worse for them both.'

'Them?'

'When the water came through to Bea's room. The whole place could have caved in. As it was, it must have been a shock.'

'Why do you say "them"? Who was with Bea?'

Anna paused for a second before answering.

'With Bea? I don't know. Maybe Wadim. Yes, I think he was in her room.'

That was what had so bothered Anna about her rescue but she had been too much in shock to rationalise last night. It had been almost ten o'clock and Antigone had been with Bea rather than asleep in her own bed. Janey did not need to know that. 'What's going on here?' She gestured to the building works.

'These contractors are just making good the damage that was done by the aggravation of that minor crack,' said Janey. 'I'm absolutely rushed off my feet trying to get everything rectified before Cally's skincare launch next month. You really couldn't have done this at a worse time, you know, Anna.' She began to bark at the contractors. 'This pool has to be refilled by the twenty-sixth, do you understand me? I don't care if it's fit to use or not, it has to look good, OK?'

'Are you sure it's safe for us to be in the house? Especially if there's going to be a party,' asked Anna. 'I mean, if there's a crack in the basement, couldn't it mean that there's subsidence or something and the whole house is at risk? I don't know much about architecture—'

'No, that's evident,' said Janey. 'Well, you must still be very tired from all the excitement. I won't keep you any longer.' She dismissed her with a wave.

While the works to make good the broken foundations of the basement were being done, Antigone and Anna were allowed to play in the grown-ups' sitting room. It was in fact much better suited to Antigone's interests than the primary-coloured playroom with its shrunken Alice-in-Wonderland-like versions of adult furniture – the tiny desk and chairs, the now redundant toy piano keyboard when she'd long since moved on to the real thing.

The air and light were so different up in this room, Anna felt as though she and Antigone were like those pit ponies that were blinded by life at the surface. The three floor-to-ceiling picture windows flooded the room with light from the (west-facing, naturally) garden, despite the constant drizzle of the end of an English spring. Anna sighed, wondering when summer would finally arrive, and with it some escape from inside these walls.

The rock-star-meets-game-hunter interior decoration of the room was so completely realised that it could have been used as background to an *Out of Africa* fashion spread, perhaps called 'Modern Mogambo' to evoke its neon, zebra-print-covered coffee table and the outsized papier-mâché stag's head on the wall.

Antigone noticed Anna staring at it. 'Don't you think it's strange?' she asked Anna.

'I suppose so.'

'It's very illogical. I mean, aren't they supposed to be trophies of things you've killed on a safari? I've been on a safari, twice actually, in Kenya. But we didn't kill anything. If we had, we could have put its head up here.'

'I think it's supposed to be a fun twist on a traditional shooting lodge. That's what Janey told me anyway.'

Antigone frowned. 'It's not so fun. It doesn't make sense to have a trophy of something that never lived. Unless, of course, you had to shoot someone in the shop to get it, I suppose.'

Anna laughed and then realised that Antigone was being serious. Antigone noticed her reaction and so laughed herself, as if pressing a replay button on somebody else's recording of real mirth. Even fake laughter seemed like progress.

They sat together at the enormous claw-footed desk by the window and began to go through the story that Antigone had written the day before. Although she'd shown a precocious ability to write poetry, Antigone found creative writing more challenging than music or maths. Anna was trying to create a toolbox of adjectives, adverbs and similes for her to call upon in times of need. They were compiling them into a list cribbed from other books, a pick-and-mix set of metaphors and descriptive words that Antigone could delve in to. It was the art of writing turned into a science, or a recipe made from pre-measured ingredients. The list had something for all occasions – 'as happy as a spring lamb', 'as rough as the sea in a storm', 'the tree's arms crept out', that sort of thing.

'Antigone,' said Anna, as she saw that her charge had been lulled into a happy blur of concentration. 'What were you doing in Bea's room the night the pool split?'

Antigone touched her ear and her eyes darted from side to side in an almost exaggerated illustration of what people do when they're lying. 'Was I there? I don't think I was. I'm not sure.'

'It's all right, I won't tell anyone.'

She looked relieved. 'Not Janey, please don't tell Janey. I might get Bea into trouble. She tells me never to tell Janey. We almost didn't go to help you, she was so worried Janey would find out. But I said we had to.'

Which explained, thought Anna, the delay between the vision she had of Bea and Antigone in their night clothes, and the feeling of Bea's mouth upon hers, administering resuscitation. 'I'm glad you did stop and help me. I won't tell Janey. If she asks, I can make up some story.'

'But that would be lying,' said Antigone, uncomprehending.

'Even so. Sometimes it's OK to lie. It's called a white lie.'

'No, a white lie is when you say that someone looks nice in what they're wearing when they don't, they look like they've forgotten to put their skirt on, like Mummy does all the time now she's got her new muscly legs.'

'Yes, but there are other sorts of acceptable twists of the truth too. Like, I don't know, when your parents told you that Santa filled your stocking at Christmas.'

'I never believed that. I always knew it would be impossible for him to go down everyone's chimneys on the same night, and some people don't even have chimneys. And how would he know if you'd been good? It's completely ridiculous.'

'Yes, but if you met a three year old you wouldn't tell them Santa didn't exist.' Anna hoped that Antigone would never come across such a wide-eyed toddler child. 'Anyway, why don't you tell me the truth and I can worry about the lying-to-Janey bit.'

'OK. I was in Bea's room that night. I go there lots. It's not like anybody even notices, since she always makes sure I'm back in my bed when I need to be, before the alarms get switched on. And sometimes, lots of the time, in fact, I don't need to be back in my bed at all because Mummy isn't here so much anyway. And now I can't go there because of the stupid swimming pool.' She clasped her hand over her mouth, ashamed at having used what her school referred to as 'the s-word'.

'Why do you go there?'

'Because I like it. I'm happy when I'm there.'

'And why don't you want Janey to know?'

Antigone frowned and then spoke with unexpected vehemence. 'I don't want Janey to know anything about me. She's not nice at all. She's like the White Witch in Narnia. That's a simile: do you want to put it in our book of words?'

'Yes, but you could make it more interesting – something like, "she's so cold she's like the White Witch", or "as ice-cold as Narnia's White Witch".'

'Oh, you think that about her too?'

'I didn't say that. But they are similes. You could say Bea is as warm as . . . what's she as warm as?'

'A heater,' said Antigone.

'Yes, a heater. It's not particularly poetic though. Try again, Bea's arms are as . . .'

'Bea's arms are as lovely as a whole jar of *cajeta*.'

'Excellent, well done, good image, but perhaps you could make it more evocative by comparing something specific – say being held by Bea is as delicious as a jar of Mexican toffee.'

'But not as sticky.'

'Was that a joke, Antigone?'

'I suppose it might have been.' She looked quizzical and then joined in Anna's laughter. Anna had never heard her joke, even inadvertently, or laugh naturally before, only giggle at her father's tickles.

'Bea's arms are as sticky and delicious as *cajeta*,' repeated Antigone, still giggling, delighting in her newfound skill, like someone who has discovered that they can play the piano without ever being taught. 'Daddy likes Bea's sticky sweet arms too.'

Anna sat up. 'What do you mean?'

'Nothing,' said Antigone, pinching her ear and her eyes darting from side to side once again.

When they went to the kitchen for supper, Sholto was already there.

'Hello, my gorgeous princess,' he said, 'and you're not looking so bad yourself, Antigone.'

'That's a joke,' Antigone explained to a blushing Anna with her recently discovered expertise. 'It's because Daddy knew we'd think he was talking about me, so he pretended that he was calling you a princess. Which you aren't, of course. But then I suppose I'm not either, actually, although a teacher at school said I was Hollywood royalty.'

'Who said that, darling?' asked Sholto.

'Miss Davenport.'

'Looks like we'll have to have words with Miss Davenport about that.'

'Exactly,' said Antigone. 'Everyone knows there's no royal family in America. If teachers can't get facts right, then they shouldn't be teaching, should they?'

'Exactly,' said Sholto. 'Not like you, hey Anna? I'm sure you always get your facts right.'

'I try,' said Anna. Speak normally, she told herself, wondering why she always underwent a wit-ectomy when faced with Sholto. 'Though I'm not actually a trained teacher since I haven't done a teacher-training course.'

'I'm sure there's more to pedagogy than a piece of paper.'

'I hope so.'

He really did have that whole twinkly older man thing down to perfection. Anna was quite aware of the fact that it was a studied charm, but it didn't stop her being charmed nonetheless.

Antigone climbed up on the stool between Sholto and Bea, who was making supper. The paparazzi shots of Sholto, Antigone and Cally on their way to Halloween parties or playing on the beach looked like an advertiser's idea of the perfect family: father with his geeky-yet-hunky Arthur Miller looks, mother with her amazing-for-forty body and their bluey-white child. Yet the trinity Anna saw before her now looked like the authentic version of a family at its best, cooking together in this glorious kitchen. Having felt warmed by the glow of Sholto's flirtatiousness, she now felt as though she was exiled from the inner circle.

'*Cuidado*,' said Bea as Antigone snuggled up to her. 'My hands are raw chicken.' She was kneading strips of chicken breasts in a marinade. The pinkness of the uncooked flesh had been glazed with a honey and soy sauce so that they quivered brownly under the low hanging pendant lights. She began to remove the strips and lie them on a chopping board, ready to be cooked.

Sholto examined them. 'Glossy, painted brown and so flawless as to be almost plastic,' he said. 'Do they remind you of anyone?'

Bea jabbed him with her elbow, while keeping her raw

poultry fingers safely away from him. She giggled at his remark and muttered something in Spanish that Sholto seemed to understand; he said something back, fluently but heavily accented, all the o's being rounded as they would be in English.

11

All Felled, Felled, Are All Felled

Jack was trying to impress Anna with his ability to flick multiple beer mats, while she demanded that he concentrate on her questions. 'Have you got anything for me – you know, from your contacts – about Janey?'

'I've got plenty for you –' he raised his eyebrows in a way that he no doubt thought of as wolfish – 'but nothing concrete you can use against Janey.'

'Shame. I just know she's up to something and I need to stop it, for Antigone's sake. Was there anything about the rest of them?'

'About Sholto and Cally? Just the usual, that he's playing away.'

'That makes me sad,' said Anna.

'That it's not you?'

'No, no, whatever gave you that idea?' Damn him, thought Anna, he's a lot smarter than I ever give him credit for. 'No, I mean for Antigone. It would be awful for her if she found out her dad was doing that.'

'Wouldn't be great for Cally either. Though that assumes she doesn't know already.'

'Surely if she knew something, she'd divorce him.'

'And let everyone know this whole perfect Cally-world

is a sham? Everyone would assume she was a rubbish shag, since being beautiful wasn't enough to keep him from straying. Wouldn't be great for Sholto, for that matter. When was the last time he directed anything good? He's already been reduced to doing cheap super-hero movies and then justifying them as "such fun".'

'He brings a certain intellectual emphasis to those films,' protested Anna. 'I mean, there was an Oedipal subtext to the one with the nuclear-powered scooter.'

'Yeah, yeah, he owes it to himself for the boy he was to make action films, blah blah blah. He'd be another jobbing director moving on to telly if it weren't for who he's married to. If they divorced it would be a disaster for all of them. The whole house of Cally would come crashing down.'

'You're right, it wouldn't be good for him. But she's an actress. Don't life experiences and tragedies give actors more emotional resources to draw on?'

'What was the last thing you've seen her in?'

Anna frowned. 'There was that thing, I don't know, the TV thing, wasn't there? The thing where she was a doctor who was on loan from another hospital.'

'Exactly. She's not an actress; she's an idea, an ideal. You won't have seen her act in anything, but you've seen her on the cover of magazines and modelling in perfume ads and reading her children's books and flashing her false eyelashes in a mascara advert. She's not Meryl Streep, she's a beautiful woman, and that's pretty useless once you hit thirty-five and your looks go.'

'But she's still gorgeous.'

'Yes, she's beautiful, but there are plenty of beautiful girls a decade or two younger than her. Her USP is that she has this wonderful, perfect life with her fabulous clever husband and the cute but crucially female child.'

'Why crucial that she's a girl?' asked Anna.

'Better clothes and hair,' said Jack, as if that was obvious. 'So she's got this amazing life and she's come such a long way from the trailer park and her drunk mother to get it and that's the special part of her brand. Take away just one little thing and the whole lot is exposed as a lie. And if Cally loses her "job", then everyone else does too.'

'Everyone?'

'Yeah, you too, love.'

'I don't care about that, I can get another one.' Not strictly true, thought Anna, but Jack needn't know that. 'What I do care about is Antigone. If this got out she'd lose me, fine, but she'd also lose Bea, wouldn't she? And her home – and probably seeing her father with any regularity. She's been doing so well recently; this would set her back months, or even years. I won't let that happen.'

'And what are you going to do about it, Miss Marple?'

'I don't know.' Her shoulders fell. 'It feels as though everyone is lying. Except for Antigone. Keep an eye out for me, Jack. But please don't tell anyone if you find out something.'

'I won't. At the moment, though, there's no one to tell. It's not my field any more. I've got a job in a bar. Just wasn't making enough on the streets any more. The paparazzi glory days are over, my friend.'

'I'm sorry to hear that. Well, not sorry exactly, but I hope something works out for you.'

'Which all means I've had to move out of the place I was renting and now I'm kipping on a friend's floor. It's not very sexy, is it?'

'I suppose not.'

'What with you living in your bosses' house and me in a sleeping bag, there aren't a lot of options, are there?' Jack put his hand under the table to her thighs. Anna surprised herself with how much she quivered at this. She put her hand on top of his, to stop it, she thought, but no, she found that she was encouraging it. He looked at her and she wanted to indicate that he should stop, but she found herself nodding – only a small nod, she told herself, as if this made it better. His hand rose up her skirt and he pulled her knicker elastic aside to push his finger inside. It was an awkward angle so she was impressed by his contortions. She gasped, oh god, she actually gasped in public. She looked around, blushing, but no one was paying them any attention. Despite the angle, he managed to find the right spot and he gently rubbed and then, arrogantly, took a sip of his pint with his other hand. She looked at him in disbelief and he grinned. She couldn't help smiling back. Sex was supposed to be serious, earnest, and he was making it seem like playing darts or some other pub game. It was a laugh, he'd say. She wanted to be indignant but she found herself giggle with the pleasure of it.

She thought of Sholto. Would sex with him be a laugh? No, it would be romantic and real and amazing because it would be born of love, not laughter, and surely love trumped every time. But if she loved Sholto, how was it that she was so enjoying this?

She moved her body forward and rocked slightly, on and on, she didn't know how long for but she couldn't bear it, oh no, yes, oh the embarrassment, oh the joy.

She rushed to the loo, where she put her palm against it to quell it, but also to prolong the moment. It seemed she liked forbidden, semi-public sex. Who knew? There had never been anything untoward in any of her previous sexual encounters. Girls at university have no parents or religious beliefs to stop them, so there can never be any sense of the illicit. Even anal was apparently on the standard menu, which was obviously a step too far for Anna. There had only been three lovers, and she knew with certainty that she'd never enjoyed any of that so-called 'proper' sex as much as that experience she'd just had, at a pub table, with Jack.

Here was a man who made her come and they hadn't even had full sex. Yet. She'd never been able to join in the stories that her friends told each other, overly seduced by television programmes of four women telling each other ever more raucous stories over eggs Benedict, but now she wanted to shout from the rooftops. She wanted to ring up all those friends she hadn't seen for a year and tell them how she'd got fingered in a pub by a man who said 'was you' and 'haitch' and how it was good, how it was *amazing*.

She dragged herself out from the toilet cubicle and looked at herself in the mirror. She was like the photo that Jack had taken of her: flushed, almost speckled with a rash of pleasure. She couldn't walk out into the pub yet, not until her face had calmed down and she had fanned away the stigmata of joy that branded her. She didn't want to disturb her make-up even more than it had already been by throwing water on it, so she looked towards the window of the tiled room. It had that wobbly glass on it that lets light in but funnels the shapes on either side of it into misshapen bubbles.

She thought she could see a figure on the other side, dark clothes separating and coming together through the pane, luminous in the street lights. She pulled on the metal clasp, not knowing whether its function was purely decorative, and was relieved that it seemed to be opening so that she could gulp some air and calm her cheeks.

As she opened it, the figure she thought she had seen on the other side darted. She saw a back rapidly retreating with an unmistakable athleticism. She recognised him as much by the feeling of thrill mixed with fear that he always inspired in her as much as by what she had actually seen.

Dan, so far from home and yet so at home anywhere.

London was too big for such coincidences.

'You keep looking behind you,' Antigone said to Anna as they walked home.

'Do I?'

'Yes. You're looking for Dan, aren't you?'

'What makes you say that?'

'Well, he's always following us, isn't he? He's there most days, I don't know why. Perhaps they don't think you're sensible enough to cross the road on your own. They don't think I am, but some people my age are allowed to walk to school on their own. I don't know any of them, but I've read about them in books.'

'I used to when I was at primary school. My mother worked so I used to let myself back in again and make myself some toast.'

Antigone sighed. 'I would love to do that. Do you think I'll ever be able to?'

She expressed such yearning in her voice that it was as though she was asking for a business-class trip to the moon. Actually, the latter seemed a more probable treat. 'Maybe.'

'When I'm nine?'

'Perhaps. I don't know, darling. You'll have to ask Janey or your parents.' Anna looked round again, but there was no Dan on her trail. She had been rehearsing her confrontation of him, but now she wondered whether it wasn't better that he didn't know that she knew. Or something. Life at Lorston Gardens was like a mirror being held up to a mirror and reflecting an infinite number of times, except that in each image something was distorted as if each of them were fairground mirrors that changed fat to thin and tall to small.

Antigone followed her gaze. 'He's not there. He was there yesterday and the day before, but not the day before that. Last week he was there three mornings and four after-schools.'

Anna looked at her in astonishment. 'I had no idea you'd even noticed. It took me months to know he was shadowing us. I thought he'd only be doing that when I started the job.'

She shrugged. 'You should have asked me. I wish he wouldn't. I wish I just walked with a parent or with you and there was no Dan and no photographers.'

'I always thought you didn't mind. You never seem to pass comment.' It was, Anna had always thought, Antigone's normality, and she'd seemed to accept it as such.

'Not making a fuss isn't the same as actually liking it. I never said I liked my life. In fact I hate it sometimes.'

As they walked into the kitchen, Anna thought of Antigone's longing to make herself a piece of toast, un-accompanied. She had so much, but it would be a long time before she'd have the privacy to pour cereal into a bowl without someone watching, stepping in, or commenting. While the girl was well versed in loneliness, she was never given the luxury of being alone.

'I wonder what deliciousness Bea has got planned?' Anna said.

Antigone smiled. 'And what secret surprise pudding I'm getting.'

'What secret?'

'Don't be silly, Anna, if I tell you then it's not a secret, is it?'

'Well, whatever it is, she shouldn't be doing it. I might have to tell Janey.'

Antigone's eyes widened. 'You wouldn't!'

'You know your mother doesn't like you to have sweet things.'

'*Puta anoréxica*,' she said, with full Hispanic flourish.

'What did you say?'

'Nothing.'

'I heard you. You said your mother was an anorexic –' Anna paused and thought – 'cow.'

Antigone looked dismissive. 'Your Spanish is not as good as your Latin, is it? Although Anorexia is a Greek word, as I'm sure you know.'

'Listen to me, Antigone, you do not go around calling your mother such disrespectful names. Nor are you allowed to eat sweet things. Whatever anybody else is telling you.'

'I'll do what I like.'

They stood looking at one another for a second, before Antigone walked ahead towards the kitchen.

Antigone sat on a stool in front of the stove as Bea stood behind her so that her arms were wrapped around the girl as she stirred a pot of something delicious smelling. Heat, love and nourishment, that's what Bea offered Antigone. No wonder she had beaten off the competition offered by Cally. As was evidenced by the behaviour of the children at school towards Antigone – fame and elegance works a treat on grown-ups, but children remain admirably immune from its charms.

'Bea,' said Anna, 'what are you planning to give Antigone for supper?'

'This casserole,' she said. '*Frijoles*.'

'That's beans in English,' said Antigone. 'People at school sing about how they make you fart.'

'Well, they're right, sometimes they pass to the large intestine in an undigested state, leading to what is more politely known as flatulence. But what else is for supper?' she said to Bea, not wanting to ruminate further on the subject.

'Fruit salad,' said Bea.

'Antigone says you give her secret puddings. Like that caramel stuff you keep hidden in the cupboard.'

Bea shrugged and continued to stir the beans, her arms still wrapped around Antigone.

'Do you want me to tell Janey?' Anna said. Bea immediately lifted Antigone down and walked towards her.

'Don't tell her anything,' Bea hissed into Anna's ear.

'Well, stop giving Antigone sweet things then. It's not fair when nobody else is allowed to.'

'I can do what I like.'

'No, you can't. You know what her mother thinks . . .'

'Her mother thinks it's OK to have sweets sometime. It's good for children, everybody knows that a little sweetie is nice.'

'No, she doesn't, she really doesn't, Bea.'

Bea smiled. 'Her mother is very happy because she is having sweets. It makes her very happy.'

As she walked out of the kitchen, Anna walked straight into Dan. 'What fresh hell?' she muttered. She could have sworn he frisked her as they disentangled themselves. She would never admit, though, that she quite liked it. Damn him. She tried to expel the image of him in his swimming trunks and replace it with the sight of his back furtively retreating into the night outside a pub miles from home.

'Fancy seeing you here,' he said to her.

What was that supposed to mean? 'You're the one who turns up in unexpected places.'

He grabbed her arm. That feeling again. Oh for god's sake, get a grip. She'd gone from being the girl who found no one sexually stimulating to the sort of woman who'd ogle a male stripper.

'Janey wants to see you.'

He's been watching too many of those gangster films again, Anna thought. 'Then why doesn't she ask me nicely? Or are you her henchman?' As the words came out of her lips, another part of the picture seemed to form. It was as if she were like those archaeologists of Pompeii that she and Antigone had talked so much of, and she kept on being given random chips of coloured stone.

'I am asking you nicely.' He leant forwards and she took a step back, to find she was now literally up against the wall. 'Or is this the way you like your invitations?' He pushed his hands between her legs and pushed up, hard.

This time the fear far outweighed any flicker of desire. She pushed his hand away. 'I know you were there. I saw you.'

'Good,' he said and walked away.

Anna was prepared to be defiant. She did what she'd seen people in films do as she stood outside the door of Janey's office. She stood up as tall as she could, breathed deeply, put out her chin and then knocked twice, rap-rap. It was a knock, she was sure, that conveyed strength, firmness, good character. She was rather surprised to be greeted by one of Janey's radiant smiles.

'You wanted to see me?' She had not decided whether to be defiant or apologetic about meeting Jack again, if this was what it was all about. But maybe Dan hadn't told her? Or maybe she'd been wrong, she hadn't seen him and she'd imagined that conversation they'd just had? No, Janey would most likely know, so Anna should just play dumb. Story of her life: she was always being told she was too clever by half, though, ever since coming to this place, she'd begun to think she knew nothing about anything.

'I just felt we hadn't had a chat for a while,' said Janey, gesturing to the sofa that ran along one side of the room.

As Anna sat down she knocked a hardcover book that had been lying across the sofa, which fell to floor, opening on a spread of interiors.

'One of my photo books,' said Janey.

'Oh,' said Anna. 'I thought it was one of those glossy coffee-table books about houses in LA.' She picked it up and realised that it was in fact one of those photo albums that organised people put together on their computers and then send off to get printed so that they looked like real books and nothing like the sticky plastic sheets and fake leather of her parents' collections of childhood snaps. As she flicked through the pages, she thought she recognised the floor-to-ceiling windows as being those of the drawing room at Lorston Gardens, but these ones looked straight out onto some gracious beech trees instead of the grass mowed into precision stripes, like those intricate hairstyles of the young black boys Anna saw and feared on the street.

'Lovely, aren't they?' said Janey.

'Yes they are,' said Anna, staring at the way the branches of the trees swept down towards the house as if about to knock on the windows. 'There's a wonderful poem by Hopkins about some trees in Oxford that were cut down: "My aspens dear, whose airy cages quelled, Quelled or quenched in leaves the leaping sun, All felled, felled, are all felled." Antigone loves a bit of Hopkins – I think for the musicality of the words more than what they actually say.'

'I wasn't talking about the trees. They were horrible, really blocked out the light.'

'You had them cut down?'

'We weren't allowed to, stupid conservation area. No, we had them moved to the bottom of the garden. They're still there, by the trampoline.' She spoke as if they'd had to re-park the car, rather than move trees that had lived so long and would outlive them all.

The room was like a shrine to the house. As well as the book, the walls were covered in tributes to it. 'I love old maps,' Anna said, staring at a detailed Ordnance Survey map that showed Lorston Gardens when it was surrounded by fewer roads.

'Yes, they're interesting, aren't they? You can see how these houses were some of the earliest in the area. They were built for rich merchants and well-to-do types. You needed quite a bit of money to buy them even then, but obviously nowhere near as much as now.'

'What's this?' Anna asked, pointing at a street or pathway on the map, which appeared to run along the back of the garden and then down the side of the house towards the main road.

'A rather troublesome right of way. We did everything we could to annex it, but the council insisted that it was some sacrosanct bridleway that existed before the houses. You'd have thought it was Hadrian's Wall rather than some stupid path. So ridiculous.'

'But I've never seen anyone use it,' said Anna.

'Well, those trees you so admire proved rather useful in the end. When we moved them, we made sure that they were positioned in a way that was perfectly legal and yet makes the pathway very difficult to cross. Even on Google Earth, you can barely see that there's a right of way. And there was nothing that the council could do about that. Nor the scooping out of the basement. They have the most ridiculous petty rules about changing a window above ground, but dig down and you've almost total freedom.' She stood up to pull down a dozen narrow-backed books from the shelves. 'Here, take a look,' she said with all the pride of a mother showing photos of her baby's early years. This analogy was apt – as Anna began to look through the photos, she realised that, like the proud mother of a precious first-born, there was no detail too small to go unrecorded.

'This photo book is about the house when we first got

here,' said Janey. She looked misty-eyed. Anna had never seen her look so emotional, lacking her usual ironic detachment. 'When I first began to work for Cally. It's hideous, isn't it?' Anna looked at the magnolia painted walls, sisal carpeting and dark burgundy full-length curtains with their pelmets and fringing and thought of her parents' house with a heave of homesickness. 'Then this is the first big revamp. That gold-tiled mirror was especially commissioned to fit that wall and then given that wonderful aged look. We decided that it was very evocative of Gustav Klimt, don't you think? You'd like that, being so cultured.'

Each book revealed another decorating fashion; it was like walking through a museum devoted to the insides of people's houses, but instead of representing the different eras of, say, a burgher's dwelling pre- and post-industrial revolution, it was fixated on the tiny nuances of décor trends in the early 21st century. It would be a very specialist historian who'd find them interesting – perhaps one who was writing their PhD on 'Lifestyle Choices of the Urban Elite: 2003–2013'. It was as if Anna was being dragged through a themed hotel – there was stark white, lush velvet, faux country house, Victorian eccentric.

'This is the big one,' said Janey. 'The digging down project.' She sighed as if remembering a golden era instead of a very muddy one.

Anna looked at photos that showed a conveyor belt of gloop being scooped from the basement of the house. She saw the row of beautiful beech trees pulled out from their earthy home and upended to flash their muddied stumps. Another photo and there they were being dragged to the end of the garden, leaving their emptied gums behind them. There was a photo of the house balanced precariously on stilts as concrete was poured into the moat of sludge that surrounded it, like a twisted fairy castle. Caterpillar-wheeled diggers crawled around the site, their scooper arms snaking from them, with the grey and brown of the scene illuminated by the men in fluorescent jackets dotted around the photos.

'It looks very fragile,' Anna said as she turned the pages.

'It's very safe; don't let any of these NIMBYs tell you otherwise, with their nonsense about water tables and chalk soils. I think it's the new frontier. Where once ambitious people looked up to the skies and built New York, now those with vision look down to the ground. There could be whole worlds down there, unimpeded by stupid petty rules about permitted development and conservation areas.'

'I suppose so. It just feels odd that instead of being in the gutter looking up the stars, it's the other way round.'

'Are you calling the basement here the gutter?' asked Janey.

'No, no, of course not,' said Anna. 'It's lovely and amazing and gorgeous.' But interesting how you don't choose to have your office or accommodation down there. No, it's just the very downstairs staff who are forced into the airless dark rooms to live like rats. For all the portholes and light wells, underground was always just that: underground.

'The only limit is our imagination,' continued Janey. 'Dig down and you can build tennis courts and ballrooms, bowling alleys and climbing walls, whole cinemas and squash courts.'

'You know a lot about architecture and decorating.'

'It's always been my passion. I should have been an architect, but I didn't want to spend that long studying. I wanted to get out into the world and earn some money. Still, over the years, I think I've practically learned more than I would at university anyway. One day, soon, I'm going to build my own home.'

Of course, thought Anna, why would she be happy to organise perfection for others when she should be doing it for herself? It must be frustrating to watch others less intelligent and driven than you, less blessed with good taste, have the money to do so before you can. Anna wondered what Janey got paid. Whatever it was, it would not be enough to afford the lifestyle she organised for others.

'Enough about me,' said Janey. 'How do you think Antigone is doing? How does she feel about Cally? About Bea?'

Here we go. Anna had almost been enjoying the conversation, but she knew the agenda would emerge once again. 'Antigone's not one for gossiping.'

'I've not been so vigilant of late,' said Janey. 'What with the party.'

'The skin thing?'

'The launch for *Callyskinetics*, yes. It's going to be here because that'll be so much more personal than some soulless hotel. The long-range forecast suggests that this interminable rain is finally going to stop. It'll be the perfect opportunity to show the world the herb garden and the flowers that were the inspiration for her natural, yet effective beauty line.' Again that tone of barely disguised sarcasm. 'She does have, as I'm sure you'll agree, remarkably young-looking skin for her age, and all through the use of her own exclusive and so organic skincare brand. It's chemical-free.' Janey looked at Anna, as if daring her to point out that it was impossible for anything on the planet to be so-called chemical-free. 'And obviously Antigone will be there, Cally's most blooming flower in the garden. And of course you'll be her, her . . . ?'

'Chaperone?'

'Special grown-up friend for the evening.'

'But wouldn't it be better if Bea was with her? She's much better at keeping her calm and –' Anna had been about to say 'normal' – 'relaxed.'

'Bea and Martina will be helping the catering staff in the kitchen. It's going to be quite the party. We probably won't be able to actually use the pool, but I think it will still look magnificent shimmering below the windows that go up into the garden, don't you? There will be a marquee from the house to the lawn with a very simple, understated English country garden theme – imagine a walled kitchen garden at a Cotswold vicarage look.'

'Are you organising it?'

'Cally feels she needs to call in professionals, party planners. She can be quite insecure like that. But it was my original vision and I can assure you it's going to be spectacular.'

'Isn't it a bit soon after the business with the pool?' asked Anna.

Janey rolled her eyes.

'I almost died!'

'Anna, really, I think there are enough drama queens in this household without you adding to them. You did not almost die and the builders are dealing with it. It was just a small crack in a swimming pool, for goodness' sake, not the San Andreas Fault.'

Anna phoned Jack, not wanting to leave any electronic trail that could be traced to her.

'Listen,' she whispered, although she was safely out of range of Lorston Gardens and was standing in the middle of open parkland where Dan could not be lurking. 'You're skint, right?'

'Yes, totally.'

'I owe you, I know I do, now that you can't use any photos from outside the house. And for all your patience.'

'I'm sure I can think of a way for you to pay me back.'

'Give it a rest. I can make it up to you, which is what I'm going to do now, but just this once. Do you know about Cally's skincare product launch?'

'Yeah, I've seen that on the wires. There's going to be a lot of coverage, plenty of it official, you know, inside job, pre-approved photos only, only getting Cally's good side, lots of semi-celebrities pretending to enjoy themselves and swearing that they use her products all the time. You get the picture. Which is more than I can say for me. If I stand outside with the boys, then I'm sure your mate Dan will be having words with me.'

'You obviously can't stand out in front of the house, but there is somewhere else you can go that I don't think anybody else knows about. But promise me you won't tell anyone. I'm not sure if it counts as trespass or not.'

'Get on with it.'

'Along the end of the garden there's a row of trees – beeches.'

'So?'

'Well, there's also this weird path that runs between the gardens, from there to the houses in that crescent on the other side. Janey wanted to annex or block it, saying it was a security risk, but the council said they couldn't because it's an ancient right of way or something.'

'Good for them,' said Jack.

'So what Janey got the builders to do instead was to plant trees right up against the path so that would seem like part of the garden and put off anyone walking along it. Nobody ever does use it because they've also put a gate up, unlocked but forbidding, and unless you knew about it you'd never know the path was there. Anyone would assume it was off limits, plus the trees are so thick you can't see the trail on any satellite pictures.'

'OK,' said Jack. 'Where do I get in?'

'There's another passage between numbers 12 and 14 of the crescent. If you go down that you come to a gate that says "Private, Keep Out", but it's not legally binding, it's like those notices saying "No Parking, garage in constant use". They've also put up some security fencing, but the council said that they couldn't make it spiked or electronic as they'd be liable for any injuries done to an intruder.'

'But I'd still be intruding?'

'But you wouldn't, that's the thing. They put one of the exiled beeches—'

'You what?'

'One of these trees that they moved from nearer the house. They replanted it illegally in the middle of the path, before it hits their garden, to stop people from walking down there and trying to see over the fence. The branches have grown over into the garden of the house, but the tree's technically not on their land. I'm no surveyor or lawyer, but couldn't you climb that tree and it would not count as trespass?'

'I reckon I could.'

'Better still, it's the one nearest the house. The party's going to be in the garden all the way down to the playground area. All the guests will be outside if the weather's good, which the long-range forecast says it will be, and nobody else will get the photos you can.' Her voice rose with excitement.

'It sounds like it's worth a punt,' Jack said.

'It is, I've scouted it out for you already. It's perfect, so long as you're careful.'

'I won't get caught – it doesn't sound like there's much they can do anyway, if it's not their land.'

'I meant, be careful not to fall when you're climbing the tree.'

'I didn't know you cared.'

'Of course I do. I wouldn't be telling you all this if I didn't. I can't believe I *am* telling you.' How far she'd come from being revolted at his suggestion that she share information with him in order for him to get a good photo. There were worse people in the Cally industry, she'd decided, than him. 'But Jack, one thing. Don't use anything that could hurt or upset Antigone. I mean it.'

''Course not.'

'Promise me.'

'I promise.'

'I can just feel your fingers are crossed even though we're on the phone. Good luck, Jack.' Why did she sound as if she was sending him off to the Normandy landings rather than his rather sordid mission?

12

A Night to Remember

A week later, Anna emerged from her rooms into the hall at eight in the morning and felt like someone standing at the side of a motorway trying to cross six lanes of speeding traffic. There were unidentified workers zigzagging all over Lorston Gardens. The floor had been covered with plastic sheeting as the various florists, decorators and planners walked through. The flowers and plants were so huge that they obscured the minions carrying them and so appeared to be walking by themselves, like pretty triffids. The marquee men could be seen through the windows, building their English country garden-style tent. Who knew that simplicity could be so complicated?

'Not since the pyramids have so many laboured over such monuments to one person,' said Sholto, who had joined her.

'Hello,' said Anna, flustered as ever. 'It's very impressive.'

He laughed. Everything foxed her in this place. People laughed and cried at all the wrong moments and she needed subtitles to understand the subtexts. 'Indeed. As are Cally's skincare products, don't you think?'

'She really kindly gave me some.' She touched her cheeks, which glistened with the heavy-duty serum she'd put on that morning and that already seemed to be causing her skin to break out in a rash of hives.

'Are you coming this evening?'

He seems to care, she thought, he really seems to care. She blushed. 'Yes I am, we all are, I think.' Some of the boldness she'd been developing came back and she said, 'Well, not Martina and Bea.'

'Of course not,' said Sholto. 'That wouldn't be appropriate, would it?'

'But I'm only there to look after Antigone. I'm under no illusions that I'm adding to the glamour,' said Anna.

'I wouldn't say that.' He gave her an appreciative look. Damn him, she couldn't calm the feeling of hope he inspired in her. The men she'd met here were like different perfumes. Sholto was hope mixed with yearning, Dan was desire with the stench of fear and Jack was . . . what was he? He was something warm and sweet, but surprising.

'Don't be fooled,' he went on, 'the party won't be glamorous anyway.'

Anna gave a gasp of disbelief 'There are sheep, real live sheep, in the garden,' she protested. 'They are sticking moss onto the walls of the house to make them look even more aged.' She gestured to Wadim, who walked past pushing a trolley with two wisteria trees on it, as if to emphasise her point still further.

'I see what you're saying, but it's all nonsense, isn't it? I mean, you could spend thousands, as we are, on a set dressed to look like an English country garden, but it will never be as good as even a pretty mediocre real country garden, so what's the point? There's something about authenticity that will always trump artificiality, however beautiful. Don't you agree?'

'You're so right.' She put some of her authentic hair behind her earring-less ears.

'I knew you were a clever girl. It's the same with the guests. Half of them will be journalists, the others will be professionals with their own agenda. Nobody will be here because they actually give a damn about some over-priced moisturiser.'

Hmm, maybe Eau de Sholto had a bitter kick. 'Don't shatter my illusions. I keep thinking it's going to be like something out of *The Great Gatsby*.'

'It will be. Nobody much enjoyed those parties either. Which you'd know if you'd actually read the book,' he said.

'I have! And I think that most of Gatsby's guests, even if they were abusing his hospitality, did have a good time. It was only the host who didn't.'

He leaned towards her. 'It's so nice to talk to someone well read and educated.'

She felt slightly faint at his closeness. 'Ditto,' she muttered. Well done, Anna, that shows him just how articulate and eloquent you are, doesn't it?

He came in closer and whispered in her ear. 'Don't change, Anna.'

She felt his breath on her neck and the arousal that had seemed to blossom, or was it fester?, inside her since coming here. They were interrupted by the arrival of Antigone in her school uniform, clutching Bea's hand. Antigone was beaming at them, while Bea wore an expression that could be described as glowering.

'Daddy and Anna, how lovely,' said Antigone. Bea retreated quickly.

'Ready? Bag?' asked Anna. 'I packed it all ready for you last night with your homework. Are you looking forward to the party this evening?'

Antigone shook her head. 'Can't you and I just run away and go to the library instead?'

Anna smiled at her. 'I'd like that very much. I really would. But we can't.'

'One day we will,' said Antigone. 'You, me, Daddy and Bea can all go and live in a great big library and never have to go to another party ever again.'

After picking up Antigone as usual, Anna was allowed to leave her with Bea and Martina, the Cinderellas in the kitchen, to go to join the chosen minions in Cally's suite for some 'girly time'. At last, she was being allowed into the grown-up rooms on the first floor, those mysterious portals into another universe.

Cally's suite, and it was very much hers rather than a marital one, covered five rooms and had the best views in the house. First there was a sort of dressing or drawing room with two sofas and two dressing tables, as if set up for group narcissism. Beyond that was her bedroom, which had passed through as many interiors incarnations as the rest of the house, before finally setting on a look that could be described as Elizabeth Taylor in a snowstorm. A hundred-carat chandelier lorded over a whitewashed world that, despite its lack of colour, was anything but sterile or laboratory-like. Cally's vast bed was extravagantly piled with a barrier of silvery silk cushions, the sophisticated women's equivalent of cuddly toys. Three doors led from the room. The first opened onto a walk-in wardrobe the size of Anna's bedroom, with clothes exquisitely curated into sections. Then there was the shoe temple, with footwear literally put on pedestals under glass domes, designed to be seen without mucky feet obscuring the view. The last door led to a bathroom the size of an average apartment, which had two of everything, like Noah's ark – two sinks, two baths, two showerheads, and then pairs of matching products on the open shelves: shampoo and conditioner, hand wash and hand cream, day and night moisturiser. Everything in this bathroom had mated for life, and yet Cally herself seemed lonely in a bedroom so shorn of Sholto.

In the centre of this mini-department store was Cally, having her hair teased and added to – with pieces that had doubtlessly belonged to some poor Russian woman – by Sandi. She, too, looked like a cartoon on a modern game of Happy Families – 'Mrs Shears the barber', never without a black cloth-wrap of scissors or her wheelie suitcase filled with sprays, dryers and irons. Lysette sat on a nearby stool, randomly throwing words in their direction: 'awesome', 'beautiful', 'fierce'. Cally was elongating her neck and then sticking her chin out and pouting into the mirror with a shocking lack of self-consciousness. Doing your mirror face, it seemed to Anna, was like going to the toilet: it should really only be done in private.

'Not only are you beautiful,' said Lysette, as if reciting the valedictorian at Cally's graduation ceremony, 'but you have a truly beautiful heart.'

'Thank you,' said Cally, graciously. Now see, if anyone compliments me, thought Anna, I can't accept it. I shrug and look away and change the subject. So nobody ever does again. 'Anna!' Cally said on seeing her. 'We are so super-excited that you're joining us. We want to give you a makeover!'

Sandi and Lysette started squealing and flapping their hands. Anna felt as though she were trapped in a modern-day update of a high-school horror movie like *Carrie*, in which the queen bees were going to get out the lipstick and then impale her on the straightening irons. The whole atmosphere of female togetherness seemed forced and unnatural, like those groups of cackling women you see in wine bars who shriek out lines like, 'Men! Can't live with them, can't live without them,' in an attempt to convince themselves that the evening is all as much fun as it's supposed to be.

'Yay,' said Anna, and tried to do the thing with the hands too, but looked mostly like a baby bird trying to take off.

'You are really so natural, aren't you?' said Lysette. This, it was clear from her tone, was not a good thing.

'Yes, I suppose.'

'Well, I think it's lovely,' said Cally. Noisy agreement

from Lysette and Sandi. 'But you could be even more naturally lovely with a bit of help.'

Lysette wheeled a clothes rail dripping in finery towards her. 'Some samples sent over for Cally.'

'I don't think they'd fit me,' said Anna.

'Obvs, but there're a few stretchy things and things that are way too big for Cally.' Lysette looked over towards Cally; Cally just gave an airy wave of an arm so toned that it had a line on it formed by a thousand triceps dips, like a ripple in sand upon the shore.

Anna gulped on the glass of champagne she'd been given and tried to sacrifice herself to the vision that these women wanted to create. Her hair was backcombed and then put up in a chignon, layers of make-up were added and dresses were held up against her, usually followed by rueful shakes of the head.

Cally had ordered that music be put on and, shedding her robe, was now dancing braless with studied abandon in a pair of tiny briefs. Her boobs didn't move much, only leaping higher when she jumped, like salmon in spring, but never seeming to go downwards on their return. Newton would never have developed the theory of gravity if he'd been watching this display rather than sitting under an apple tree. Anna was trying not to look, but then she realised that you didn't strip to your panties and whip your hair if you weren't an exhibitionist, so she felt entitled to a good long stare. She should be less perfect in real life, but she wasn't. Lysette went to join Cally and they did some bumping and grinding that was supposed to be risqué, but looked about as sexually abandoned as a smear test.

'Woo-hoo!' said Lysette, waving her arms in a circle above her head before shimmering her body up and down Cally's nearly naked one. Anna knew that she wouldn't even do that with her best friend, before remembering that she didn't really have a best friend – or any friends these days. Perhaps Lysette, Sandi and – gosh – Cally were her friends. For a moment, she pictured getting up and pressing her body against theirs and making the whelpy-whoopy noises too, but even the thought of it made her feel nauseous.

Lysette stopped dancing and came back to her carrying one of the larger items of clothing in the collection, a silver sheath that Anna imagined would be very loose on Cally, but would be skintight on her. Anna realised she was expected to try it on in front of everyone else, but fortunately years of putting on her swimming costume under her towel had given her good training in the art of dressing without undressing.

Even Cally's thespian talents couldn't disguise the fakery in her gasp of admiration when Anna put on the dress. And yet, when she looked in the mirror and saw herself, six inches taller than usual thanks to some borrowed heels and the high hair, with the layers of shimmering and shading to create planes and contours on her face, she couldn't help but give a genuine noise of approval. 'Gosh,' she said out loud. Of course, her own benchmark had been set pretty low on the grooming and make-up front, which is why she suspected that these women had been so desperate to give her a makeover, but actually she did look pretty. Inadvertently she found herself making a face that reminded her of someone. Of course, it was Cally; she'd copied her mirror face. Chin out and down, pouty smile on her lips, engaged eyes.

Lysette and Cally high-fived each other in the manner of a female 21st-century update of Professor Higgins and Colonel Pickering. 'You are hot, baby,' said Cally.

'Yeah, hot, babe,' echoed Lysette in her flat London tones.

Anna wanted to accept their compliments, but too long had she practised the English art of disabling them. 'Oh no, well not me, all your work though, that's amazing. Thank you for that.'

She looked in the full-length mirror. The months of snacking on edamame beans and miso soup, coupled with the running and the swimming in the now drained pool, had paid off. She wasn't as tightly toned as Jude or Cally, but she was not bad for a 'civilian'. She couldn't stop herself from smiling at her reflection.

'Aw bless,' said Lysette. 'She's so chuffed with her new look.'

'Maybe I'll regret it,' said Cally, checking her own reflection, which even in its still unvarnished state was evidently superior. 'After all, now you've got brains *and* beauty.'

She looked genuinely, as opposed to dramatically, melancholic for a moment, before shaking that perfectly peachy ass once again.

Beautification was also taking place in Antigone's room. The little girl was having her hair brushed by Bea, who did so with a languid tenderness. Anna had been struck by the almost sexual intimacy in Cally's room, not the faux-lesbian floor show, but the almost shocking physicality of a woman putting lipstick on another. Here she felt equally embarrassed to intrude on the moment. Not for nothing was the word 'grooming' used about all this business with the hair and skin, as well as the process that innocents go through at the hands of sexual predators: the compliments, the drink, the coaxing.

Antigone frowned at Anna, who gave a self-conscious little twirl. 'You don't look like you. You look like my mother or Janey or someone like that.'

Anna giggled, a sound she didn't recognise as coming from herself. It was as though they'd replaced her voice box while applying three sorts of blusher to her cheeks. 'I'll take that as a compliment.'

'It's not,' she said. 'You look strange.'

Some of the buoyancy Anna had gained along with the expensive designer dress escaped, but she had only to look in the mirror for a whoosh of it to return. She wanted to see the men of Lorston Gardens and she wanted them to see her. In her mind they had become combined and blurred, but all of them – Sholto, Dan and Jack – inspired the same unfamiliar feelings within. Sholto, Dan and Jack, that's how she always thought of them – in that order. Was there a hierarchy? Did Jack's low standing come from the fact that he was the only one to have shown any interest in her, or was it his lack of professional status that dragged his ranking down?

'Do you know what, Antigone? I think I look . . .' Anna paused. 'Hot.'

'Hmm, you probably are,' she replied. 'That silver material looks like it might be a bit sweaty. It's like chain-mail, isn't it, like the armour we saw at the Tower of London. You look like you're off to fight a dragon.'

'I do believe you've made another joke. OK then, do I look fierce? Lysette says I'm working a Joan-of-Arc-meets-Barbarella vibe.'

'That woman can't really speak English very well,' said Antigone, shaking her head. 'Nor any other language, I expect.'

'On the other hand, I must say you look lovely.'

Antigone shrugged. Anna had noticed that those mothers at the school who were most influenced by current fashion dressed their children in a style of studied timelessness. While the women catwalked the school run and talked about 'Autumn slash Winter' as though it were a real season, their children were stuck wearing clothes last seen in a C. S. Lewis adaptation. They shopped in darling little boutiques that were named after the offspring of whichever banker's wife owned them. Their children's casual off-duty wear consisted of glossy bobbed hair, Kirby-gripped into unforgiving side partings, double-breasted navy peacoats and shoes that predated the invention of Velcro fastenings.

Antigone's dark green party dress had smocking and embroidery across her chest, which acted as binding against her precocious budding, a Peter Pan collar and a sash tied in a perfect bow around her waist, or the place where her waist might be. On her feet were patent leather, buckled shoes, while her hair had been tonged into the ringlets of a 1940s child star. Her height and the way she already had those first signs of adolescence gave the whole look something of the *Whatever Happened to Baby Jane?* about it, or poor Judy Garland with her breasts strapped down in *The Wizard of Oz*.

A wolf-whistle pierced Anna's musings.

'Daddy!' cried Antigone, running into his arms and being twirled like a girl greeted by a returning soldier of a father.

Sholto put her down and turned to Anna. 'You look phenomenal.'

'Thank you.' I can do it, I can accept compliments. She pulled a face before she could stop herself. 'I can't really take any credit, it was all Lysette and Cally's work. I was a bit like those paper dolls you can cut out and then add different clothes and hairstyles to.'

'I don't think of you as a doll,' he said. When he frowned he looked exactly like Antigone. It was strangely appealing on a grown man. 'You're far too bright for that. And you,' he said to his daughter, 'look absolutely gorgeous. Can I be the man to escort you two beauties to the party?' He put out a hand to Antigone and his arm to Anna. Antigone giggled in that way she only did for him and Bea, while Anna tried to retain the poise that she'd hoped she'd borrowed alongside the silver dress.

Anna felt giddy as she held onto his arm, needing to lean against it to steady herself. Was it him or the heels that were making her so unsteady on her feet? She barely spared a thought for Bea, whom they left picking up discarded clothes in Antigone's room, wearing her normal outfit of man-made fibres and a wipe-clean apron.

Anna's feelings for Sholto had always seemed ridiculously infantile, but dressed in the heels of a grown-up woman, she felt that maybe she hadn't been so deluded. She staggered a little and wondered whether her outfit was too old for her, much as Antigone's was too childish. Sholto gave her a reassuring smile and she found herself leaning further into him.

'Here we go,' he said, 'unto the breach.' He handed Antigone to her and was gone, standing by Cally who was resplendent in a tiny white dress that showed off her flawless legs and the colour of her skin, as different from goose-bumped pink English whiteness as a lush Mediterranean tomato is from a tube of double-concentrate puree.

Anna's moment of triumph evaporated. She was staff. Not the catering staff, admittedly, but she should still not forget why she was there. She looked around and was quickly assailed by familiar faces. It was like being trapped in Madame Tussaud's after closing time, there were so many celebrities with a slightly waxy hue to their skin, who stood almost unmoving in their signature poses, exactly as though captured for posterity. 'Look at all these famous people,' she whispered to Antigone. 'It's like we've fallen into the television.'

Antigone sighed with weariness.

'All right, all right, I know it's not a big deal to you,' said Anna. 'It's not to me either.'

The photographers called out to Antigone as photographers are wont to do, except a little more politely than usual.

'Oh my word,' Antigone said. 'I suppose I better had.' She dragged herself off to her beckoning mother and stood stiffly between her parents for the photographers, not flinching at the explosion of clicks and flashes.

Anna's phone buzzed in the impractical clutch bag that she'd also been lent for the evening. She looked at it to find a text message from Jack.

'*Am loving my treehouse.*'

Anna realised that, having shown her new improved self to Sholto, she now wanted to be on display for Jack. 'Come on, Antigone,' she shouted over to her as the photographers moved on. 'Let's explore.'

The lawns had been covered by a layer of disconcertingly realistic fake grass to compensate for the sogginess of the preceding weeks of rain. In the absence of a red carpet, the set dressers had created a green one, more perfect than anything that nature could offer. Real grass, it had been agreed, was just hopeless for women in heels, who'd sink backwards into the quagmire and might even look as if they were wearing flats, heaven forfend. No, as ever, the artificial was so much better than the real thing. She supposed that the party planners would rather have created an enormous glass dome above the whole of Lorston Gardens, like one of those holiday camps, and been able to control the temperature with a gigantic thermostat.

'Look, Antigone, stalls,' she said, pointing to 'ye old

country fayre' atmosphere that had been constructed atop the almost neon of the AstroTurf. There was a 'home produce' stall with mini lemon drizzle cakes and jam jars wearing gingham mob caps, a coconut shy and an ersatz Biggest Vegetable Competition populated by genetically modified marrows. This was all to suggest that Cally's skincare range was made with lavender plucked from the herb pots by her bare hands, rather than a reconstituted version of a supermarket moisturiser.

The early evening sun shone for the first time in weeks, as if the set dressers had at last been able to extend their artistry to the skies above. The repatriated beech tree glistened with early summer leaves, its branches sweeping regally over the lawns from its roots in the secret passage. Anna peered up at it, feeling a warmth at knowing that somewhere within its foliage, Jack was ensconced. As Antigone was fawned over by the actors playing country vicars and Women's Institute members, she texted him.

'Can you see me?' She smiled up at the leaves of Jack's tree as she sent it.

'You look beautiful,' came the reply, with a picture. She looked at it and for once it seemed to match the way she was feeling perfectly. She shimmered in the low sun and was framed with the pale green foliage. She looked, yes indeed, actually beautiful. All the other photographs of herself she'd ever seen made her cringe. Proud parental shots where her puppy fat spilled, Facebook shots taken by drunken friends that looked ripe to be stolen by tabloids in the event of any future misbehaviour, those terrible ones that Janey had shown her from the security cameras. Only Jack ever produced an image that looked like her best self.

She looked up to the leaves again. It was odd to be seen but not to see, but she supposed she should be used to it by now.

Anna felt a small, dry, ungloved hand find its way into hers, skin pressed to hers. She looked round to find Antigone beside her, standing nonchalantly as if this was an everyday occurrence. She hardly dared acknowledge the hand for fear of scaring her away, of giving her the 'rubbing velvet' feeling that so nauseated her. She gave it the smallest squeeze and they looked at each other with what felt like complete accord. She filled with love for Antigone. It was a physical and unavoidable sensation that bloomed within her, making her grow taller than even her heels allowed, all because she was holding the hand of this extraordinary child for the first time while being gazed upon by a man who seemed to love her. Only then did she realise how lonely and untouched she had been all these months and how much she had craved affection. She was like one of the flowers in the water-logged gardens, finally feeling the sun on their stalks and blossoming picturesquely at just the right moment.

It was as though the assembled guests felt the same as they thronged outside, happy in the rare sunshine, as only those who live in such a rain-drenched country could ever be. Cally had brought some of California to them, like a bride for whom the sun was always going to shine on her special day. Gladdened by the unfamiliar warmth, the strange mix of fellow celebrities, journalists and professional partygoers seemed seduced into believing that they were indeed attending a village fete circa 1911, one of those golden summers before the First World War. They began to throw coconuts, try out their strength on the hammer, eat the miniature scones passed around by the absurdly good-looking waiters and waitresses.

'I love you, Antigone,' Anna said. She couldn't stop herself and felt a stab of mortification, as though she'd said the words prematurely to a casual boyfriend.

Antigone looked thoughtful. 'Do you know? I love you, too. You and Daddy and Bea. Yes, I do love you too.' She had that quizzical, shocked look that she wore on the rare occasions she made a joke.

Anna felt like skipping through to the special 'wild meadow' area of the fete and spinning Antigone round and round. Men found her beautiful, this special child adored her; if there were small animals they would scamper towards her and the birds would fly down to perch on her arms. She was magnetic.

The partygoers were hushed so that Cally could address them. Sholto stood behind Anna and Antigone, his arms around both of them. It was paternal gesture, Anna knew that, but she wanted to bottle up his touch for ever. Finally she was living that glamorous life of parties and perfect men that she had dreamed of.

Cally stood on a pedestal garlanded with wild flowers, wringing her hands and glancing around with mild panic, the sort of look that actresses practise before award ceremonies, the 'Who, me? Little old me?' routine. Anna felt a flash of irritation.

'Thank you all so much for coming, it means so much to me,' she began with a perfect balance of endearing nervousness and eloquence. 'People are always asking me for skincare tips and I tell them, you know, lots of water, sleep and physical exercise.' She looked towards Sholto as she said this and gave a stagey wink. 'But really I know how difficult breakouts and sensitive skin can be, and I wanted to give the world more than just advice. So, by turning to my beloved garden, I've developed a really natural but super-effective skincare range. I want the world to glow. And I want my darling daughter to live in a society where young girls can have perfect skin without horrid chemicals. So I dedicate the range to my gorgeous girl, Antigone, and my equally precious husband, Sholto, whose love is my real beauty secret.'

As the partygoers turned to toast them, Anna felt Sholto's arm drop away from her, but the other remained tightly around his daughter's shoulders. They were standing above the portholes of glass that let light into the pool and spa area beneath. Anna had a brief worry that anybody standing below might be able to see up the silver sheath of her borrowed dress. She caught sight of Bea staring at them from the picture windows of the drawing room. Yes, we do look perfect together, she thought. If only Jack could take a photograph of this scene, she was sure it would be every bit as lovely as it felt in her head. She turned her head towards the beech tree to smile once again, before feeling a stab of guilt that she should be looking so happy standing so close to another man. But she loved Jack too. She loved everyone that night. She loved herself.

She thought she saw the branch wave in response and then the earth move. Literally, the earth seemed to keel, though she swore she hadn't drunk more than two glasses of champagne.

Then it rolled some more, so that her heels faltered and a noise – not screaming, but a collective gasp of shock and confusion – then amplified into a higher pitch that sounded like nothing she'd ever heard before. Before she had even realised what was going on, a thought scratched its way across her brain: it's happening again. The same lurch out of control, the panic yet peacefulness, the consciousness of fear without actually feeling it. Then the grass, the gloriously fake grass, lurched as if someone were tugging the carpet of green, the magician's trick of pulling the tablecloth while leaving the crockery still standing. Except the people weren't still standing, they were falling and tumbling. Her hand let go of Antigone's and she thought how sad that they should only just have grasped each other and then lost the grip so soon. She had an acute awareness that she might never hold Antigone's hand again, and then that she might never hold anybody's hand again.

There was no calm any longer, not inside her head or outside. Screams everywhere, not like those you hear in horror films but more atonal, lower, higher, so many different sounds but still all so human, just not the sound you ever hear – an orchestra of keening tuning up but never reaching harmony. The ground gave way completely now as if sucked by the devil's hoover down into some watery pit.

Anna hurtled like an elevator down a shaft before coming to a stop. She had landed by the swimming pool, along with dozens of other guests, some of them lying prone like parodies of sunbathing tourists. Things – she hoped they were things, not bodies – floated in the water, alongside the striped awning from one of the fairground stalls.

The air was sliced with the sound of crunching glass. She thought it was the champagne flutes but then realised it was far too loud for that. It was the windows in the basement; all those windows built to convince you that the subterranean layers were not troglodyte caves but as light and airy as a Mediterranean villa.

She was fine, she was fine, there was nothing broken. Antigone, where was Antigone? Then the floor went from beneath her as the pool seemed to burst its banks. It was like the time she'd been sucked into the vortex, but this time it was the whole swimming pool, all a thousand tonnes of water, that was falling into itself.

With that, everything seemed to go. The basement levels folded in on themselves, the foundations shot through by some natural or unnatural disaster. Columns fell into one another; the earth gaped as if trying to reclaim the space that had been stolen from it by the grasping claws of the basement diggers. The sounds were so loud that Anna could no longer distinguish the shattering glass from the collapsing columns, the screams of horror from the anguish of pain. They were all so unfamiliar to her but she'd hear them forever. She knew she had to get out of the house. How was she even inside it, since she had been standing in the garden? She looked around frantically to see that there was no garden, at least not that area of the garden nearest the house. It was now in the basement, its real grass and fake grass crumpled and crumbled into the gloop.

She began to stagger to the promised land above ground, a cliff above the sea.

'Anna!' She heard a voice over the screams, its familiarity making it distinguishable amid the cacophony. She turned to see Antigone, her face streaked with mud, tears and pain.

She scooped her up, surprising herself by being able to lift her, and then began to pull away from the water and marble and high-end light fittings. Having fought against the water once before gave her the strength and knowledge to do so again. She felt as though they were escaping from a tidal wave and had come to the bottom of some cliffs, where at the top was the bit of the garden that had survived, the bit of the garden that had been unscooped, left undug, that had remained as it had been intended when the house had been built a hundred and seventy years earlier. It was three metres above her and she could see people running across its promised heights.

'Help!' she called to them, lifting Antigone up as someone more precious than herself. A child, she's a child, she wanted to shout, but nothing came out. Not just any child, she might have said, a famous one.

'Antigone, grab the towel!' a voice called.

Anna looked up to see Sholto leaning over the cliff edge, holding one of the once white fluffy towels that had been used as casually as tissues in the times before all this. She pushed Antigone up further, using all her strength to lift her from her calves and then push those feet, still clad in stupid, pretentious little-girl shoes, onto her palms, so that she could reach the towel.

'Please, Antigone,' she shouted, feeling her knees buckle, not knowing if the unsteadiness was from the weight upon her or whether the floor was going to collapse again as the water swooshed in waves, one against another.

She looked at Sholto and saw fear in his eyes. It looked so different from what she'd seen in disaster films that she realised actors were rubbish. What she saw in his expression was not dramatic – it was dead and deadening. She carried on pushing Antigone until at last she reached up for the towel and the load lightened. She watched Antigone's legs disappear over the side and waited for the towel to come back down to her.

'Sholto!' she screamed, but there was nothing, no towel nor man. She kept calling. He must be coming back for me, he's taking Antigone to a safe place and then he's coming back for me. Count to ten, slowly: one banana, two banana . . . She reached ten bananas and realised that she had to help herself. She began to claw at the wall of mud and marble that stood in her way, sticking her newly painted nails into it so that they became varnished with filth. She couldn't get a grip without help from above or below. She looked around for someone to give her a shove, but there was only panic and confusion. Those guests had always been strangers to her; she had just thought she knew them.

She began to wonder if she hadn't got it wrong, that she should be looking for ways to help others rather than to help herself, but people were ricocheting away from her. Think, think, think. Aren't you supposed to be clever? That old chestnut. Just then, she felt something flap against her head. A piece of the bunting from one of the village fete stalls had been thrown down to her. Sholto, surely: she knew he wouldn't abandon her! She looked up, expecting to see his face, but instead saw one even more familiar to her, always handsome, now beautiful.

'Jack!'

'Grab it and hold it tight.' His face strained as he pulled her up.

'Thank you,' she said, her voice polite with shock as she reached the top and edged away from the crumbling front.

'Pleasure,' he replied. 'Antigone told me you were still down there.'

Anna looked around her, trying to find her other saviour. She spotted her being dragged away from the scene by her father. She ran over to them.

'Good, you're here,' Sholto said. 'You can persuade Antigone that she has to get away. She's so stubborn.'

Anna stared at him in disbelief, wondering whether she'd imagined her own abandonment. She was nothing, a mere human stepladder for Antigone's escape, and now a further aid to the child's salvation. Parents are supposed to be unselfish, aren't they? That's what Cally had said to her in the pool that night. But although they're prepared to sacrifice themselves for their children, they'll quite happily sacrifice others too.

'I wanted you, Anna,' Antigone said. 'I won't go without you. And now I won't go without Bea!' She had extricated herself from Sholto's grip and was now standing rigid, with her lips pursed in determination.

'Have you seen Bea?' asked Sholto. He sounded desperate.

'She was in the house. I saw her in the drawing . . .' Anna's voice tailed off as she looked towards where she had last seen Bea. The walls of the house were still there, the original early Victorian was standing, as if to lord its superiority over these 21st-century innovations. But there was nothing behind the walls; they had become a façade, like a stage set – as unreal as Tara in *Gone With The Wind*. The elegant floor-to-ceiling windows were empty, like eyes that had been gouged out. Anna looked round, disorientated. It was as though someone had come into your bedroom and rearranged all the objects, just to convince you of your madness.

'Look after Antigone, I'll go find Bea! Get away from here, get her as far from the house as you can,' Sholto said.

Anna turned around to try to find Jack, who was still leaning over the precipice, helping others as he had helped her.

'Jack!' she screamed, but he didn't hear her over the rest of the noise. She stood still, not knowing where to go.

'Move, you stupid girl,' said Sholto. 'Save Antigone.'

She ran clutching Antigone's hand to where she thought safety lay, the only place she knew, towards the beech tree where she hoped Jack would return. It too was standing tall and mocking against the morass of new-fangled materials that swirled behind them.

She pressed herself and the child against the base of the tree. 'Antigone, are you OK, my darling?'

The little girl nodded, her characteristic calm for once giving Anna some comfort.

They looked back towards the house, which seemed to have stopped moving, though the sounds continued to ring out.

'It's stopped,' said Anna. Where was Jack? She wanted him to be safe and then – she surprised herself with the thought – she wanted him to profit from the chaos. She wanted him to adopt the hard morality of a war photographer, snapping the starving child with its distended stomach or the soldier clasping a blown-off leg. She wanted the world to know that this had all really happened, and why shouldn't Jack be the one to show them? Even then she knew that she needed proof, too, of what she had witnessed, to convince herself that it had been real. But most of all she wanted him to be OK, for any photos he'd taken to be with him, not recovered from a lifeless body lying in the wreckage at the bottom of the pit.

She crouched down to hug Antigone. She clutched at her as tightly as she'd ever held anyone, seeming to offer comfort but in fact taking it for herself. 'You're OK, you're OK,' she murmured again and again into her white-blonde hair, but what she meant was 'please let Jack be OK'. Antigone clutched her in return and the girl who was so advanced intellectually and physically, now seemed so tiny and young pressed against her.

Antigone whispered, 'Bea.'

'She was in the house, I'm sure she's fine. Look, the house is still standing.' They looked over to see a crack rippling through the building. The house was still there for the moment. Where was Bea? Where was everyone? Janey must be feeling like a bereaved mother. Anna imagined her clutching her photo books and weeping over the ruination of her baby, perhaps throwing herself into the muddy slurry in a suicidal gesture of together-ness with her greatest project.

'Mama!' screamed Antigone. Anna looked round for Cally but saw only Bea running towards them, plaster dust caked into her hair. She pushed Anna out of the way to grab Antigone and held her tightly in her arms, whispering those words again, '*Mi hija, mi hija.*' Sholto came up behind them and wrapped both of them into his arms so that he, Antigone, and Bea looked like a set of Russian nesting dolls. Anna looked at Bea's brown arms contrasted against Antigone's pale ones. My daughter, my daughter, she kept saying in Spanish. I don't understand, Anna thought, how can it be? And yet somehow it made perfect sense, made everything comprehensible. She looked at Sholto, who looked back at her and nodded, as if reading her thoughts. Yes, he was saying, yes.

'How?' she mouthed at him.

He sighed, still clutching Bea and Antigone as though they were the most precious people in the world to him. They *were* the most precious people in the world to him.

Anna, exiled from Antigone's inner circle, left in search of safety and Jack.

13

Putting Down the Bunting

The carriage driveway was crowded with ambulances and fire engines, their flashing lights illuminating the wet and wounded who wandered in a daze, their party finery obscured by mud and hospital blankets.

Nobody paid Anna much attention since she was unharmed, physically, and the emergency services were too concerned with those who were obviously damaged.

She wanted to ring Jack, but she'd lost that minuscule clutch bag that held her phone. It wouldn't have happened if she'd been wearing trousers, or a jacket with proper pockets. Stupid bloody designer borrowed dress and stupid clutch bag. It would now be lying buried in the hardening mud below the house, preserved like those dice-playing Pompeians, a useless, impractical bag with no strap and no room inside it, a perfect symbol, like high heels, of the way women were expected to be conveyed across the world by men and taxis. Perhaps the phone was still working, its ringing muffled by mud, and Jack was trying and trying to contact her? Please let him be all right. Why hadn't she insisted that he come with her and Antigone? She had let herself be dictated to by Sholto instead of making sure that Jack was out of danger.

Jack had risked his life to save strangers, while Sholto hadn't even bothered to save her.

She went back to the garden, but was prevented from moving nearer to the gaping home by the red and white barriers that had been hastily erected by the emergency services.

'Go home,' said a fireman as she tried to peer over them. 'Nothing to see here.'

Home? She didn't have one any longer. Home is where the heart is, they say, and yet her heart was as lost as one of those pieces of swimming pool mosaic; it had slid off to some subterranean Neverland. It was with Jack and it was with Antigone, and she knew where neither had gone now. She didn't even know if Jack *could* go anywhere.

'Do you know what happened?' she asked the fireman.

'The basement collapsed.'

'But why?'

He shrugged.

'Is everyone all right?'

'She's fine.' He emphasised the word '*she*'. Well, that's OK then, so long as *she's* fine. 'People have been taken to hospital. We won't know anything until a proper cross-check is done of the guest list against the names the police have taken and those of the patients at the hospital. Sorry.'

If your name's not on the list, you're not coming in. This was some sort of VIP route to hell, a cesspit of a roped-off area. People would one day boast of having been or not been there.

She walked out of the front of the house, round to the secret passage that ran beside it and came to the bottom of the beech tree. No one knew about it, so there was nobody there to stop her from climbing it. She'd lost her heels when clambering up to safety with the bunting thrown down by Jack, and the bark was rough on her bare feet. But the evening had inoculated her against pain and she managed to shimmy up to the branches that she'd scoped out in advance for Jack's eyrie.

She'd been right – the view was superb from up there, and the gentle sway of the branch as she shifted along it felt reassuring after the nauseating roll of the ground. She felt safe. Safe but cold, yes, freezing – damn this stupid dress. It should feel precarious to be balanced up there in the branches, but now to be grounded was to feel rootless. Everything had been turned upside down.

It was dusk, but the bright lights of the emergency services were like those used by film sets; they'd blind you if you went too close. It only increased the air of unreality, that this wasn't a real disaster, but somehow one choreographed by a director and expensive special effects, that those doctors, paramedics and firefighters were actors pretending to be heroic (except, of course, they weren't quite good looking enough for celluloid). She imagined what Jack had seen from up in the tree only an hour or so ago. He would have seen all those guests milling about with their pretence of enjoyment, their 'look at us, what larks we're having' at the coconut shy. He would have seen her, twirling in her silver dress, then holding Antigone's hand, shimmering with love and light, convinced that she was wearing a cloak of fabulousness by having been lent those clothes by Cally.

There would have been the good-looking workers teeming away to make the party planner's vision real. Everyone had gathered together to celebrate moisturiser. Fucking moisturiser.

Go home, the fireman had told her. Her rooms were probably fine since, as far as she knew, the excavations hadn't extended under the garage. They, the staff and owners of Lorston Gardens, would all be evacuated and sent off to different places. They would never live together again; that era was over and everything would be different from now on. She couldn't go back to her parents' house; she couldn't face the humiliation of her return, where her only chance of paid employment would be to don the high-visibility tabard of the charity collector once again. She had failed to keep in contact with her friends from university, who had separated off into those who'd got their fancy jobs and their flats, or marvellous self-contained areas at their parents', and those – like her – who didn't have such connections and comforts to rely on. She had at last been forced to give up her childish fantasies about Sholto. He had proved beyond any doubt that he didn't care if she lived or died.

Sholto and Bea, she thought. Bea and Antigone. Having seen them together in the face of disaster she knew that they were a family of sorts, but she couldn't quite work out how they fitted together or where that left Cally.

A little inventory: Bea, Antigone and Sholto were fine – she'd seen them all. Cally, according to the fireman, had survived too. Without a phone she couldn't check the internet to see if any celebrities had been among the casualties. Martina, what about her? Not that her fate would make the news, nor that of Lysette or Jude or Wadim. Dan, what about him? Despite his rudeness and parody sinister air, Anna imagined him doing something heroic, saving people with his top inexplicably removed, photos of him making the papers and his name. And Janey – she who was always so ever present had been so suddenly absent when the world folded in on itself. Had she made it, or was her fate so intertwined with the basement that she could not survive its destruction?

Anna was so tired and cold. She wanted to fall asleep, right there up in the tree. People did stranger things. During some floods in Africa, a woman had given birth up a tree, so surely she could sleep in one? She was so exhausted she could sleep anywhere. Right now, she could fall asleep and wake up in the morning to find that everything had been cleared up, as though it was no more than the mess of cigarette butts and empty glasses from a normal party.

'Anna!' A shout – real or a dream? She started and looked down from her perch.

'Jack! You're alive!' He was more alive than anybody she'd ever seen, the mud and the mess that clung to his face and clothes making the fact of his survival more visual.

He made a rueful sound that was half snort, half laugh. 'You too. Come on, get down from there.' She clambered to the lowest branch before jumping down into his waiting arms. They felt strong, she supposed from carrying all that camera equipment, but also stronger than they had been before, as if a night of running around trying to rescue people had made him steely. She collapsed into him and allowed herself to be held, finding that something stirred within her despite her tiredness.

They hugged in silence for a few minutes before she asked, 'How did you know I was here?'

'A hunch. I kept trying your phone and I was worried when I got no answer. Jesus, it's a relief to see you.' He looked up at the harbouring branches. 'It's a good view, isn't it?'

'I suppose. Jack, what on earth happened here tonight?'

'I don't know. Nobody does yet. It was all just confusion.' He shuddered.

'I'm so sorry; it's all my fault you were even here. You should have run away with me and Antigone. You idiot for going back there with your bunting.'

Jack smiled. 'The hero, accessorised with floral-patterned bloody bunting.'

Anna giggled and then felt ashamed to be laughing when people might have died. 'Did you get any photographs?'

'Anna! I can't believe you of all people are asking me that.'

'Well, did you? I'm not judging. I think you should have got some. We need to know what happened here.'

'A few, yes, and some film – I just left my phone running on video.' He pointed to the phone attached to his arm by a runner's strap. 'Thing is, until I know how bad it was, if anybody, you know . . . I don't feel I can use it. It might be like a snuff movie. I need to have a proper look at it and then probably hand it over to the police.'

'The police?'

'Yeah. They'll need it as evidence.'

'Of what?'

'Dunno. Buildings don't just collapse like that. There must be malpractice of some sort, I guess.'

'Could it be terrorism?'

'What, against the decadent Western actress? It's possible, but from what I gathered at the scene and from a couple of phone calls to the news desks, it seems more likely that the building work to that big old basement was a bit dodgy.'

'Do you know,' said Anna, 'Janey told me that those upside-down houses with multi-levelled basements are called iceberg houses. Because there's more underneath than on the surface. An iceberg, lots of people swimming and drowning while wearing their party dresses.'

'Like the Titanic, you mean? Very apt.'

'Indeed,' said Anna. 'The basement was never right; there were cracks and faults all along. I'd noticed them. It was always dripping down there.'

'Well, if that's true, someone will be prosecuted. Manslaughter, if anyone ends up dying.'

'Who's responsible though?'

'The builders, the project manager, whoever contracted the work, the architect . . . I don't know. If there is some sort of prosecution, the film I took from up there might help to explain it.'

'Why do you think it collapsed?'

'Combination of rain, bad foundations, digging down too deep . . . ? I'm not an expert. There's talk about water tables and the fact that the trees had been moved. You know, the beeches. One of the firefighters told my mate that their roots might have been stabilising the house and that moving them was dangerous.' He shrugged. 'You did look lovely, by the way.'

Anna laughed and found that once she started, she couldn't stop, and then she began to cry. The permanent confusion she had felt since coming to this house seemed to have bubbled over to a point where she knew nothing about anything and everything she'd previously believed had been wrong. As Jack held her beneath the beech tree, she wondered how she could ever have found Sholto attractive. She pulled away in order to look at Jack. He was as weary as she was.

'What now?' he asked.

'I don't know,' said Anna. 'I'm homeless.'

'I'm living at a friend's flat while they're off abroad for a few months. We can get a taxi. Reckon we've earned it.'

'So you've got a proper bed now?'

'And you're not living here.' They paused. It was one of their moments. 'Come on, doll, you can help me look through all the footage I collected.'

The flat was in one of those appealingly urban early 20th-century blocks, originally designed to house the respectable poor, but now eminently desirable for their cool East London addresses. Anna had assumed the flat he was staying in was a male friend's, but the photos on the wall, the silk cushions strewn around and the collection of yoga mats in the corner suggested otherwise.

'Whose flat is this?' she asked.

'She was Ellie when we were together, but I think she's now called Harmony. It's her spirit name or something. She's in India trying to find herself.'

An ex called Harmony with a bijou wooden-floored flat – this didn't fit into the picture that she'd built up of him. She was pretty, too, this Harmony/Ellie person, though narcissistic. Who covers their walls in photos of themselves doing the downward dog pose in a bikini? Anna realised that she knew almost nothing about Jack – not even basic first-date stuff, like where he'd grown up or how many brothers and sisters he had. She had become, she realised, so embroiled in the workings of Lorston Gardens that people outside of it were like bit-players whose lives were worthless. She had only been interested in him when he could help her find out more about the house; she'd never even asked him about where he lived.

He connected his phone to a laptop and they sat side-by-side watching the footage. He'd managed to hold his camera very straight as he'd filmed; there was none of the wonkiness she'd have expected, even when he evidently hopped down from the tree. Even at the remove of a few hours and through the filter of film, the horror of the noise and the confusion pierced her. She shivered as she realised that she might be watching real people dying. How many times had she watched grainy footage from Middle Eastern war zones or African famines on the news and she'd never once had any compunction or guilt? These people, these wealthy Western people in their expensive clothes, had lives that were worth more to her.

He'd missed filming the beginning, the moment where the grass had begun to roll, so he connected up his camera and began to scroll through the pictures. There she was, laughing in her silver dress, the early evening light giving her the aura of an angel. She had been right, he had captured her at her loveliest. He'd clicked to take this image so many times that scrolling through them created an animation, like in a basic flicker book. Then a few dozen of minor celebrities talking to other minor celebrities, framed at the edges with the leaves of the beeches. Then a set of photos of her and Antigone being hugged by Sholto during Cally's speech. Behind them, Anna could see signs of anxiety on the faces of the staff as they looked towards the basement area. There must have been something to alert them to what was about to happen, as there was definitely movement away from it, as if what they heard had compelled them to edge away. People can have a sixth sense that tells them not to get on the plane, not to go to the beach that day, not to climb that mountain.

They went back to the footage. Once Jack had jumped down from the tree, he'd attached the phone to the strap on his arm facing forward and allowed it to film. She felt nausea bubble inside her as she saw the camera peek over the ledge and down into the pit, with her face staring up in confusion at the bunting that had been thrown down. Then she saw amputated footage of herself being pulled up and then their brief conversation on being winched to safety. She had to look away as she watched Jack going back towards the danger, especially when the camera lurched as the ground collapsed again beneath him, almost throwing him into the pit.

She heard his voice, the London accent that she had so derided, calming people as he dragged them to safety. She began to lose count of them as she heard him shouting instructions with detached calm.

Then there was a scream as a girder swooped into view and in a few split seconds whizzed towards the camera. Even though Jack was sitting safely behind her, Anna put her hands over her eyes and ducked, it was whirring so near. It landed what must have been a few centimetres from Jack and obscured the picture until he had jumped away from it.

He sat in the chair next to Anna's, watching the film, and his face became mottled with red and white splodges. This was what terror looked like. How many of us ever get to see our moment of near-death?

'I'd known it was close,' he said, 'but not that close.' He began to shake. That calm bravado he'd exuded was pure adrenalin and it was now beginning to wear off.

Anna leant over and clasped his head to her chest, just as she had done earlier with Antigone. She stroked his hair and said, 'you're all right,' over and over again.

He pulled away. 'I need to send this footage and photos to the police, there might be something in it that will help them.'

'Shush, they're not going to need it now. They'll be taking statements, checking up on people in the hospital, that kind of thing. We need some sleep.' She looked at him, wondering if she'd see that look in his eye, but all she saw was exhaustion.

She led him to the bedroom. He took off his shoes. She had none to remove. He took off his trousers. She was only wearing underwear and the borrowed dress so, overwhelmed with shyness, she left it on as if it was the old nightshirt she always slept in. Having felt so tired that she could have fallen asleep up a tree, she now felt a mixture of alertness and exhaustion, as if she'd been mainlining high-energy drinks. She lay rigid next to him, her sleeplessness not helped by the scratchiness of the metallic dress and the way that her skin bristled with his nearness.

She was tired, muddy and confused. She only liked to have sex in seriousness; it needed to be *special*. She shouldn't be wanting him just because they'd just been through the most extraordinary night of their lives, especially since it had been extraordinary for all the wrong reasons. Sex should be preceded by a nice dinner. Her stomach growled. It had been a long time since the mini-scones at Cally's fayre. She glanced over at him. He was awake too and she felt something in her stomach that wasn't hunger, at least not for old-fashioned baked goods. She must be confusing the fear for lust, cortisol for oxytocin. It was all wrong.

The dress bit at her skin. She sat upright and pulled it over her head, revealing a bra that was more about creating a clean line under the silver than exciting a man. No matter, he turned to her and put his hand to her chest. She undid the bra and clasped his hand, not knowing whether she wanted this moment to last or whether she wanted to move on eagerly. She shivered.

'Are you cold?' he asked.

She shook her head and put her leg across him in order to bring her lips to his. They had kissed before but this felt different. This time it was not an end, but a prelude. He tasted of chewing gum and coffee. She ran her hand through his hair; it jagged on a clump of mud that had crusted into his thick curls. A surge of desire rippled through her and she fumbled towards his shorts. They were satisfyingly shaped, thank god. Would he be too tired? Was she too tired? What was she doing? They should be sleeping, talking to the police, contacting the house, finding out if everyone was safe.

He kissed the nipples now unbound from her bra and then her lips again. A grapple with his wallet and then at last he was inside her and it felt somehow harder than those boys from Oxford, with their stroking and whining and brevity. Soon she felt herself screaming. In her confusion she didn't know why and wondered whether it was all the fear releasing itself, but then she realised no, it wasn't. She straddled him and pushed herself against him, like she'd never done before. She'd always lain there like Ophelia drowning, her hair arranged picturesquely on a pillow, but now she grabbed and she tussled and she shouted instructions, her voice knowing what she wanted when her conscious mind was unsure.

When it was over, she lay back, desperate to distance herself a little from him, whereas before she'd been happy to spoon away with those boy-men.

'Jesus, Anna,' said Jack. 'I've waited so long.'

'Sorry,' she said. 'I hope it was OK after all that wait?' She cringed, did she have to be quite so unsexy? She was supposed to say 'worth the wait?' rhetorically, or something, knowing the answer full well.

'What do you think?' He grinned.

'Personally, it was really good. Actually, it was better than anyone else. Not that there've been many others.'

'It was flipping fantastic, girl.'

She turned onto her side and shimmied closer to him. She felt as though she had been opened along with the ground beneath their feet at Lorston Gardens. She thought she'd remain awake, given what had happened and the strangeness of the bed, but she found herself falling into dreamless sleep.

14

Missing Persons

'Anna, wake up, you've got to get up.' Jack thrust his laptop into her arms. 'You've got to look at this.'

She struggled to take in everything at once, her eyes darting all over the screen of a newspaper website. Predictably the 'carnage at Cally party' was the lead story, of course, and how fortunate that there should have been so many photographers on the ground. The sight of all those beautiful people amid the chaos was strangely photogenic.

'You need to ring someone,' he said. 'You're on a missing list, see?' He clicked to an article with lots of names and a telephone number. Anna wasn't sure whether it was for an official body or for the newspaper to solicit some 'I was there' stories. Janey and Dan's names were on it, but no others that she recognised, except hers. Her name in lights, this time not just the 'nanny'.

'My parents!' she said. He handed her his phone. What a selfish, horrible person she had become to be off having sex without thinking of her parents and their worry. And then she astonished herself by smiling at the thought of it. If you are going to have selfish horrible sex, then it should at least be very good, selfish horrible sex. 'What time is it anyway?'

'Five thirty. But they're not going to care.'

Five thirty a.m. It was only 12 hours ago that she had begun to get ready for the party.

She punched in the only number, other than her own, that she knew off by heart. It only rang once before being answered. 'Mum, I'm fine,' she said quickly, news that was greeted with weeping relief. 'I'm at a friend's house and I'm absolutely fine. Yeah, a bit shocked. Of course, let me speak to him.' She mouthed 'my dad' to Jack, who was rubbing her leg in a way that was half comforting and half erotic, made shamefully more so by the fact it was so illicit, given that she was talking to her parents after a near-death experience.

'I'm sorry,' she said to her mother and then to her father. She was sorry for everything, for the worry that they had felt, but for all that had gone on before; for never calling them, for moving out and on so completely once she'd started work at Lorston Gardens. She was sorry for ever having compared her mother unfavourably to Cally's maternal charisma, for ever wishing that their house and life had been more like the glamour she'd briefly and vicariously enjoyed.

She put the phone down and turned to Jack. 'Dad's just pointed out to me that I need to let someone at Lorston Gardens know where I am, but I don't have any numbers on me.' She uselessly patted the virtual pockets on her naked self, which emphasised how amputated she felt without her phone. 'And Janey's on that list of missing persons anyway.'

He carried on rubbing her leg and then moved his hand up. She pulled him towards her.

'Is this 9-11 sex?' he whispered in her ear. 'You know, desperate survival sex and then you're going to disappear?'

'I don't know,' she said. 'Does it matter?'

Jack, of course, knew exactly which police station to go to.

'Can I speak to Cally and Sholto?' Anna asked the police officer who had been assigned to them. She'd insisted they call her Kirsten, which felt over-familiar.

'We'll let them know you're safe,' Kirsten said.

'And Antigone, I'd really like to speak to Antigone. We were together, you see, when it started to happen. It might be traumatic for her.'

'She's with her parents.'

'And all my stuff, everything I own,' she looked down at the rolled-up jeans, T-shirt and flip-flops she'd borrowed. Somehow, when she'd seen models in 'boyfriend jeans' in magazines, they had looked a whole lot better than this. 'It's all at the house. Can I go there?'

'The building's still being stabilised, but I'm sure we can arrange for some of your clothes and possessions to be picked up.'

'All right. I just wanted to make sure everyone knew I was safe. Is everyone else OK?'

She nodded.

'Janey? I saw her name on the list in the papers.'

'She's fine.' Kirsten paused. 'We believe she's fine.'

'Where is she?'

'That's a good question. We were wondering if you'd be able to help.'

'Me?'

'Were you aware that she and the driver, Dan McClaren, were in a relationship?'

'A relationship?'

Kirsten couldn't hide her impatience. 'Yes, they were having sex with each other.'

Of course. Forget damaged Cally and ageing Sholto, Dan and Janey were the house's true alpha couple. She had only ever seen the possibility of Janey and Sholto, blinded as she was by her own yearnings. But it had been there for her to see all along. 'I didn't know, actually, but I can well believe it. It wasn't official, if you see what I mean. They were never openly a couple.'

'And now they've both disappeared,' continued Kirsten. 'I'm sure there's a reasonable explanation, but we'd be very keen for them to get in touch with us so that we can hear that explanation first hand. How well do you know Janey?'

'Not really well at all. She's quite unknowable.'

'Do you know anything about her family?'

'In a way, we were her family and Lorston Gardens was her family home.'

Kirsten rolled her eyes. 'That's all very sweet, but where would you guess she might be?'

'You're making it sound like you need them to – what's

the expression they use on the television? – help the police with their inquiries.'

'If you like watching cop shows, then you'll also know that I am unable to tell you more.' She gave a quick conspiratorial grin. 'But yes, we would like them to help with our inquiries. Do you know anything about the Stewards' financial arrangements?'

'The Carpenters, you mean? Not a lot. I think that Janey was the centre of everything.' Well, not everything, thinking of Bea. 'Have you checked out her office?'

'Her office at the house?' Kirsten asked with audible disdain. 'You were there last night, weren't you?'

'Oh yes, I see.' Although she had witnessed it, Anna could still not quite believe that much of what she'd known as Lorston Gardens was now condemned to its watery grave. 'What's left of her office. There were files upon files and photo books in there. If you can find her computer, I'm sure it's all on the hard drive. I think I remember her saying something about the accounts.' Priya, of course, Priya knew about the accounts and that was what had got her sacked. She filed away that thought to tell Jack later. Kirsten could find out about Priya soon enough, but she wanted to make sure that Jack got to her first. 'Janey kept detailed records of all the building work, so maybe you can get some clues as to what went wrong with the basement. What did go wrong with the basement?'

'It's too early for us to say. Your friend Jack's footage is certainly helpful. Look, you're tired, go away and think about it.' About what exactly, wondered Anna. 'And do let us know if you remember anything about arrangements at Lorston Gardens being odd.'

Everything about that place was odd.

Jack set off armed with his photos and footage, for a meeting set up with Priya, who seemed eager to sell her side of the story. What's more, she said she could supply him with an interview with Wadim as well.

'Thanks for that,' Jack had said to Anna. 'I owe you.'

'Not as much as I owe you. And I'm sure Priya will be delighted with any contribution to her university fees.'

He left her with his key, some cash, and the address of a hotel where his contacts had told him the family could be found. 'The family': Cally, Sholto and Antigone; that perfect picture-book family, two parents and a girl-child. Or, so they thought. Anna wondered which permutation she would find, how the Happy Families cards had been shuffled this time.

She took a taxi to the hotel, which was already swarming with paps.

'I know you!' shouted one of them. 'You're the nanny.'

I'm not a nanny, she intoned to herself wearily, I'm a tutor stroke mentor. I was, anyway. She gave a half-hearted wave and fought her way into the hotel. She'd hated the leering glass gaze of the lens, but she had a brief surge of future nostalgia for it.

After protracted negotiations and phone calls, one of the receptionists took her up to the penthouse suite. The door was opened for her and she entered to find Cally and Antigone sitting on a sofa with Sholto standing behind them, as if posing for a story on how they'd put their house hell behind them.

Anna couldn't hide her surprise. The three of them together, alone, as she had never seen them at Lorston Gardens. She realised then that this had not been what she had expected after all. She had so many questions, none of which she was allowed to ask, so instead she stood dithering at the door.

Antigone leapt up and ran to her. Anna crouched down with her arms out, hoping that the closeness of the night before had not collapsed into the mud along with all those carefully chosen objects and fragile structures. She held her breath as Antigone threw herself at her with such force that she was almost knocked backwards. It felt as though they were saving one another once again. Antigone's cheeks were so smoothly pressed against hers she wondered how she'd ever been so physically rejected by her. It was as though her charge was trying to make up for all those times they should have hugged but did not.

'You saved my life,' said Antigone.

'And you saved mine.' Anna began to cry, still unstable from all that had happened.

Sholto still stood behind Cally, sitting regally on the sofa. 'Thank you so much, Anna, for all that you've done. And especially for yesterday.'

She shrugged. 'Anyone would have done the same. I would never have left her there, you don't do that to people you love. And you know I love Antigone.'

'We all love Antigone,' said Cally.

Yes all right, thought Anna, you don't need to say it as though it's a competition. 'I've got your dress,' she said, holding up an inelegant plastic bag. 'I lost the shoes and bag, though. Sorry.'

'That's OK,' Cally said, as if this was a generous concession on her part. What was the alternative – that Anna's wages be docked?

Sholto busied himself with room service while Anna sat, cuddling up with Antigone, on the sofa near Cally.

'I'm sorry to intrude on what must be a private time,' Anna said. 'But I feel a bit lost, I suppose. I don't know where I'm supposed to go and I need to get my things from the house.'

'If it's money you want, I'm sure it can be arranged,' said Cally.

'No, no. It's not that, really it isn't.'

'That's good, since we can't access our accounts at the moment anyway.' The woman who couldn't order an egg-white omelette by herself was no doubt finding Janey's absence akin to a bereavement.

'It's simply that the last time I saw Antigone was when it was all happening, and I just needed to be with people who were there,' said Anna. 'I needed to know she was all right.'

'There are plenty of photographs where you could have seen that she was fine,' said Cally tersely.

'But it's not the same,' said Antigone. 'Photos aren't the same as seeing someone properly. Photos are nothing.' She snuggled closer to Anna. Last night Jack; now Antigone. Anna was lapping up the physical affection after having been starved of it for so long. She didn't ever want to be so lonely again. She wanted to have the touch of those she loved on tap.

'Right,' said Cally tersely.

'Is everyone all right? Martina, Bea . . . ?' Anna glanced at Sholto.

'Everyone's fine. Well, there are a couple of catering staff unaccounted for. Polish, I think,' said Sholto, as if this made their disappearance less troublesome.

'What about Janey and Dan? The police say that they're missing.'

'Don't you worry about them,' said Cally. 'I'm sure they're more than all right.'

There was a pause that Anna decided to fill with the words, 'I should go.'

'No!' said Antigone. 'Please don't go. Mummy, can Anna stay in the hotel until we go home? Can things be like they were before?'

'Nothing is like it was before,' snapped Cally. 'We're going back to the States. I never should have left.'

'Cally seems to be under the illusion that she's living in a Henry James novel, peopled by honest Americans and decadent scheming Europeans,' said Sholto, giving Anna one of his special conspiratorial looks. It no longer worked.

'Jesus, Sholto, can't you just give it a break with your literary crap?' said Cally. 'We're really grateful to you, Anna, but your contract, along with all the other Brit employees, is now terminated. Don't worry, we'll give you one month's notice.'

'But Antigone – and it's my home, and I—'

Cally shook her head. 'Your home? You think you're the only one suffering here? We've lost everything, don't you understand? My whole life slid down with that house. Don't you see that? Everything I've worked for.'

Anna wondered what happened when you defined your life through your possessions and then they were all destroyed. 'I know it must be awful. But I lived there and lots of other people did too, and we count. And Antigone's lost all her things as well – I don't think she should lose me too.'

'You?' said Cally.

'Mummy, please don't send Anna away.' Antigone clung harder to her. 'You're always doing that. Please, I need her.'

'Sholto, take Antigone into the other room. Why don't you get that drawing you did to show Anna, sweetheart?'

Sholto prised Antigone off Anna and took her away.

Cally leaned forward and said quietly, 'What on earth makes you think I'd let you anywhere near my daughter?'

'What do you mean?'

'Your days were numbered anyway; we'd already planned to get rid of you. I know what you were doing to her, you twisted little bitch.'

'What? I was teaching her Latin.'

'Latin and low self-esteem. Making her feel shit about her body, goading her about her . . .' She paused. '. . . big bones.'

'What? I never . . . I mean, once or twice I told her to exercise, but that was because you, *you*, Cally, said I had to do that. You were worried you were going to have to put her in a corset or she would let you down by not being tiny. It was all about *your* image, not hers! It was you that made me tell her to exercise more and to eat less.'

'Janey,' Anna and Cally said together, and there was a brief moment of accord.

'Jesus,' said Cally. 'What sort of a person bullies a little kid? On top of everything else.' She sighed. 'OK, so Janey was a liar, but she wasn't lying about the company you keep. Bringing that man into our house. A pap!'

'Jack, his name is Jack. He came to my rooms – my rooms and nowhere else – once. And I swear, he never took any pictures of the house or sold any stories, whatever Janey might have told you. He's a good man.' Anna was distracted by Sholto returning to the room with Antigone, who was clutching a brace of paintings. 'Jack,' she continued, 'is the sort of man who risks his life to rescue people he doesn't even know.'

'Let's have a look at your fabulous paintings, Antigone,' said Cally.

'They're very good, aren't they?' said Sholto.

'Yes, they are, they're amazing,' said Anna, looking at the thick oils showing mud criss-crossed with red bodies and colonnades. Amazing but deeply disturbing. She clutched Antigone's hand in remembrance of the horror.

'You're not going to leave me, are you?' said Antigone.

Cally looked at Sholto and gestured towards the door.

'Look Anna, I'll take you outside, we can talk about it.' He gave her an imploring look.

Antigone threw herself upon Anna. 'No!' she sobbed. 'Please no. They'll send you away and I'll never see you again. Please, no.' She wept snotty tears onto Jack's T-shirt.

'Of course I'll still see you, shush, my love.'

'No, I won't. I'm never going to see Bea again. They're sending her back to Mexico.'

'That's not true,' Cally snapped.

'It is, she told me and she told me the truth. It was our secret; I'm not supposed to tell you that I know. You're not my mother so you can't have me. Daddy and me and Bea, we're going to live together. You can come too, Anna, and we can all be together.' Antigone clutched on harder and this time it took both Sholto and Cally to peel her off.

'Get her out,' Cally screeched at Sholto as she restrained Antigone with the arms that had been strengthened by a thousand two-hour workouts. 'And make sure no one sees you.'

Anna wanted to stay with Antigone, but found herself being bundled to the door in a daze. Sholto gripped her arm and pointed her to a fire exit, which led them to the back stairs and out into a back alley, beside the bins stinking with the compost of the wealthy.

'Drink?' he asked. 'We need to talk.' He gave her one of his smiles, but she no longer found it disarming.

'Aren't you worried someone will see you?'

'They aren't interested in me. You know that.'

They found a basement bar round the corner. It was the first time she'd ever been alone like this with him. How many times had she fantasised about it?

'Anna, you're still under contract so you know that anything I say to you now is in confidence? My wife is pretty litigious. You will be bankrupt for the rest of your long life if you mention any of this to anyone.'

She nodded.

'I think you know something or suspect something and I feel that I ought to clarify it so you don't speculate any further. I would hate for you to tell your friend Jack some half-baked theory. And if I tell you the truth, then you have no choice but to remain silent. We will not be black-mailed over this, not again. So, what do you think you might have seen?'

'Seen?'

'The night of the collapse? Or maybe it was before.' He examined her face for a reaction and then his face was transformed with relief. 'Don't worry about it, Anna. Clearly we've made a mistake. You'll get your money and your things and then I think we can forget all about it.'

You're not getting away that easily, she thought. 'I think, somehow, that Bea is not just someone employed to look after Antigone.' It was more than that, but she couldn't say it – somehow she believed that Bea was Antigone's mother, but she couldn't work out how. She would not have been sure, but his paranoia only confirmed to her that she'd been right to see something in the way that Bea, Sholto and Antigone had embraced after their escape from the fall of Lorston Gardens. She knew she'd just have to say it out loud. 'I think Bea is Antigone's mother.' She blushed. It sounded utterly ridiculous although inexplicably plausible in her head.

He sighed. 'You're right.' He paused and breathed deeply. 'Bea is, sort of, not really – well, you could say she's Antigone's mother. Yes, she is in a way. Not biological mother though, obviously, you only have to look at them to know that.'

'Antigone doesn't look much like Cally, though.'

'Yes well, that's because she isn't her biological mother either. That's some Harvard student who's also a part-time model. The best eggs that money can buy.' He gave a rueful laugh. 'That's the clever thing, you see, this way you get to choose the perfect genes from a catalogue and the perfect vessel in which to carry them. They're not necessarily the same thing. The sort of woman whose eggs sell for the most money is not the sort of woman who'll also let her body be an incubator for nine months. The perfect eggs mixed with my imperfect sperm.' He gave a little self-deprecating smile to which Anna remained stony-faced.

'But I saw pictures of Cally pregnant.'

'And, no doubt, the ones where she snapped back into shape after just six weeks with a figure that looked like it had never been pregnant. Have you ever heard the story of the warming-pan baby, Anna?'

'I think so. James the Second, wasn't it? People said that the real baby had died at birth, so they smuggled in another one in a warming pan to pretend to be the heir. Something like that.'

'Clever girl. This is some kind of modern equivalent. It's not Cally's fault, she did want to be pregnant, she really did. She was desperate for us to have a baby together. I don't think she believed it was possible that she couldn't; whatever you think of her, she's always believed that with hard work, money and medical help you can achieve anything you want. And if a doctor doesn't tell you what you want, then you pay another. But they all said the same thing. She hasn't had a period since the Reagan administration. Hardly surprising, since she has no body fat.'

'Couldn't she just get some body fat? Most of us find it quite easy.'

'We tried everything. She even made the ultimate sacrifice and put on some weight, but still nothing. Worse, they kept on publishing photos of her with the extra weight next to headlines saying, "Baby Joy for Cally" and "It Must Be Twins". And when that didn't work, Cally wasn't going to let biology stop her. We looked into adoption, but Cally really wanted to have the whole pregnancy experience and present to the world our perfect baby.'

'But she didn't. You just said Bea was the one pregnant with Antigone.'

'"Gestational carrier" is the correct term. We did try to implant Cally a couple of times but they never took. The thing is that the perfect woman up on a screen isn't necessarily the perfect woman to carry a baby.'

'So you found yourself a poor Mexican woman with child-bearing hips instead.'

'That makes it sound callous, but she was well remunerated.'

'That's all right then.'

'Anna, please. This is why we've had to maintain this charade, because people like you are so judgemental.'

Anna put her fingers to her temples. 'Let me get this straight. You got your hot Harvard eggs and mixed them with your, you know, in an IVF clinic and then paid Bea to get implanted, get pregnant and then to give birth, presumably with no drugs in case that damaged Antigone in any way. Oh god, I bet Bea wasn't allowed even a cup of tea or an aspirin for nine months. All the while, Cally was wandering about with a fake belly strapped on and talking about her cravings for macaroons. You contracted out the contractions. That, I get. But what's Bea doing still working for you?'

He looked very tired and suddenly so much older. 'That's where we maybe went wrong. We knew that breastfed children have higher IQ levels than those fed with formula. So we thought it would be best for Antigone's intellect and immune system to give her breast milk. It seemed a bit crazy to have taken so much care over her genes and gestation and then not care what we fed her. There are milk banks, but it seemed so much easier to get it from the source and we knew that Bea was healthy and disease-free and we could monitor what she ate, so—'

'Bea breastfed Antigone?' Anna didn't have much experience with babies and the whole idea of anybody breastfeeding was a bit icky, let alone a baby that wasn't exactly yours.

'God no, she expressed milk, which the day and night nannies would then feed to Antigone. And Cally and I would do too, of course.'

'But Antigone's hardly drinking breast milk any more, so why did Bea stick around?'

'Cally didn't like having Bea in the house, obviously. She was a constant reminder of her failure to get pregnant herself, and she beat herself up about it all the time, blamed herself for getting so thin, thought it might be the implants or the diet pills. So we got rid of Bea when Antigone was little. With a very healthy severance package, of course.'

Anna shivered. Severance, what a word to use. She knew that for both Antigone and Bea it would have been exactly that, a severing of the ties between them. 'But she came back?'

'We've only ever wanted the best for Antigone.'

Or for Antigone to be the best. The perfectly designed, laboratory-tested, best baby in the whole wide world.

'She was miserable without Bea. Her speech stopped entirely and we were worried that she might be autistic, or that somehow this trauma would make her so. I don't know. But Bea was willing to come back and Antigone's always just been easier, more normal somehow, with her close by. Cally doesn't find Antigone very easy.'

'Good things in life rarely are. You wanted a special baby and then you worried that you got one with special needs. Special enough for you?'

'Anna, this isn't like you, you're being so harsh. I'm trying to be honest.'

'No, you're not. You just want to get this off your chest with someone who's legally obliged to stay quiet about it. And someone you thought would be so unquestioningly adoring that you wouldn't have to ask questions of yourself.'

'That's not true. I've always liked you and respected your intellect, Anna.' He put his hand over hers, the hand that had not been extended to her when she was facing death only the day before. She pulled hers away brusquely.

'And I take it Janey knew all this?'

He sighed. 'Yes, she did, inevitably. She began working for us when Antigone was a baby and she saw Bea breast-feeding her one day. She wasn't supposed to do that, she was supposed to express her milk for others to give, but she disobeyed us and gave it directly and Janey saw and worked it out.'

'And she was using this information against you? Was she blackmailing you?'

'Not exactly,' he said. 'But it's one reason all our staff contracts are so stiff. I wouldn't say she was actually blackmailing us, just using the information as leverage. We never really realised it at the time, but now that she's gone—'

'Gone where?'

He shrugged. 'I don't know. Nobody does. But she made herself so essential to us, to Cally, especially, that we let her get away with a lot of things that we shouldn't have. She had – has, I suppose – this way of becoming so central, so all-powerful, that rather than questioning it, you just become filled with fear that she'd leave. Do you know what I mean?'

With sudden clarity, Anna realised she knew exactly what he meant. 'Yes. She did something like that to me. She set me up so that I was in debt to her, reliant on her to keep my job. Instead of being angry with her, at first I just felt really grateful.' She had thought it was just a terrible coincidence that the nocturnal ramblings story had come out of the same night as Jack coming to her rooms. Now she knew better. 'But she didn't know about you and Bea, did she?'

'There is no Bea and me,' he said. 'She's the surrogate for my daughter. People use surrogates all the time.'

'I'm not talking about that.'

Sholto rubbed one eye vigorously. 'What do you mean?'

'You were sleeping with Bea. Or doing stuff, other stuff, maybe not sleeping with her.' He shook his head but did not deny it. 'I'm right, aren't I? God, I've been such an idiot, I think I knew all along that it was you and Bea, but I let myself be fooled by appearances. I let myself believe that beauty was everything, when it's not, is it? Not when it comes to sex. Does Cally know? Is it some other icky physical duty that you and she just subcontract out to a third-world woman for a generous package?'

'I didn't pay Bea, I mean, not for that,' he protested.

'No, you're right. I've seen the way she looks at you. She's in love with you. And with Antigone. She sees you as a family.'

'Me too, in a way. It's really hard for me. There's a

connection between us – she's the mother of my child. Well, she isn't, but I was at the hospital at the birth and there at the clinic when she was implanted. It just creates a bond between us.'

'That and the shit-hot blow jobs she gives.' He looked shocked. Not half as shocked as Anna felt. Gosh, where did that come from? She couldn't believe she'd said that out loud, but had felt jolted into it by remembering what she'd overheard in the changing rooms that time, knowing now that it had been Sholto enjoying Bea's ministrations. She visualised Bea, kneeling as a supplicant to her boss, hiring out her womb and mouth and vagina for a ticket out of poverty.

'It's not like that. I do love Bea. She's so good and warm and kind. I love Antigone so much and so does Bea and somehow that love just goes round and round the three of us.'

'So are you leaving Cally for her?'

'No, of course not.' He looked shocked at the sugges-tion. 'Cally and I are a team. It's not perfect, but it works. Without her brand it would be so hard to get my films made. I'm an auteur, I can't function without my work, you know that, and it's just so difficult to get funding for serious projects these days. But in partnership with Cally, well . . . We're just better together. She needs me too – her brand's a bit tarnished at the moment, what with everything that happened yesterday. Poor thing is really missing Janey, who used to fix everything. Cally's pretty hurt by her abandonment.'

'I'd have some respect for you if you'd at least mentioned

Antigone in your list of reasons to stay with Cally,' said Anna.

'Of course, she's the number one reason. It goes without saying.'

'You think you're so much better than Cally because you've got an education and you don't tart yourself about to get publicity. But you're much worse than someone who does that, you're someone who lives off someone who does that. You're so convincing too, I believed the whole charade, bought the idea that she was the shallow idiot and you were so noble.'

Anna stood up to leave and he grabbed her arm. 'Remember, you're not allowed to tell anyone. You've signed a contract. We will sue you for every penny you're ever likely to earn.'

She shook him off. 'I won't tell anyone, but not because of your threats or the money. Because of Antigone. She's all I've ever cared about. You're going to pay me off and you're going to pay off Bea, but you won't stop us from loving her and her from missing us.'

'I'm sure you're replaceable.'

'You're right. I probably am. But Bea isn't. And how long do you keep replacing the people Antigone loves? That's not the way it works, Sholto.'

Tags: Antigone sad; Antigone angry; Antigone awesome; Antigone fat; Antigone boyfriend; Antigone girlfriend; Antigone phone; Antigone boots; Antigone badly dressed; Antigone tantrum; Antigone birth; Antigone hair.

Antigone every adjective every noun stop.

Antigone every emotion most of them bad stop.

Antigone gay; Antigone ugly; Antigone paralysed; Antigone hermaphrodite; Antigone coat.

Antigone dead?

Yes, in a way, she is.

Parents lie.

That's a pretty good summary of childhood. Father Christmas, the tooth fairy, storks, God, Buddha, whoever . . . they're all made up. And as children we know that most of the time you're lying for what you believe to be good reasons, despite the fact that you're always telling us to tell the truth. Yes, we get that. But do you have to take such contrived pleasure in lying to us? Do you need to make us leave out some brandy and mince pies for Father Christmas and then tell us that you heard him come in? Really, was that embellishment strictly necessary? Do you have to say that the tooth fairy needs our canines to help her build her pearly kingdom?

Yes, we all have to face these discoveries, disappointments and disillusionments, but most don't find out that their mother isn't the person they were told she was. And not only is the person you've been told is your mother not your mother, but neither is, strictly speaking, the person you thought of as your mother. Instead it's someone else entirely, a shopping list of genes you never get to meet.

They seemed to relish the lies. They said more than they ever needed to create the illusion. Did Cally really need to pose with a fake belly on for all those photos that dotted the walls of Lorston Gardens? Did she need to tell me how bad her morning sickness was? Did she need to tell the world how she'd breathed me out because of all the yoga she'd done in pregnancy? Other celebrities adopt children or have them born to surrogates and don't have to lie about it, but she couldn't do that, oh no, she had to use her remarkable powers of reinvention on me as well as herself.

I was going to say that Bea told me the truth, but she didn't, she told me her own version of it. Bea told me that she was my mother, which was truer than Cally being my mom, but not exactly unvarnished either. It wasn't even as though she did a big reveal, she just always called me *hija* and when we were alone I'd call her *mama*. She never had to tell me not to tell anyone, I just knew, just as I knew that she must be my mother in a way because of the love that I felt for her. At the time, I cared not about the mechanics, but only about the love. That's what a mother is when you're eight, it's the person you love most in the world, the one that you want to crawl back inside, the one that's always there for you. Of course, I knew about where babies come from, but somehow I managed to divorce this knowledge from the reality of my own birth.

None of it really mattered when Bea and Anna left. Left – ha! They were banished. Exiled for loving me, for being too good at their jobs. They were hired as parent substitutes in their different ways and they made the mistake of loving me, which was never part of their contract. Worse still, I loved them back.

15

Dodgy Foundations

So long as Anna had neither home nor phone, she felt as though she didn't exist. She might have had her name taken off the list of missing persons, but her sense of self had vanished. The police had retrieved her passport and basic possessions from her rooms, but Lorston Gardens remained cordoned off and unsafe, an enormous crime scene marooned atop mud. Nobody was exactly sure what the crime was, but that didn't stop the newspapers and websites from making their accusations.

No home, no phone and no Antigone. She'd wake up feeling OK and then have a thud of disappointment when she remembered that she'd probably never see Antigone again. She'd catch herself wanting to tell her things, lesson-planning, ripping pages out of *The Economist*, watching nature documentaries that they could discuss, books that they could read together.

Even when she had lived inside the house, Anna had kept herself informed via the tabloids and gossip sites written many miles away. Now they were her lifeline to her previous world and she read them voraciously, with full credulousness, despite knowing better than to believe them.

Jack was off out of the flat every day, having been given a fat contract by one newspaper as the man who had the best photos and insight into a world that had now sunk. This left Anna alone with the internet, leaping from site to site. She knew she should try to begin her new life, but at the moment she was trapped in a pale, virtual reflection of her old one.

At first the news was all about the night itself. There were lots of eyewitness accounts and tasteless references to tsunamis. It was fortunate for all involved that the party should have been so well attended by attention seekers and fame hunters, all of whom were happy to tell and sell their stories. Within a few months, Cally's launch would become one of those legendary events at which thousands claimed their attendance, like the Beatles' gigs at The Cavern Club, or those who insisted their ancestors came to America on the *Mayflower*.

There was some coverage of the lives and deaths of the two − Lithuanian as it turned out − kitchen staff who'd been killed. There were extra drinks fridges in the basement and the women had been crushed on their way to fetch more champagne for the guests. There were grainy photographs of them culled from social networks, their faces shiny with the happiness of holidays, graduations and parties, the events that get pictured and displayed. There was a reverence in the reporting of their tragedy, but − Anna couldn't help noticing − a faint sense of disappointment that amid all those notables, the only deaths should be of two nobodies. One of them was blonde and pretty, though, which was something.

What Juste and Viktorija's deaths did achieve was a change in the narrative. Enough of the facts, now the bloggers and the newspapers needed someone to blame. Cally was the perfect target, having committed various unforgivable misdemeanours such as wearing a bikini into her forties and her teeth being just too white. That and her being American, like some grey squirrel that never really deserved a place amid the native red ones of the British Isles.

Initially she had been presented as 'brave Cally' emerging from the hotel. She wore respectful dark colours, covering her flesh and perfecting a look that could be described as 'hot but modest Amish wife'. Anna knew where the family was each day as easily as if she'd attached a tracking device to them: first they were at the hotel, then they decamped to their country house. Then, nothing. She guessed that at some point they'd move back to the States as Cally had suggested, but there were no sunglass-wearing shots of them walking to airport departures, no sidewalk fashion ones in New York, and an absence of 'Cally Goes to the Wholefood Shop' shots in LA. Jack was right, if a star didn't want to be spotted, it was surprisingly easy to facilitate.

A week after the basement collapse, the focus shifted. 'Police hunt for missing PA' went the initial headlines, not daring to openly accuse Janey of anything quite yet.

'Did you really not know that Janey and Dan were a couple?' Jack asked her.

Anna shook her head. 'It's quite dense of me, but when you're in the house, you're so dazzled by Cally and Sholto that you forget that other people can have relationships with each other, you can only imagine them in a relationship with one of those two. It was like they were the stars and we were only the supporting cast, never allowed in the picture without one of them.'

'So who was with them?'

'What do you mean?'

'Well, no one has yet come forward to say that they were shagging Sholto, whatever the rumours.'

'Shagging Sholto . . . it's almost poetic,' said Anna.

'Don't change the subject, darling. Can't you think of anyone or anything that might have led Cally and Sholto to want to get out of this country as soon as possible? Are you sure you don't know about anyone in the house doing it with someone inappropriate? People are still talking about Sholto having a lover of some description, but no one's come forward to sell their story. It would be worth a fortune.'

Anna paused. She thought of Bea's supplication at the lap of Sholto and that combination of love and smugness that she had radiated when around him. Anna owed little to either Sholto or Cally and their hypocritical promotion as the perfect couple.

'Come on, Anna,' said Jack. 'Think – did you ever notice anything or anyone behaving in a suspicious way?'

She opened her mouth, but then thought of Antigone and her pinched little face and her snowy white skin, the odd workings of her mind, what went on inside her and what went on around her. She saw the headlines as if they were real, ones that no child should ever have to see about their parents, biological or otherwise.

'No,' she said, looking at Jack. 'Nothing. Really nothing. You know I'd tell you if I did.'

Then the headlines changed again, away from the supposedly sympathetic plea for Janey's safe return. 'Cally PA Took Millions', 'Janey on FBI Most-Wanted List', 'British Tourist: "I saw Janey in Guatemala".'

Then there was the 'My Janey Hell by Sacked Accountant', illustrated with a photo of Priya wearing a very stagey wronged face and an utterly gorgeous, but modest, outfit. Anna was glad to hear from Jack quite how well remunerated Priya was from selling her story. It seemed only right that she should have enough to cover her tuition fees and more.

In lieu of photos of Janey in whichever tropical paradise she was deemed to have been spotted that day, the newspapers found a seemingly inexhaustible supply from their archives: Janey standing behind Cally at events; snapped alongside Antigone or Sholto outside the house; running alongside Cally and her trainer, looking gorgeous in expensive kit; Janey walking behind Cally at the airport; Janey doing something innocent like holding a sheaf of papers with a caption now asking 'What Is She Doing With That Paperwork?'

Dan was less easily illustrated, but it didn't matter, for he wasn't as pretty as his partner and, anyway, everybody knows that the woman is always the villain in such part-nerships, the brains behind the operation, your Lady Macbeth, your Imelda Marcos, your Elena Ceauşescu. There were some much-used photos of Dan when he was a footballer, which suited the angle of the dim stooge behind the avaricious lady.

They had both vanished. With all the technology there was these days, the scanners and satellites, they had still managed to disappear as easily and thoroughly as Lord Lucan.

'Janey: By the Family She Shunned', 'Sex Secrets of Cally Thief', 'PA with a Taste for the High Life'. Those were the headlines, and a thousand more, but it seemed to Anna that none of them had any sense of what Janey was actually like. She couldn't claim she'd ever really known her either, but she knew enough to dismiss this picture of a crazed shoe-lover, consumed by consumerism.

'Think,' Jack said to her again, 'did she ever tell you anything that gives you any clues?'

'To what?' said Anna, 'where she is or about what she has done? Allegedly done?'

'Either.'

She stared at the screen, her eyes aching from having been looking at it for so many hours, her fingers arthritic from the repetitive scrolling and clicking. 'Nothing concrete. It's not shoes she loves, though, I know that much. It's houses. She loves beautiful houses. If I was going to guess where she was, it would be in some hot place with relaxed planning laws and she'd be spending the money on building her own stately pleasure-dome. Do you know how much money she took yet? Apparently the accounts are labyrinthine.'

'They're definitely messy. She set up so many different accounts which all fed into one another, that nobody had any idea where the money might be.'

'Surely she will have left an electronic trail?'

'You'd have thought, wouldn't you?' said Jack. 'But it turns out that embezzlement is actually pretty simple. You set up lots of different accounts, some of them genuine, others for your own benefit, and it can take years to disentangle. Every time they get to one account they find it's empty and leading off to another dozen, which in turn lead off to another dozen. For example, she set up a shadow account in the name of the builders' firm, where she'd put in the payments, then whack off ten per cent before passing on the correct payment to them. But she was also getting ten per cent back off the builders as part of a kickback if she agreed to hire them in the first place. She was getting her commission from both places. You think about it: the work on that house cost millions and she got, what, twenty per cent of that? The builders claim that she bought direct from the suppliers, rather than through them. All the materials were supposed to be top-end, but it turns out all the structural bits and pieces were cheap knock-offs. Then, with every payment to the staff, the same thing would happen. If anyone ever cottoned on, she'd get them sacked.'

'Like Priya,' said Anna.

'Exactly, like Priya. Except Janey pretended it was because she'd broken some clause in the contract about not having sexual relations with other members of staff.'

'And Priya couldn't bear for her family and fiancé to hear about that. But she knew the accounts were dodgy all along.'

'Double whammy for Janey in that sacking someone keeps the rest of you scared, plus gets rid of anyone who might suspect something. Poor Priya, it turns out she was being paid a pittance, but Janey was charging for her as if she were a trained accountant,' said Jack. 'They reckon she was also skimming off great chunks into an account called "Lorston housekeeping", which as it happened had nothing to do with the house, but Cally never questioned the money leaving her account into an account with that name.'

'It was a bit dim of Cally.'

'And your man, Sholto, don't forget him. Neither of them kept tabs on the household accounts. That's what they'd employed Janey to do. Plus she probably knew stuff about them that they wouldn't want to get out. When I think about those pictures I took of her with Sholto, it makes total sense that she had something on him – or even both of them. Any ideas?'

Again Anna paused, preparing to deny him a second time. She tried to stop her eyes from darting as Antigone's had done when she had lied to her. 'No, sorry, I can't think of anything. Is it really Janey's fault that the house collapsed, though?'

Jack shrugged. 'Well yeah, difficult to pinpoint exactly, and the builders are getting prosecuted anyway, but they say it was all Janey's idea to cut corners and buy cheap materials and not do the foundations properly and all that malarkey. It might be that they're trying to shift the blame onto someone else, but so far it looks like they might have a case.'

'I don't think she's evil and intended the building to collapse.'

'Yeah, but nobody ever does, do they, but they're still responsible. If you're an employer and you don't get your machinery properly serviced and it then slices off the arm of one of the workers, then the old "I didn't mean anything bad to happen" hardly lets them off, does it? Same with Janey.'

'I suppose. I think she did love overseeing everything and being all-powerful. And the decoration bit, she had a taste for that. But I suppose it being well made was all a bit irrelevant, since she probably knew she wouldn't be around to see it in a few years' time. It was like a stage set, impressive to look at, but not built to last.'

Before long, the papers wheeled out the 'experts' who could tell the public exactly what Janey was thinking (in the absence of the real Janey telling her own story). The psychiatric profiles used words like 'psychopath' and 'sociopath', explaining that she would be feeling no guilt towards her victims, a woman compelled to steal from all those she met. A lot of it seemed overblown to Anna, but elements rang true. Janey was so smart, so imbued with a sense of her own superiority, that it would have pained her to have to work for those she felt to be so much less deserving than she was. It explained that perpetual smirk she wore, the way that anything respectful towards her employers was clothed in silent ironical quote marks.

Even then, Anna didn't think that Janey had gone into the job intending to steal quite as much as she did. She was certain it had not been planned from the start. From what she gathered from the profiles, Janey's background was modestly comfortable – parents in Surrey, a grammar school girl, rejecting university in favour of getting out there and earning from a young age. But working in the City and then for Cally had broadened the horizons of her materialism. Anna suspected that Janey had started small, borrowing money when she needed it for those darling suits of hers and for presents for Dan, but had discovered that not only could she get away with it, but that she liked it. She'd have had that shoplifter's buzz except that, rather than outwitting some dim security guard, she was stealing from Sholto and Cally, the so-called perfect couple who were too stupid or too rich to notice the thousands, then tens of thousands, then hundreds of thousands, then even millions that were going missing. Just as readers of the news these days were now luxuriating in the downfall of two such smug celebrities, so Janey must have felt enormous pleasure at siphoning off their earnings. Anna could imagine Janey snarling at Dan: 'They think they're so clever, don't they, but look, they're idiots. We're the clever ones,' and Dan saying something like 'Yeah, doll, you're the business,' and then having really hot Bonnie-and-Clyde sex. Maybe on a bed covered in bank notes.

There are lots of things that can happen to the children of the famous, so many ways to go wrong. I've made a study of them through history (you can't stop me researching, you see).

I've read all those misery memoirs of kids who grew up in the so-called Golden Age of Hollywood. They're all: poor me, Mommy made me wear gingham and blow out the candles on my birthday cake for a photographer from *Picture Post* and it wasn't even my birthday, boo-hoo. And I'm thinking, you reckon you had it bad? One photographer fawning over you in comparison to the hundreds or even thousands that have tried to steal bits of me? I've read about the 1970s, and apparently women used to get shouted at by builders saying stuff like, 'Cheer up love, it might never happen.' They were allowed to do that and everything. And then all the women complained and the builders weren't allowed to do that any more and were given special awards for being so nice as to not shout out remarks about their bodies. Well, nobody told anyone to stop doing it to me. I was some sort of special case. Imagine my world as being one enormous old-fashioned building site and everyone on the street is like a builder scratching himself and eyeing me up and shouting stuff where even the compliments sound like insults. That was my life.

Have you ever been on holiday somewhere poor where the market traders and hawkers harangue you constantly, always asking, 'Buy something, one dollar,' and things like that? And it makes you want to stay in the air-conditioned calm of your luxury hotel? How it makes you despise the locals and feel that they all want something from you? Again, that was my life.

Anyway, I digress. My studies of those who've graduated from the school of celebrity offspring a few years ahead of me show that when the average celebrity kid grows up, the career options are as follows:

Drugs, obviously. Loads of them, followed by rehab, possibly trailed by a documentary or reality TV crew to chart your interventions, relapses, one week sober, etc.

This is so unimaginative and unoriginal. It is never going to be my fate. I don't even like coffee much, I think I OD'd on it all those years ago with those damn frappés.

A lot of them become actors themselves. Their first job is playing their mom while younger or the little girl narrator in their godfather's blockbuster. Then they complain that it's been 'so much harder for them to get a break in the industry' because of their name. Hilarious.

There's this new vogue for sex-change celebrity offspring. That never appealed, really, though I guess I can respect their choices. It's just I can't see why you'd bother. I've always felt that I'm more me than just a girl. The sex bit of it, too, that confuses me. Not that I've done that myself – I'd like to be able to blame my parents, but I don't think it's that so much as never finding anyone very attractive. The whole thing sounds so yeurgh to me. And when my Hollywood peers get a sex-change, they go from straight to gay or the other way round and it's so confusing and mixed up – like they go from straight girl to gay man or gay boy to straight woman.

The next option, absolutely the favoured and certainly easiest form of rebellion at the moment, is to become enormously fat. Not a bit tubby, or failing to do the necessary workout to ensure your body is bikini ready, but really trailer-park morbidly obese. You can then 'show off' your euphemistically called curves in inappropriate and unflatteringly tight clothes. The biggest way to stick the finger up at your beautiful mother is to not stick your finger down your throat after a really massive Krispy Kreme session. I couldn't even do that one right – my body's not real fat but then it's not real skinny either. It's exactly like the bodies of most girls my age, size normal, which doesn't garner any attention.

Then there are those jobs that everybody thinks they can do, those roles where the only qualification is chutzpah, where if you say you are a 'whatever', then you are. That's all you need to do, announce yourself. They're all professional versions of things that everybody manages to do quite well at home without being paid for the job. DJ – programming your computer with some tunes; photographer – taking some arty snaps with your digital camera; shoe designer – ability to pick out heel sizes from your closet; brand consultant – I can write my name on a piece of a paper. Oh, and my favourite, children's author with someone else doing the illustrations, but unfortunately Cally got there first (I'm sure you've all read her classic, *The Little Girl with a Little Bit of Everywhere*, about her own experiences of dealing with racism).

Here's a list of jobs my peers never seem to take up: doctor, teacher, social worker, lab technician, Nobel prize winner, farmer, call-centre operative, accountant . . . and so on.

Age sixteen, and I've already taken the most rebellious path of all.

16

The Disappearance of Antigone
Steward-Carpenter

Anna had thought about Antigone every day in the eight years since they'd last met. A Latin phrase, the sound of a violin, the shadows cast by an avenue of trees; they would all spark off a memory. As the years went by, she could dismiss them more easily, but she'd still search the internet intermittently to try to find out what had become of her. Eventually, the overwhelming urge to find out more began to wane to a mild curiosity, and Anna's electronic searches became more infrequent.

The world had become a place where everyone was a star. Once, it was only celebrities whose photographs were public property, whose utterances about diet and culture had an outlet, whose movements and whereabouts were known to people outside of their family. Now anyone could have that lifestyle, everyone had a loud-hailer and it was up to them how loudly their voices were amplified.

But there was one freakish, young person whose life remained mysterious and undocumented. That was Antigone. Her position in the world compared to her peers had reversed since she and Anna had lived together at Lorston Gardens. Now Antigone was the mystery, while everyone else blogged and tweeted and shouted about their lives, telling the world where they'd got their 'look' from and how delicious a certain brand of low-fat yoghurt was #yum, and look at this photo of the sushi I had for lunch. But of Antigone there was no recent news, only the old photos from those London days.

Anna supposed that the years from eight to 16 are a no-man's land for celebrity children or, more accurately, a no-girl's land. Before eight they're cute and it's a human instinct to coo over pictures of babies and toddlers. But then once their breasts begin to bud, it becomes less acceptable to stare at their images, and publishing photos of an 11-year-old girl in the twilight of childhood before the age of consent is not something even the most scurrilous of websites wants to be seen to do. Anna supposed it was just a coincidence that the time since those months at Lorston Gardens happened to dovetail with these ghost years for the celebrity girl-child. She assumed that when Antigone hit 16, there would be a rash of pictures of her in a bikini on the beach with the comment that 'she's all grown up now'. They, whoever they were, would decide that, overnight, Antigone had crossed some arbitrary line beyond which it becomes acceptable to perv over her flesh.

And yet, when the time came, the photos never appeared. Sixteen-year-old Antigone remained as anonymous as before and Anna realised that perhaps she would never know what had become of her charge. It was as if

Antigone had disappeared along with Janey, both of them in some obscure place with no cameras. The two of them had vanished that fateful week.

One day, Anna's phone rang.

'I can't believe you still have the same number,' the voice on the other end said without preamble. It was familiar even after all these years – deeper and with an American accent, yet the tone of both knowledge and curiosity remained undimmed.

'And I can't believe you still remember it,' Anna said, in shock that she was reviving a conversation after a gap of eight years.

'Do you know?' the voice continued, 'I ran it through an algorithm that a friend of mine at college created and it turns out it *is* a prime number after all.'

Anna hadn't had many dates in her life, but she supposed this was how one might feel. She sat in the same hotel foyer where she had been interviewed by Janey all those years ago, now waiting to meet the girl she'd been employed to look after.

She worried about being stood up. She hadn't really got to the bottom of what she was doing here in London and how a 16-year-old was allowed to fly alone to the other side of the world. Then she became anxious that even if she did show up, Anna wouldn't recognise her, given that it had been half the child's lifetime ago since they'd last met, since they had clung to each other in another hotel room.

But as soon as she walked in, Anna realised how silly that thought had been; that even had she been wearing a balaclava, she'd have known her by her posture, the slope of her shoulders, the way that her head swivelled to take in the surroundings, that unique mixture of self-sufficiency and vulnerability. Anna stood up to greet her, feeling her legs buckle as she did so.

Antigone walked forwards, still with that same smile that looked as though it had been taught and she had only learned to use it with much practice. Her skin retained its bluish paleness, but in between the sprinkling of spots it glowed with the radiance that serums promise but only youth can give. Her hair, once almost neon-white, had darkened to a dirty blonde, while the much-scrutinised body was now unworthy of scrutiny. It looked strong and practical, lacking the remarked-upon fat of her childhood but not presented for delectation now, clad as it was in jeans and a jumper. She carried an expensive-looking leather bag, but had such an air of the varsity geek about her that she looked as though she should really be accessorised with a pile of books clasped to her chest.

They stood for a second looking at each other and then Antigone stepped forward and put her arms around Anna. They hugged, no longer as a woman and a child, but as two equals, standing at the same height. Anna felt such happiness and relief that she wanted to shrink and become enveloped by Antigone, just as she had wrapped her arms around the girl while Lorston Gardens fell about them all those years ago.

'It is so great to see you again,' Antigone said as they sat down. 'I've missed you.'

'Really? I've missed you too, so much. I sort of assumed that nannies or tutors just got forgotten about the minute they walked out of the door and got replaced with this week's model.'

'Mostly I do forget them the minute they walk out the door. There have been quite a few, let me tell you. But there was something about that time that I keep going back to, do you know what I mean?'

'Yes, I do,' said Anna. 'I feel as if everything changed then.' She smiled as she realised that they were speaking as peers, that she could now have out loud all those conversations she'd had in her head.

'Exactly, like those books about girls coming of age, you know, *Bildungsroman*,' Antigone said with an exaggerated German accent, 'when they go, "And from that summer, nothing was ever the same again." Ellipsis.'

'What did it change for you?' asked Anna.

'Well, obviously, we moved back to the States and I never saw you again. My family house collapsed in a spectacular and public way, along with a lot of what I thought I knew. I stopped going to normal school and went to a special college for gifted kids and it was OK, I kind of liked it because it meant I was no longer special.'

'It's good that your parents stayed together.'

'You mean Cally and Sholto?'

Anna nodded, unsure of how she was supposed to refer to them.

'Don't worry, Anna, I know the full story about where I come from. Yeah, I suppose they officially stayed together, though spent less and less time together in reality. Didn't stop them doing endless articles about how their marriage is stronger than ever and our love is built on stronger foundations than the house was yada-yada.'

'And you never saw Bea again?'

Antigone smiled. 'Oh no, I saw Bea. Plenty.'

'Really? How come?'

'I've always known that Bea was my mom – felt it deep down – but it took a while for me to work out how I was conceived. You know, the mechanics. I know she's not my biological mom, but you know that's the least of it, of being a mother. Once I knew, I told Cally that if she didn't let me spend time with Bea, I'd tell the world that she'd lied about being pregnant with me. So then when I lived away at boarding school, Bea lived nearby. When Dad came to visit me, he could stay with Bea too.'

'As a couple?'

'Sleeping together you mean? Yes, I presume so. I know you're thinking, why would he be with Bea when he's married to the so-called most beautiful woman in the world, but I think they're like properly in love.' She wrinkled her nose in a way that suggested to Anna that she had yet to fall in love herself.

'And your mother – I mean, Cally – didn't mind?'

'Not so much as everybody knowing that she bought a baby and lied about it.'

'That's blackmail.'

She nodded. 'Learned it from the mistress. I learned Latin from you and how to be a manipulative bitch from Janey. Oh, and how to make *cajeta* from Bea.'

'Oh Antigone, you're making me feel sorry for Cally.'

She shrugged. 'By the way, I'm not called Antigone any more. I'm Rosie, Rosie Carter. Rosemary was Sholto's mom's name and my middle name and Carter is just Carpenter with the 'pen' taken out. God knows I love a Greek myth as much as the next classicist, but "Antigone"? Really? The daughter of Oedipus and his mother? Come on. And nobody ever pronounced it right. Worse, it made me just so ridiculously googleable. Is that a word?'

'A newly coined one maybe, a neologism.'

'I love the way you talk.'

'Thanks. I did google you a lot, you know.'

'But found nothing, right? Antigone Rosemary Steward-Carpenter was the daughter of Cally and Sholto but I buried her years ago, maybe in that stupid spa room at Lorston Gardens. She doesn't exist any more. It turns out that it's really quite easy to disappear and start over. Cally always tried to teach me that being in the public eye was a burden I had to carry for the rest of my life, but I don't, not at all. There's nothing of Cally left in my name. Or me.'

'She wasn't so bad.'

'No, she wasn't. She isn't. I still see her. We're fine. Of course, I committed the ultimate rebellion by becoming a nobody, but she and Sholto are OK with it.'

Anna felt a pang of sympathy for poor Cally, she was always poor Cally and she found her head always cocking to one side in pity when she thought of her. 'Is she happy now, do you think?'

Antigone shrugged. 'She's got money, which is what she most needed. She's not divorced, officially, which is something she's pretty proud of too. She managed to survive the wreckage of that night at Lorston Gardens, which I gather was a triumph of PR. I don't know, she's as happy as she ever was, I suppose.'

Anna thought back to that desperate, proud look Cally always wore, like someone arriving at a party full of strangers and trying to convince herself that she felt confident. 'Which was not very happy, really,' said Anna, sadly. 'Still, you seem to have your life sorted. You seem so normal.' Of all the scenarios that had played in her mind, she'd never expected to see this gorgeously generic-looking girl, with her seemingly well-adjusted attitude. Suicide, drugs, burnout: those were likely outcomes for someone as odd and famous and as oddly famous as Antigone, but not this. This sort of normality.

'I know. I'm not a freak any more. Well, I am at college at only sixteen and most of the students are four years older, but even that's not particularly freaky. Have you seen some of these Asian kids? There are eleven-year-old Chinese girls who are working on postgrad-level stuff. I am totally not the weird one with the hot-looking mom any more. I'm not weird and she's not my mom. Brilliant!'

'I'm so happy for you and your utter normalness. I think,' said Anna. 'I, like most teenagers, spent all my time convinced that I was either exceptionally superior to all the idiots who surrounded me or that I was exceptionally hideous and unworthy of love. Never normal.'

'I see what you're saying – that actually my normality makes me different from most truly normal teenagers? Hmm, interesting idea. But I'm not really normal, am I? Just more normal than you would have ever expected.'

Anna laughed. 'I've missed our discussions.'

'I still remember them. Wow, I so don't want to sound sentimental, but really you spoke to me like nobody had ever done before. You made me think that the thoughts inside my head should be harnessed instead of suppressed. That kept me going. You were the first person who told me that I was more than just my parents' daughter, do you remember? It was that time when Miras came over and we were bouncing on the trampoline.'

'Miras, yes, that young frequenter of the world's hottest clubs, flaunting his jailbait gorgeousness. He's not exactly disappeared, has he? In fact, he's hard to avoid. But I don't remember saying anything like that to you. It's true though, and I always thought it. You were always very *you*, even at that young age. You were always more *you* than anyone I've ever met.'

'You helped with that. You made me realise that who I was didn't have much to do with who my parents were. Or who people thought they were. This is me:

super-smart, hanging out with all the other smart kids, but no longer being seen as some stupid celebrity child. It's amazing.'

'Oh Antigone – I mean, Rosie – you sound . . . why, *happy*.'

'I am. I think so. I don't really know, you know I've never been so good at all that stuff, but I'm not unhappy. I feel like me. Rosie: the girl you can't find photos of on the web. I never felt like that other girl, Antigone, the one with the fancy coats and frappés and hairstyles. Cally is never allowed to be seen out with me now or she'll blow my cover. It's like a witness protection programme for celebrity kids. She says it's sad for her, but she can still see me in private if she wants. I'm like those tribes-people who think that cameras can steal your soul. They do, you know: a little bit of me died every time my picture was taken. Jeez, those paps.'

'Like Jack,' said Anna. 'I'm sorry if he ever stole your soul.' She thought about him with a painful nostalgia. He had saved her life, and not just by pulling her out of the morass at Lorston Gardens. With him, she'd enjoyed sex for the first time and realised how closely allied it was to laughter. She didn't want to sound like those novels that Antigone had mocked, but that summer he had made her a woman. 'He wasn't a bad person, really he wasn't,' she said.

'No, Jack's all right.' Antigone smiled. 'He was the only one who ever said please and thank you.'

'I don't know how much your parents told you, but Jack and me, we were involved.'

'Yeah, I knew that. Why do you think you guys split up?'

'We stayed together for a couple of years. We were happy, but I made a choice that our relationship couldn't really survive. I couldn't tell him something because I couldn't trust him, and the fact that I had a secret meant that I knew he couldn't trust me either.' *I chose you, Antigone or Rosie or whatever your name is, I chose you over Jack.*

She had loved him so much, but their relationship had been based on foundations as shaky as the basement swimming pool at Lorston Gardens. Moments of happiness with him were always soured by the knowledge that she would never tell him the truth about Antigone's birth. 'The thing is,' continued Anna, 'once a pap, always a pap. Although that's not technically true any more. He lives in San Francisco now; he went just after we broke up to do something with apps and photos and phones. Something techie and clever like that. He's doing really well, I gather.'

'Yes, he is,' said Antigone, smiling. 'As are you, I gather. You're a teacher, right?'

'Yes. It turned out I was quite good at it, especially teaching outliers, you know – those at the extreme ends of the IQ scale. How did you know?'

'Doh, just because I'm not all over the web, doesn't mean I can't use it to find other people.'

'True; everyone's on there, even me. Well, everyone except you and Janey. We'll never know what became of her.'

'Oh, I know what's happened to her.'

She said it with such an air of defiance that Anna immediately started thinking thoughts that came from reading too many thrillers. 'What do you mean?'

'Your face! Are you thinking I murdered her or something?'

'No, of course not. Just wondering how you know.'

'It's a bit of a story.'

'Which I'd love to hear. Especially if it ends badly for her. I hated the way that she became a bit of a folk hero after it all, people trying to make out that she was some sort of Robin Hood figure. Sure she stole from the rich, but I don't think she ever gave to the poor. And those girls, those waitresses, the ones that died . . .'

'Nobody ever remembers them,' said Antigone.

'I do,' said Anna with a shudder. It could have been me, she always thought, it could have been me.

'Well,' said Antigone, 'here's the strange thing. Janey was always keen to keep in contact with me. She used to email me, regularly, laughing at me, telling me she'd seen my photos and how fat I still was, saying that she'd never get caught.'

'How horrible,' said Anna. 'Like those letters that serial killers send the police, boasting about how they're so much cleverer than they are.'

'Yes, that's exactly what it felt like.'

'Couldn't the police trace her from the emails?'

'They tried, but they never managed to, as she sent them from cafés and fake accounts from a variety of different countries. She was right: she *was* so much cleverer than them. Then I stopped even telling the police about the emails.'

'Why? Because they never managed to find her?'

'A bit, but mostly because I did kill someone off.' Antigone left a dramatic pause. There were some ways in which she was Cally's daughter. 'I killed off Antigone Steward-Carpenter.'

'When you changed your name and fell off the internet?'

'Exactly, then I was a bit stuck. As much as I wanted Janey to get punished, if she ever got caught, everyone would know about me again and the whole photographing and blogging and discussing my looks and my outfits would start again.'

'Your parents must have wanted you to report her, though.'

'Not really. It took Cally ages to get her image together after the house collapsed. She and Dad were made to look like idiots. The last thing she wanted was to dredge it all up again. I mean, if Janey was ever put on trial, there would be lots of stuff about how Cally didn't notice that millions of dollars, sorry pounds, had vanished over the years. That makes her look pretty careless and would rather destroy that I'm-just-like-you-guys persona she'd cultivated. Even now, nobody really knows quite how much Janey siphoned off. It was crazy amounts of money, and it's so embarrassing that Cally and Sholto were so naïve it about.'

'I can see that,' said Anna. 'Much as I'd like to see her punished, I suppose I can take solace from the fact that if she was sending you emails she must have been bored witless. Imagine how tedious your life must be to write mean emails to a child? And imagine how even more bored she must be now that you've denied her that small pleasure. Her whole life was about pulling all our strings, leaking stuff to the press and pinning the blame on someone else, blackmailing people into obedience or loyalty, punishing others just because she could. She needs an audience and, unless she's found a new one, she'll be miserable.'

'So you think me changing my email address was punishment enough?' Antigone smiled.

'Perhaps. I don't know, it's something though.'

'It's not enough, come on, admit it.'

'OK, you're right. When I've not been wondering how you've been doing, I've been fantasising about seeing Janey's face in a police mugshot.'

'There's a part of her, though,' said Antigone, 'that would quite like that. The attention, the glory, the adulation from people who think she's some sort of counter-cultural heroine. She'd be unbearable.'

'So what would punish her?'

'I had to think about it and then I realised, Janey's quite like Cally, but a cleverer version, that's why she was able to play her so brilliantly.'

'What do you mean?' asked Anna.

'She's like Cally in that the thing that she'd most hate would be to be poor. Poor and anonymous would be even worse.'

'Yes, you're right. And she is anonymous. But she's

rich, isn't she? She's got all the money she stole and I imagine her in some amazing glass-plated house in Belize.'

'She *did* have all the money she stole,' said Antigone.

Anna felt the hint of a warm giggle billow inside her. 'Antigone . . . Rosie . . . go on.'

'The worst thing that could happen to Janey would be if someone stole all her money from her, just like she stole money from us. And worse, she wouldn't be able to do anything about it, would she? I mean, she could hardly report it to the police.'

'But how can you steal it back when you don't even know where she lives?'

Antigone smiled again. 'You need to find someone who can put you in touch with the world's best hackers and isn't afraid to do things that aren't exactly legal.'

'Right? And who would that be?'

'It's someone you know.'

Anna frowned, confused.

'Weren't you just talking about someone who lives in San Francisco and works with technology?' said Antigone.

'Jack? You've been in touch with Jack?'

Antigone nodded. 'He's been so helpful over the last couple of years. He has some very useful friends who were only too happy to hack into some offshore accounts and start stealing money from them. They loved pitting their wits against someone as smart as Janey. It's amazing how easily they can do something that seems to be totally beyond the expertise of the police's tech team.'

'Did Jack keep the money?'

'No, of course not. He paid off his hacker friends, obviously. But today there are some charities that promote universal female education that are very grateful for Janey's generous contributions. Actually giving the money away turned out to be the biggest challenge. There are all sorts of money laundering laws we had to get round. Jack was great about that too.'

'Do you think you've cleaned her out?' said Anna.

'Maybe. I don't know. There are some accounts in Dan's name too. It's hard to tell since we don't know how much money she had in the first place. But she's certainly got a lot less now.'

'Antigone, sorry Rosie, that is absolutely brilliant. You're brilliant.'

'Jack is brilliant.'

Anna felt a jagged envy that the two people she most missed in the world should have been having this high old time together. 'Yes he is. He was always kind. He sometimes tried to hide it, but he really was kind.' She'd been out with other men since they'd split up, reverted to type by hooking up with earnest fellow teachers and graduate friends, but they'd seemed so wan in comparison.

'He'd like to see you, you know,' said Antigone.

'Really? I'd like to see him.' Anna sighed. Too much time had passed, too many secrets.

'He knows all about me, you know,' said Antigone. 'Bea. I told him. He's never told anyone else, I know that because it's never come out. That was your problem, wasn't it? Silly Anna, you could have trusted him.'

'Yes, perhaps I should have.' *But it's too late now.*

'He's not with anyone. Which is surprising, because those tech guys out there are like rock stars, especially with that accent, but he's not got a girlfriend.'

Anna felt herself flush with excitement. This is ridiculous, I'm not that girl any more, she thought. I can't go back, even with this permission from Antigone. 'So much time has passed. Just look at you, you were half the height you are now when we got together. You were a child.'

'But I'm not that different on the inside. Look at us, here talking. It's just like it used to be and I'm so happy.'

'Me too. So happy.' It was true, Anna had not known how much she had missed her until now.

'See,' she said. 'You can pick up where you left off.' The child-woman known as Rosie but who would always be Antigone to Anna, leaned over and held her hand.

Anna looked around the hotel foyer. Women in office-wear chinked glasses of Prosecco. An interview seemed to be going on between a middle-aged man who was tapping aggressively on a tablet as he spoke to a nervous-looking woman – girl, really; the age that Anna had been when she'd first come here. Two mothers bounced well-dressed babies on their knees as they swapped stories.

Nobody looked round to stare back at them.

*

When at last they decided to leave the hotel, Anna concentrated on enjoying the satisfaction of feeling an old love revived. So, she thought, this is to be a girl-meets-woman love story, rather than boy meets girl. That will have to be enough for me.

'Can we not leave it so long next time?' she said to Antigone, wondering where they'd both be in another eight years.

'Hell, no. You'll never get rid of me now.'

They walked out into the dusk and Anna had the strange sense that they were being watched. It had once been such a familiar feeling, but one that she no longer experienced, that it revived in her a sort of nostalgia, like the smell of school corridors or sun cream in winter.

'Hello there, Mary Poppins.'

Startled, she looked across the road to where the voice came from and saw him.

'Jack,' she said. He had changed less than Antigone, but the Californian weather had done his complexion a world of good and he was no longer accessorised by a camera.

'And hello, Rosie,' he said. His London accent was undiluted.

'Glad you could make it,' said Antigone.

'Thanks for the tip-off.'

The three of them stood on the street and Anna half expected him to start entertaining them with some magic tricks. She looked from Antigone to Jack and back again. She thought of Janey, poor and anonymous in some distant land. She thought of Bea, still living someone else's life, and Cally, the envy of the rest of the world but a misery in her own one.

And finally, she thought of herself, and how all these years later, she could bury the past into the rubble that remained of Lorston Gardens. Maybe some magic had taken place here, after all.

Acknowledgements

Huge thanks to Arabella Stein for her support and humour. Oh, to have an agent for all aspects of life. Thanks too to all at Abner Stein, especially Ben Fowler.

Everyone at Hodder for their professionalism, charm and courtesy. Francesca Best transforms manuscripts for the better, while Karen Geary and Becca Mundy are wizards of publicity. Sarah Christie is an innovative designer, as is evident when holding this book. Much gratitude, also, to Sharan Matharu in editorial and Naomi Berwin in marketing.

Penny Isaacs brought more than a beady eye for detail in her copy editing, she also had invaluable suggestions and thoughts.

William 'Silly Billy' Tibballs is a talented magician who generously shared some ideas for card tricks. Another man who does magic is Chris Jones of Jones Associates Architects. He found it painful to come up with suggestions on how to build a house badly, since in real life he does the opposite, and I'm very grateful to him for wincing his way through to the right fictional ways to build wrong buildings.

Ali Knight is my library partner and whinge sponge when I'm finding it hard going. Thank you and apologies for all the times I've said, 'I just can't think of . . .'

Sara Keeny and Ania Szablewska have helped with childcare and other tasks on the home front for which I am eternally grateful.

Hopkinsons and Carruthers are wonderful to have in my life, as are all the friends who offer practical and emotional support. I hope you know who you are.

And, as always, Alex, William, Celia and Lydia have provided love and distraction.

Christina Hopkinson

THE PILE OF STUFF AT THE BOTTOM OF THE STAIRS

Mary Gilmour feels as though her life is going down a plug hole clogged with cornflakes and Play-Doh. Her job is part time but housework is full time, and she has no time at all for her two young sons.

Mary is convinced that there is only thing standing between her and organised contentment: his name is Joel and she's married to him.

Since star charts have worked on improving the behaviour of their children, she designs an equivalent for her husband: a spreadsheet detailing every balled-up tissue, every sock on the floor, every wet towel on the bed.

Joel has six months to prove that his credits outweigh his debits. Or else . . .

Out now in paperback and ebook

HODDER

Christina Hopkinson

JUST LIKE PROPER GROWN-UPS

'You don't really grow up until you either have a kid or one of your parents dies.'

Glamorously carefree and nearing forty, Tess shows no sign of settling down. That is, until she drops a bombshell on four of her friends: she's pregnant, and has chosen them as godparents.

Yet while they rally round the single mother, each one is struggling to face the realities of adulthood. Sierra may be only twenty-three but her mother is so irresponsible that she's had to grow up fast. Michael is too busy searching for Mrs Right to worry about collecting the essential accessories of spice racks or investment saucepans, while Owen eases the pain of a mid-life identity crisis with a string of unsuitable fiancées. Only Lucy has the trappings and offspring of a proper grown-up, but is terrified of ageing.

On a challenging and hilarious journey through birth, Botox, bad sex and beyond, all five friends must discover that while growing old is inevitable, growing up is optional . . .

Out now in paperback and ebook

HODDER

Do you wish this wasn't the end?

Join us at www.hodder.co.uk, or follow us on
Twitter @hodderbooks to be a part of our community
of people who love the very best in books and reading.

Whether you want to discover more about a book
or an author, watch trailers and interviews, have the
chance to win early limited editions, or simply browse
our expert readers' selection of the very best books,
we think you'll find what you're looking for.

And if you don't,
that's the place to tell us what's missing.

We love what we do, and we'd love you to be part of it.

www.hodder.co.uk

@hodderbooks

HodderBooks

HodderBooks